EVERYDAY
HORRORS

STEVE RASNIC TEM

Their farm lay in a wide, flat valley bordered by ancient elevations to the east and west. These worn ridges weren't high as mountains go but there was no way over them. The nearest town was a ten-minute drive, but the brothers rarely bothered. They had what they needed, nothing of much value: a few head of cattle for milk and the occasional cut of beef, a dozen or so chickens, a pig, a goat, a garden with corn, tomatoes, beans. A small inheritance dispensed slowly by a local banker paid most of their modest bills. They resented his babysitting, but there was nothing they could do. Mother had been wise enough not to trust them with a lump sum.

Their valley was beautiful in the way most desolate things are beautiful, with nothing obvious to mar the impression. So much sky overhead and what's not to like in a sky? The ground beneath was unremarkable but whole, unlike the region of strip mines, long inactive, a few hundred miles away...Here the world didn't turn into lovely shades of brown, but grays and blacks and the dullness left after the color leaks out of leaves and stems.

Aubrey spent most days sitting on the front porch, away from Brother Jeff, indulging his visions, that other, less useful thing he inherited from Mother. Jeff, otherwise unlucky, had been spared their family's special way of seeing. Aubrey was convinced if he didn't periodically discharge his phantasmagoria he'd become as disconnected as Mother was at the end.

CONTENTS

EVERYDAY HORROR

Their farm lay in a wide, flat valley bordered by ancient elevations to the east and west. These worn ridges weren't high as mountains go but there was no way over them. The nearest town was a ten-minute drive, but the brothers rarely bothered. They had what they needed, nothing of much value: a few head of cattle for milk and the occasional cut of beef, a dozen or so chickens, a pig, a goat, a garden with corn, tomatoes, beans. A small inheritance dispensed slowly by a local banker paid most of their modest bills. They resented his babysitting, but there was nothing they could do. Mother had been wise enough not to trust them with a lump sum.

Their valley was beautiful in the way most desolate things are beautiful, with nothing obvious to mar the impression. So much sky overhead and what's not to like in a sky? The ground beneath was unremarkable but whole, unlike the region of strip mines, long inactive, a few hundred miles away.

Aubrey had been home a year after decades away. As autumn progressed darkness closed in earlier with each passing day. Here the world didn't turn into lovely shades of brown, but grays and blacks and the dullness left after the color leaks out of leaves and stems.

Aubrey spent most days sitting on the front porch, away from Brother Jeff, indulging his visions, that other, less useful thing he inherited from Mother. Jeff, otherwise unlucky, had been spared their family's special way of seeing. Aubrey was convinced if he didn't periodically discharge his phantasmagoria he'd become as disconnected as Mother was at the end.

Suggestions of death and dismemberment journeyed across the darkening dome of sky. Symphonic wraiths gathered for meaningless consultations. They all had something to say, but Aubrey struggled not to listen. He saw and heard things normal people's senses could not perceive. Like a dumb mutt plagued by an invisible dog whistle. It was all quite useless and beyond interpretation, although sometimes he found these appearances entertaining. At least half the secret to living sanely was learning how to fill the time.

"If you're done seeing stuff we should get back to sorting," Jeff said from the other side of the screen door.

Two things brought Aubrey back to the farm: to help bury their mother and accompany his brother to his doctor appointments. "The doc says you should be there, because you'll hear everything he has to say, and I might not." That's how Audrey learned of Jeff's cancer. Jeff still refused to speak the word. "Do you think Mother knew? I think she knew. She must have."

Inside the living room, boxes were stacked almost to the ceiling, labeled KEEP or BURN. Most of the boxes said BURN. Aubrey hadn't lived here in forever, so as far as he was concerned most of the house's contents were properly Jeff's. But Jeff said, "I'm not going to cheat you, not now," and insisted they go through everything together.

Jeff picked up a battle-scarred toy truck. "Yours or mine?"

"I have no idea. It might have been Dad's. What's the difference?"

"We'll call it yours. Keep or burn?"

"Burn."

They'd been doing this for weeks. Aubrey said he didn't want anything. He told Jeff whatever happened—he couldn't say after you die—he'd be moving on. Jeff persisted. "We have to do this. Dad always said you have to clean up after yourself."

"What did he ever clean up? He ran off, left us all high and dry."

"He couldn't listen to Mother describing every awful thing she saw in her head. Can you blame him? At least you have the decency not to share everything you've learned about Hell."

Aubrey said nothing, listening politely as Jeff continued to rant. His brother was in obvious pain. Jeff's skin began to blacken and peel away, the tissues underneath swelling and bursting. His mouth writhed open as his face began to melt, lips shrinking back and teeth exploding, jaws snapping open to release clouds of steam. For weeks Aubrey had watched cancer eating his brother, filling Jeff's belly with fluid, wondering if he had been here if he might have seen it developing, and gotten his brother to the doctor in time. But this wasn't cancer. Unlike his brother, Aubrey believed in neither heaven nor hell, so what kind of new misery was this?

"Wait. What are you looking at, Brother? What are you seeing?"

"Nothing. I was trying to remember the last time we saw Dad. You're older, maybe you remember better?"

"No. No. I know the look. You and Mother—I know both your lying looks. What the hell did you see?" Jeff was out of his chair, hovering over Aubrey's head, fists raised. He'd lost so much weight, and yet it hadn't registered with Aubrey before now. How could that be? Seeing so much, yet not seeing this obvious transformation?

"Nothing! Get back in your chair. Let's finish this pointless ritual so I can get out of here. I didn't see anything." Jeff clamped his forearm onto Aubrey's neck and went down, pulling Aubrey out of his chair and onto the floor with him. "Are you crazy? Wrestling? Let go dammit! Are we kids now? Is that what we are? Are you eight years old? I don't want to hurt you!"

"You think you can hurt me? You're a fool if you think I can't beat you!"

They rolled into a stack of boxes and the boxes came tumbling down, covering them both with things to keep and things to burn. "Dammit, Jeff! Now we have to start this whole deal over."

At least Jeff allowed Aubrey to make his choices quickly this time, so after another couple of days they recouped the lost time. The Keep collection was much smaller than before, consisting of a few of their parents' wedding photos, an old pull toy he remembered from his kindergarten days, and a water-damaged copy of Ovid's *Metamorphoses*. There were a lot of old boy's toys around, guns and plastic soldiers, tiny military equipment. They'd always liked army stuff. Every day had been filled with pretend dying and killing. Now Aubrey couldn't recollect the attraction. Burn burn burn.

"Do you think having another female around would have made things easier? A sister ..."

Jeff looked at him. "Don't you remember? Mother said we couldn't have a sister. She said we would've killed a little sister with our roughhousing."

"I hated when she said it. But it wouldn't have to be a sister. It could have been a wife or a girlfriend for one of us."

"That seems unlikely, Brother. Don't you think? You live too much in your head to have a girlfriend. Just like Mother. It must come with the territory, when you have that second sight." Jeff's face and arms were layered in bandages. Some had bled through, but he refused to let Aubrey change them. He didn't see the point. Aubrey himself was in similar shape. They could have been killed beneath that avalanche of boxes. He hadn't changed his either. He avoided mirrors.

"Second sight is like precognition, remote viewing. What I have, what Mother had, isn't all that straightforward. I used to think I saw the future, but when the future came it wasn't always exactly what I'd seen. Sometimes it wasn't even close. I see potentialities, worst case scenarios, but I also see the now we don't like thinking about."

"Mother said it was like a horror movie every day. Everyday horror. She said she never wanted to get used to it, but she did. She said sometimes she made up things even worse in her head and she'd see those things, just to distract herself from the horror every day." He stood up and went into one of the bedrooms. Jeff couldn't stand sitting in one place. Aubrey could hear him in there tossing things around. A man sick as he shouldn't be tossing things around. Jeff came back dragging a couple of trash bags with swollen sides. "You left a lot of clothes behind. And we still have some of Dad's old ones. They might fit. You should go through them."

"Burn the lot. No telling what's gotten into them, all these years. Bet they smell."

Jeff opened a bag and stuck his face in, jerked it away. "They sure do." He piled them near the Burn boxes. "I don't want to die, you know." He was still looking away.

"I know. Don't snap at me, but remember the doctor said there were treatments which might give you a few months."

"A few months of puking and fuzz brain. I want to be clear so I can think about things. I should be thinking about things. But hell, I don't know what to think." He turned around. "Are you going to be sad when I die?"

"Of course, I'll be sad. How can you ask such a thing?"

"Well, I guess it's a good thing somebody will be sad. I think I want to be cremated, if you don't mind."

"Why would I mind?"

"Some people don't like to think about it, the body burning like that. Damn, I don't like to think about it. But it seems clean, don't you think? Not like this mess here." He looked around. "God, how did we let things get to be such a mess? It won't bother you, seeing me burning?"

"Hell, Jeff. Such a question. You'll be in a box, inside a furnace. I won't see."

Jeff sat down in a chair. "I wish I hadn't asked. Now I'm seeing it, inside my head." Aubrey saw Jeff, dead, slumped in the chair, his mouth hanging unnaturally open, his flesh disappeared from parts of his body. He tried to think that's not Jeff, that's just his body. Jeff has gone on somewhere else. At least that's what you were supposed to think if you were a religious person. Thinking like that was supposed to fix it. But Aubrey wasn't a religious person, and he couldn't think that way. Jeff's corpse started speaking again. "Is that what you see, me burning like that? Is that what your sight shows you?"

Aubrey recalled the steam issuing from Jeff's mouth like annihilated thought, vaporized language, and didn't know how to answer. "It's what the saints possessed, some of them. They had visions of heaven and hell and felt compelled to testify, when maybe they should have kept their mouths shut. They suffered as a result."

"Are you saying you're some kind of saint, college boy?" Jeff was suddenly moving aggressively around the room, lifting a bundle of newspapers into a rusted wheelbarrow for the bonfire. Their mother collected newspapers for decades, read them and kept them as confirmation of the terrible things she witnessed.

"Not at all, but you know that. I'm just trying to explain."

"Oh, I know. I stayed here with Mother while you left to find yourself. You went to college, and I stayed here with the crazy."

Aubrey glanced up at Jeff. "You didn't kill Mother, did you? If you did, I could understand. Her delirium, dementia, whatever you want to call it. I know she was suffering. The death certificate just said heart failure, and it would have been easy—"

"Hell, Brother! You think I'd kill our own mother?"

"Under certain circumstances. I might have myself, if she was suffering. If I were scared enough. And if she was telling you all those awful things she saw. It might have been too much."

"Too much for her heart, you mean. It was her heart, Brother. I didn't murder our mother! You're just like she was, aren't you? Paranoid and crazy."

"It isn't crazy. Maybe the visions drove her crazy, but the sight itself? Not crazy."

"Whatever. You got the college education. I got lots of stuff to burn." Jeff took several wheelbarrow loads out to the pile in the yard, then began shifting bags and boxes at a frenetic pace. Aubrey sat watching him, Jeff's body appearing to fall into pieces, cuts of meat. At one point pieces of Jeff were hauling other pieces of Jeff out to join the rest of the bonfire fuel. Aubrey got up to help a couple of times, but both times Jeff pushed him aside, almost knocking him down.

Jeff held up a bundle of old letters. Aubrey blushed in recognition. "These old letters of yours to and from various women. I see some letters from you that were never mailed. You knew Mother kept them didn't you? She kept everything having to do with you. So, what do you want to do with these confessions of unrequited love?"

"Some were requited, thank you very much." Jeff must have read them. "Go ahead and burn them." Aubrey was getting angry. He needed to leave.

He went out the door and past Jeff who was busy throwing objects higher up on the pile. His brother was going to give himself a heart attack. Aubrey didn't understand how he had the strength in his condition.

"Walking to town," he threw back over his shoulder. "I'll bring you back a treat!"

He passed a couple of the cows in their fenced enclosure. One turned and gazed at him with its huge, lazy eyes. It began to separate into a slow-motion avalanche of living cuts of meat, its tortured tongue expressing a suffering Aubrey could only imagine. A chicken trotted over to look, its almost severed head dangling from a thin strip of skin. The everyday facts of life were brutal if contemplated too long.

It was unusually cold, but following his dramatic exit Aubrey didn't want to return for a jacket. The road away from the farm appeared broken, whole stretches missing. It hadn't been like that before. He'd gone to town just last week for some chicken feed and a few groceries. There had been some old barns, a few out-buildings, an aged wooden fence, but now they were missing. He saw evidence of a grass fire—the black burn stretched for miles. He could see piles of dead prairie dogs, thousands of them, more than a few generations worth. He spun around. He should have been able to see the farm from here, but there was nothing but more burn.

A hundred years from now. Maybe less. It was hard to tell sometimes if you were looking into the future or the past.

The wind picked up, grabbing dirt and spreading it throughout the sky. The disrupted soil beneath his feet revealed more bodies, some of them human.

The wind blasted across the fields carrying debris from far off places: tons of burnt paper, rags, street signs from cities hundreds of miles away.

"It a beautiful place, here where we grew up." He'd said this to Jeff just the other day.

Jeff laughed at him. "So, you are crazy, just like Mother."

Audrey tried to control his anger. "Look at the sky. Those fields. If you'd lived in the city like I did, you'd appreciate this more."

As suddenly as it came up, the wind fell away. Audrey gazed at the sky. Birds appeared to be floating rather than flying. Aubrey wondered if that was what they looked like when they dreamed.

He hated being out here alone. He picked up the pace until he was practically running, anxious to be around people again.

He was relieved at how normal everything in town appeared. People jammed the sidewalks, and most of the parking spaces were full. He realized he didn't know what day it was. Maybe it was a Saturday when people from outlying farms came into town to shop. So many couples, many hand in hand, touching. He should be pleased to see such things. But he never was.

Even on his good days Aubrey didn't like looking into people's faces. He was naturally shy, but he always had some anxiety about what he might see within a particular arrangement of features. He didn't want to see their troubles. He didn't want the facts of their mortality rubbing him in the face. But he couldn't always avoid looking. Some of the passersby appeared to speak so rapidly their lips wandered in and out of focus.

He went into a small drugstore and bought some of Jeff's favorite cookies, some chocolates, and some of the bubble gum they'd liked as kids. A peace offering, he supposed. Jeff might say, "You're just buying me all this stuff because I'm dying." That would annoy Aubrey, but at least he was prepared for that kind of response. The clerk's face disintegrated and spread all over the glass countertop.

Some of the townspeople had wings. They kept them folded and tight against their backs, although occasionally a gust of wind or some burst of emotion would make the wings rise and flutter. Now and then he would stumble upon a pair of empty shoes on the sidewalk or in the street. It thrilled him to imagine the possibilities.

If he could have spent the day walking around and observing until some of these people took flight he would have, but he knew such behavior would draw unwanted attention. He saw more when people stared at him. He saw too much.

He witnessed a couple kissing on a bench. Their faces melted together and one of them—he wasn't sure which—began to scream. The result of too much intimacy perhaps. Or maybe something else.

An elderly man stopped him on the sidewalk, pointing to something in his mouth. Aubrey leaned in closer as the man opened wide. There was a fish inside the man's mouth exercising its fins.

Hands appeared over people's shoulders and yanked them out of the world.

The horror was always there, churning beneath the surface. He couldn't always see it, but he often caught a whiff of its stink.

When Aubrey got back to the farm he was amazed by the size of the burn pile. The middle of it was taller than the house itself (and how was that possible?), and it spread yards beyond the house's width, resembling a giant wing the way it tapered toward the ends. It was a conglomerate of everything they had ever owned and kept, back at least until their grandparents' time. He was overwhelmed by what Jeff had put together, something much more than a pile of assembled junk. It was an art piece looking quite capable of taking flight.

He went inside looking for Jeff but couldn't find him. He called his name with no response. It occurred to him Jeff might have worked his own body into the burn pile. Aubrey was racing toward the door when he heard, faintly, "In here."

"Where?"

"In here." The voice came from Jeff's room.

He tapped on Jeff's door. "I'm not allowed in your room, remember?"

"Just come in."

Aubrey eased himself inside. It was a small room, his brother's bed filling the space. Jeff lay in the middle of the bed wearing an assortment of ragged clothes. Aubrey wondered what he'd done with what he'd been wearing. Those clothes had been perfectly fine. His brother resembled a giant rotting cabbage. Jeff said, "Let me sleep another half-hour. Then I'll be ready. I promise. I'm not dead yet, but I think I'm on my way, don't you think?"

"Only the young and the crazy don't know they're going to die."

"I'll take that as a compliment."

There was a hole in the ceiling over Jeff's bed, with a considerable water stain surrounding it. So many trash bags had been stuffed inside the cavity they were falling out. "How long has there been a leak?"

"It's been that way for years. A few more days won't matter. Every fall and winter I stuff a little more plastic into the hole. I use a bent coat hanger to spread it out a little. It's not pretty, but at least I rarely get wet." Aubrey was ashamed his family couldn't manage a necessary household repair.

The night before the burn the winds coming off the ridges and across the valley felt different. The sky itself looked unusual, a bit lower than normal, like a ceiling on the brink of collapse. The brothers stayed up all night sitting on the porch, watching, and waiting. There was no reason to do the burn on the day Jeff selected for it, except he insisted. "It's the right day. You only have one chance for a right day."

They watched a light rain begin to fall. It was hard to tell for sure, but it appeared to be raining upwards, as if the weary ground were weeping into the sky.

"Sorry, but if it keeps raining we'll have to do the burn another day, maybe even next week," Aubrey said.

"It'll stop raining. But if everything's wet we'll just add gasoline. There's some in the cow barn. That's where she kept it."

"Jeff, I always thought you were the patient one. It can wait."

"I just need to see it done is all."

In the distance lightning carved the sky into lace. The cows left the barn and went out into their enclosure, gazing up at the display. You don't see such things every day. Aubrey wondered if it was common. The cows swayed and moaned.

Aubrey woke up on the porch the next morning, cold and exhausted. Jeff stood out by the pile, shrouded in his disintegrating clothing and a tattered blanket: a giant, decaying bird. He turned around and gazed at Aubrey. "I think it's dry enough, but I sprinkled gasoline all through it. Mother kept a ton of cans in the barn. What was she thinking?"

"You know the metal stuff isn't going to burn!" Aubrey shouted back.

"Of course, I know the metal stuff isn't going to burn! I'm not stupid, college boy!"

"Don't ruin it now. We've been getting along pretty well."

"All that metal is old and rusty. If it gets hot enough it'll break and fall apart. At least it'll be easier to throw away."

"Right," Aubrey said, although he had serious doubts. "Get away from there. I made a torch last night. I'll light it and throw it in."

Jeff moved to a safe distance, then started running around, dancing and shouting "Light it light it light it!" Aubrey started to laugh. His brother had always been this big, dopey, unhappy kid. His tremendous weight loss enhanced the bird resemblance. He looked like he might fall over any second.

Aubrey lit the torch, ran up within a few feet of the pile, tossed it in, and retreated. The wing went up in flames with a giant whoosh. It looked like it really would depart the ground. Then here and there across the wing's span there were pockets of explosion. "Did you toss full cans of gas in there?"

Jeff may have answered. Aubrey couldn't hear him over the noise. A massive detonation sent the firebird soaring, one wing tip lighting up the house, the other dipping low enough to touch the outstretched wing of that sorrowful and foolish, dying and dancing bird, in a vision so extraordinary Aubrey could recall nothing close to matching it.

FISH SCALES

Sometimes sorrow falls into such a deep place it cannot escape.

When Charlie saw the first evidence of vandalism at the summer house—gouges in the front steps, the screen door ripped away and in pieces, the inner door off its hinges and lying inside—he sank onto the porch and wept. It had been a terrible year. This house, which he had been unable to visit in almost five years, was to be a haven.

The vandalism was not typical. He wasn't sure he could even call it vandalism, as nothing had been taken, and the destruction didn't seem so much deliberate as incidental.

He studied the front door lying in the entrance. There were prints all over its surface as if it had been walked on many times, but it was hard to say by what. The impressions overlapped in a vague wallowing pattern strewn with sand.

The furniture was pushed into the corners, and plants had been dragged in from the beach dunes several hundred yards away, sea oats and beach grass for the most part, along with cane and broom sedge, mashed around until they'd knitted together into a sprawling nest filling the space. The walls were festooned with streamers of dead Spanish moss scavenged from the nearby magnolias. Water and mud had been tracked in. A few of the floorboards were still wet and rotting and would have to be replaced. Everything stank of the sea.

He cut a long stick and poked around for critters, rattlesnakes, copperheads, maybe a fox or a weasel or a sleeping alligator, or possibly one of the squatters still hiding in the debris. He was vaguely disappointed not to find anything, which meant all that remained were the weeks needed to clean out the house, assess the damage, and make repairs.

It could have been worse. A few chairs and some broken ceramics had to be thrown away. Wall and floor repairs, wood and plaster replaced. There were deep scratches everywhere: in the floor, the wooden furniture, even in one corner of the ceiling. He had no idea from what. He spent days puttying, filling, staining, and painting. He kept the windows open and the smell slowly dissipated, but he could still detect its presence in random locations, at the bottom of a drawer or the back of a closet, underneath the bed.

Charlie hadn't done such work in years and it exhausted him. He took frequent breaks to sit on the porch and read from magazines he'd collected during his wife's final illness. "Skin Hunger" was the title of this particular article. He'd never heard the expression before, but he certainly knew the feeling. He read with growing embarrassment how touch is the first sense we acquire, how in experiments baby monkeys chose emotional nourishment over food, how infants who weren't held enough sometimes stopped growing and died, how that physical ache for another person's touch—he threw the magazine on the trash pile. The sub-tropic climate in coastal South Carolina wasn't a good place to collect magazines. After a while they began to smell.

Charlie hadn't much cared for the summer house when they first bought it. It was a ruin that would require years of work. He'd never found the ocean soothing, and the television reception was nonexistent. But Linda wanted this place badly, and Charlie would have done anything for her. Over twenty summers he designed rooms and built furniture exactly the way she'd wanted them. He got used to turning on the TV only so they could watch movies on the VCR. She always followed the stories better than he would have expected, but he had to describe the non-speaking parts for her. He enjoyed the task and became quite good at it. He also came to like the white noise of the ocean on their long afternoon walks.

"If you want to marry, you'll have to find yourself a blind woman." His father told him that when Charlie was just fifteen. The old man wasn't trying to be cruel. He was a simple man trying to give his son practical advice.

When Charlie told his wife the story, waiting a year into their marriage because he wasn't sure how she'd take it, Linda hugged him so fiercely he thought he might break. Then she laughed. "Well, I guess he was half right." Linda wasn't completely blind, but blind enough.

Charlie was born with Ichthyosis vulgaris, "fish scales." He had a relatively mild case, mainly on his forehead and the left side of his face, the palms of his hands. More severe cases sometimes involved the whole body, so he considered himself lucky. He used ointments and a sponge to remove scales every few days.

Much of the past year Charlie woke up with blurred vision. Sometimes the blurriness lasted until lunch or after. He worried it might be a new progression of his disease, but not enough to see a doctor. He'd had his fill of doctors. They wouldn't tell Linda how long she had, though he was sure they knew. None of their treatments worked and they promised her she wouldn't suffer. They lied.

Some days there was ambiguous movement in his peripheral vision. Turning his head, he couldn't find it. Maybe whatever it was had a talent for stealth.

He speculated whether this disturbing inexactitude was the way Linda saw things. She could see the individual leaves on trees, although her doctors said that should have been impossible. But she couldn't make out facial expressions unless she was extremely close, so she usually touched or held onto him when they talked. He'd gotten so used to that it seemed the only reasonable way to have a conversation.

At least once an afternoon he stood in front of the bathroom mirror and splashed water over his face. Sometimes it helped. "Wake up!" he'd say to the mirror. "You need to wake up." There were nights he fell asleep wondering if he'd be blind the next morning.

If he could see well enough, he'd recreate those long walks to the cove at the end of the trail. It had been Linda's favorite thing. At one time it might have been a wonderful spot for sunbathing and swimming, a private hideaway tucked away behind the rocks. But it hadn't been kept up. Thick underbrush grew almost to the shoreline and the water looked a nasty green. Some days you could see a film floating on top of the water, translucent and sac-like, a container with things moving around inside. He didn't like to swim under the best of conditions. No chance he'd venture into this.

From the summer house the trail meandered among the pepperbush, oleanders, and cabbage palms to the cove and a bit beyond. Each time he walked it he searched for signs of disturbance. The environs looked pretty much as he recalled from five years before, but the path was a little wider than he remembered, and swept relatively clean, as if subject to a regular stream of traffic.

He was surprised by the scarcity of wildlife. In summers past he and Linda had seen fox along the path, the occasional wild pig, and closer to the water brown pelicans, herons, gulls, osprey, plover, and on the beach itself a few ghost crabs. He'd point them out and describe them the best he could, researching the animals to do a better job for her. But since he'd been back no animals of any kind had made an appearance, not even the smaller birds.

Maneuvering through the world with his blind wife had been a kind of dance. Linda could see well enough in the city the regular landmarks and her cane skills kept her from getting lost. But out in this semitropical landscape she needed his arm and his elbow to guide the way. Now he thought he might have taken the closeness, the grace of it, too much for granted. Some days he missed it desperately.

Sometimes on these walks by himself Charlie thought he could hear voices in the tall grass, or in the trees, or somewhere in the curtains of vine, and he pondered if they were from those missing animals, their voices distorted because of some barrier or illness. They sounded like people speaking an unfamiliar language. He reminded himself the human brain makes things up all the time.

One afternoon when he got back from his walk, he noticed how flattened the vegetation was around the sides of the house. Investigating further, he observed the flat areas were more pronounced beneath the windows, and there were scratches in the siding, broad trails of grit and something oily leading up to the sills. He couldn't remember if he'd checked here before. Now he felt he'd been irresponsible.

Over the next few days Charlie experienced several flare-ups of his disease. This sometimes happened with a change in environment, or from added stress. The scales had not increased their spread on his face, but they felt thicker, and at times they cracked so badly he had to use heavier creams, and the areas burned as they hadn't since childhood.

With the flare-up of his symptoms he wasn't surprised by the increased intensity of his dreams, swimming with fish and gazing eye to eye, fascinated by how their armored flesh kept the liquid within separate from the liquid without. Someday he knew they would lose that barrier completely, becoming all eyes and fleeting movements. Attuned to the most subtle indications of danger—a temperature change, a shift in the spectrum or angle of light, some vaguely perceived failure in the environment—they swam unbothered through their silent domain. He woke up with the sun blurring his vision, his scales ablaze from their first contact with early morning light.

In the months after Linda died, Charlie hid in their city home, avoiding people, even old friends. He never answered the door or the telephone. He didn't want to be around those who'd known her, who'd want to talk about her, who wanted to ask how he was doing. Some days the doorbell ringing and the telephone ringing felt so abusively persistent he took to his bed and stuffed wax plugs into his ears.

Neighbors and friends came to the house, beat on the doors, tapped on the windows, walked around the outside calling his name. Finally, the police came to his address to do a welfare check and forced their way inside. Everyone wanted to talk to him about Linda, but that was the last thing Charlie wanted. That's when he sold their city home and moved here.

Most nights at the summer house Charlie stayed up late, all the lights turned off as he sat on the porch in the dark, staring and listening. There was usually moonlight, so the open area in front of the house had a silver radiance. And there was always movement out in the brush, just beyond his ability to see. But he could hear it, the branches brushing together, the leaves murmuring, the occasional rustle of the grasses. All those missing animals, he supposed, or the fish having grown legs and come to visit. Or maybe just wind. When he was a little kid he imagined lizards were just a kind of fish with legs, but his mother told him that many of them were related to the birds, and their scales related to feathers, which both thrilled and disturbed him. Flying lizards could do a world of damage, he'd imagined, if they decided they weren't your friends.

Deep in the night he was awakened by some sound, a temperature change, a shift in the spectrum or angle of light, some vaguely perceived failure in the environment. He kept his eyes tightly closed in case someone was in the house watching him, and strained to listen, seeking auditory clues as to whether he'd heard the usual house sounds, or if something else were at play.

It was difficult to tell. Anxiety made him breathe harder, and sometimes he could hear his own heartbeat as a throbbing pulse in his ears, and he knew from experience occasionally when he woke up he was still half-sleeping, still chasing the tattered ends of a dream.

He heard another sound, a kind of shifting, followed by a pause, and then another shifting. He thought about chancing a quick peek at his surroundings, raising his head ever so slightly from the pillow. He tried to open his eyes but could not. As sometimes happened, they were glued shut by sleep. He didn't want to lift his hands to rub them. He didn't want to draw attention to himself at all.

After some effort he was able to part his eyelids enough to see something, a glimmer of ambient light, of shape and shadow. Once or twice he detected a smooth glide of movement, something pulling itself out of view, but it still might be his eyes caught in sleepiness, still adjusting to the dark, and he was imagining he was seeing more than he was physically capable. Maybe he had become the blind one.

He remembered how Linda's doctors said she was always able to see more than she should have. Her doctors said she saw the almost impossible.

Charlie remained perfectly still, measuring what he could see in slices, maybe for hours. He wasn't sure what kind of impression he was trying to make on whoever might be watching. When he was a kid, he imagined the night creatures might think him dead if he lay still enough, and so they wouldn't bother him. The logic of this now escaped him. A dead body was easy prey.

Around dawn there was a clear change in the tenor of things. The shadowy movements increased, and there was a nebulous smell, not entirely unpleasant, which Charlie associated with hurry, or maybe the fear of being caught.

His own body, however, was working against him, as he desperately needed to pee. At his age the urge could only be put off for so long without an embarrassing accident. When he couldn't put it off any longer, he sprang out of bed, arms waving, shouting "Ah!" at the top of his lungs. He staggered into the bathroom, still not seeing all that well, but aware of fuzzy movement around him, perhaps trying to get out of his way. Of course, he was highly agitated, and kicking clothing and bed sheets around, so any sense of other occupants in the house might be pure delusion.

As he sat there, he rubbed his eyes with both hands and felt bits of something coming off, tissue or dried material or flakes. He held them in his palms and blinked. When he was able to see clearly, he studied them. It was bits of his skin, his scales, his fish scales. But larger, flatter, more delicate than usual. He took one and held it between thumb and forefinger up to the bathroom window. It was iridescent, like a butterfly wing or a fish's scales. Something dark floated across the other side of the window, a bird taking flight or something falling off the roof.

Later he walked through the house, examining everything. He wasn't sure, but some furniture appeared to have been moved, some things lying on the floor he'd last seen on tables, and the front door was open a few inches. Charlie couldn't remember a time he'd failed to lock the front door. In the kitchen he found those nasty wallow prints again, on the counter by the sink.

He got dressed and left the house, heading for the cove. Along the way he saw random gouges in the sandy path, broken branches, and smashed plants near the edges. He didn't know if these disturbances were recent, or if things had been like this for a while.

When he got to the narrow beach he stopped and stared at the spread of open water. The water itself was still a variegated green, but the film had been disrupted. Sections had been torn, allowing tangles of dark marine vegetation to well up from below and spread across the surface. As he looked along the shore, some of this dreary vegetation appeared to have been dragged out of the water. From the curled pieces of film, it was obvious how substantial the membrane over the water had been—inches thick and rubbery looking. At the edge of the beach directly opposite him, something thin and bony with flappy bits, resembling an old piece of filthy insulating foam with sticks attached, appeared to be trying again and again to pull itself out of the water, finally disappearing beneath the surface in defeat.

Charlie waited. He could hear the breeze moving through the grass and brush around him. He could smell the growing stench of the sea. He couldn't hear any birds, or any other kind of creature. The skin on his face burned, as did a few random spots on the palms of his hands. When he held them up those spots glistened like jewels buried in his flesh. But here and there blood welled, and the ache he felt could no longer be denied.

During those last few weeks of Linda's life, he was helping her in and out of the shower, washing her, brushing her hair, even brushing her teeth—such a delicate operation to brush someone else's teeth. This was before she became too weak to get out of bed. Sometimes she'd ask for lotion or for him to massage a sore muscle, and that was practically the only time she spoke, until that afternoon shortly before the end, when she'd asked him, "Who is going to take care of you after I'm gone?"

The remainder of that day she became so quiet and passive, unlike her usual self, as if part of her had already passed on. He remembered the way the light fell on her, the shadows and the highlights making of her face an expressionless mask.

What was left of her was pale, with shadows under her eyes, under her chin, reinforcing the subtle impression of her ribs. At a certain point light appeared not to stick to her. And then a few days later, those men in their dark formal suits were carrying her out of the home they had shared for nearly forty years.

He made his way back to the summer house, climbed onto the porch and gently eased himself down. He stretched out and stared at the roof supports overhead. They were badly warped. He thought maybe he had forgotten to paint them. Clearly, he shouldn't stay at the house anymore. He should call someone, maybe at the natural history museum. He didn't know if South Carolina had a natural history museum, but didn't every state have some such institution devoted to the mysteries of the natural world?

He could check himself into the hospital for rest and recovery. Stress only exacerbated his condition. He hadn't seen one of those specialists in years. Maybe progress had been made. Maybe he could get these scales removed entirely.

He moved his head around on the rough boards trying to get comfortable. He kept glancing over there by the chair where he'd kept the magazines. He felt like reading something helpful, but maybe he'd already thrown everything helpful away.

Some of his skin burned, and some was cold to the touch. It didn't feel like his own skin. He used the hand with the fewest blemishes to vigorously rub the other arm, massage warmth and life back into it, but it didn't seem to help.

Charlie was having trouble seeing again. Ambiguity encroached from every side. A membranous veil dropped over his eyes.

He could hear them moving around, going inside the summer 'house, surrounding him. They smelled of ocean and sun and dead things, but when they finally touched him, he did not shy away, not even when they began touching his face, or his scales.

The way they caressed his face, he considered they might be blind. They read him like he was braille.

GAVIN'S FIELD

He remembered little of his father. He wondered if this lack of information was deliberate, and mutual. Sometimes a memory would surface and he'd be seduced into obsessive examination until he managed to bury it again.

Gavin was due to take possession of his father's estate in early November, but New England had a devastating winter which delayed the move until the following April. He'd never visited his father in Vermont, never considered living there, but he had nowhere else to go. They'd been distant since Gavin Senior left his mother, and exchanged no more than a few letters the past thirty years. As a teenager Gavin searched his mother's house for a birth certificate, adoption papers, anything to prove this cold man couldn't have been his father. At the end, neither was familiar with the man the other became. His father's death brought unexpected opportunity. He had no idea how he was supposed to feel about that.

He wasn't notified of the death until well after the funeral, not that he would have attended. Although he might have obtained some satisfaction in seeing the old stranger lowered into the dirt. He wasn't informed of the cause of death, nor did he care to inquire.

Gavin nursed his aging gray Toyota wagon over the fog-laden roads of New England, periodically stopping to fill the radiator and add oil, or for a break from the stench coming from the exhaust system. He loved the green stretches, broken up by a web of intricately-fitted stone walls. He admired the quaint architecture, the tidiness of the close-together villages, the friendly feel of the region, hoping Disleigh Township would possess some of those same qualities.

The first and only sign for Disleigh was a small wooden plank bearing the name with an arrow, almost obscured by the bushes where the narrow lane joined the main road. The right-of-way was neglected and overgrown, with both dead and living vegetation crowding the ditch lines. A mile in he had to dodge his first dead animal—a small deer. There would be three more—two large dogs and a cow. Each time he stopped and looked—no blood or visible injuries. Numerous trees were scarred with obscure graffiti. Some had been roughly crossed out. The distance between houses was much farther than he'd expected in this part of the country. Many appeared abandoned and overrun with brownish weeds, skeletal bushes, and dead limbs. Inside the door frame of a collapsing structure a naked couple smeared with mud embraced. Flustered, he quickly turned his head away. He convinced himself he could not have seen this. His mouth was cracked and dry—he wished he had brought some water.

The car became unbearably stuffy, so he rolled down the window despite the vehicle's noxious smell. A loud explosion of bird song drove him to shut it again, their raucous noise dismembered. He tried again a half-hour later. This time the sounds resembled human voices, still unpleasant, but he found himself straining to understand.

An ornate metal marker announced the Disleigh town limits. More dilapidation followed, a few old buildings torn apart by dying trees, cavernous interiors suggestive of filth and corruption. No one walked the streets or appeared in windows. His father's house fronted a circular lane in the heart of town. It was much larger than he'd expected, the ashen exterior square and solid, if a bit beaten in by age and weather.

Martinson, the lawyer, waited on the narrow brick walk in front of the house across from a small park and its scatter of iron benches and maples. An elderly man in a floppy blue hat sat on one of the benches staring at the two men.

"That's Whitby. Your father called him the town watchdog. Apparently he has a good loud voice if he sees something amiss."

"These other buildings ... have neighbors? Some of them look empty."

"A few businesses, a few residences, a few vacant buildings. A real mix." He rattled the keys in his hand. "I was going to tell you I've got two keys for you. The silver one handles both the front and back doors. The old red one unlocks that gate in the stone wall behind the house, the one that says Blackburn's Field on it. Blackburn was the first owner. He built this house before there was even a town."

"So I have a field? Like a garden?"

"No, it's all forest now, like it was in the beginning. Trees so packed inside them low stone walls I don't know why they haven't pushed them over. I doubt you could walk more than a few steps before the undergrowth stopped you. I wouldn't venture inside there, if I was you."

"No problem there. I've never been a nature person."

The lawyer looked up at him curiously. "Really? Well, you'll be a long way from any city here. What do you plan to do with yourself?"

The question embarrassed him because he had no answer. "Still trying to figure that out I suppose."

"Well, whatever—it's all yours, and here are the keys. Enjoy it." Martinson shuffled toward his car.

"Wait! How do I reach you if I have questions? Do you live nearby?"

The lawyer turned and sighed. "Phone number is on my card attached to your copy of the will. I live in Connecticut. I visited your father a few times here, but that's the extent of my familiarity. Some of the shops—" He gestured around the circle. "Well, the owners would know more than I do. Locals. Ask them."

Gavin forced an awkward smile. He'd never been good talking to people. "Okay. Well, can you at least tell me about the stone walls? I saw so many of them driving in."

"Oh, they're everywhere in New England. I have some near me. They even run through the forests. I have no idea why. It really makes no sense."

After the lawyer left, Gavin looked for Whitby across the street but didn't see him. Some watchdog ...

The town was silent but for the sound of running water. It was overcast and hadn't started raining yet, but multiple rivulets trickled down the patchy grass driveway into the cobbled street. Gavin supposed it might be the last remains of melting snow, although there was no snow visible. He crouched for a better look. There was an unexpected thickness to the stream: sediment and debris, the occasional wooden splinter or twig or tightly curled black leaf, buttons and pieces of cloth, worms and dead insects, what looked like but couldn't be hair, what looked like rounded and polished slivers of bone.

He heard a meowing, turned to see a number of cats flowing down the cobbled lane in a loose sort of formation. A few of them carried shreds of some sort of skinned carcass in their mouths. One turned and stared at him boldly, a squirrel's head dangling from its jaws by a narrow band of skin.

The mist transitioned into a needle-like rain. He struggled with the lock at first, and then pushed the heavy door in on the cramped wood-paneled hall, dark with dust and grime. His heart sank at this first glimpse of filth, but he had to get his few belongings inside.

The rain increased in intensity as he struggled with the paper and plastic sacks, the floppy cardboard boxes, dumping them just past the entrance way. Halfway through he stopped and stared past the edge of the house, a large trash bag full of random clothing in his arms. There was a kind of music, one rising sharp note after another. He could see the edge of the woods a short distance behind the house, that rusted iron-gate and the unreadable sign, the low walls cobbled together out of large flat stones. The tops of the trees—many of them browned and dead-looking—were bending and separating from some serious wind which somehow had not yet reached him.

The sound of laughter made him turn around. Whitby was across the street, grinning with hat off and waving some kind of bye-bye, rain running down his face and through his beard as if he were melting.

The low-ceilinged entry led into a dank living room crowded with faded furniture, the light through the clear stained-glass windows illuminating trails of debris winding between the crappy antiques. Glass-fronted cabinets lined the walls, too dirty to see inside. A plume of visible dust preceded him into the largish dining room. Both rooms were full of dust-furred bric-à-brac that he would examine at some point, although for now he couldn't imagine touching them. The house required cleaning skills well beyond his. The estate came with some money—he hoped it was enough to hire a short-term housekeeper.

He did what he could that first day, wiped out some shelves and drawers, put clothes away, made up his bed, and cleaned the bathroom until it was tolerable. He went to bed as early as possible. He may or may not have heard more of the raucous birdcalls and discordant music, but they just as well might have been dreams.

The next morning with no instructions for utilities, garbage pickup, or just where to buy groceries, Gavin waited until ten a.m., then went out to find his neighbors.

The first few shops were closed and derelict. He came to another whose door was locked, but a bald man hunched over a desk was visible through the display window. He was busy applying labels to small bottles of dark powder. Gavin knocked on the glass and the man looked up with a smile that suddenly froze. Gavin waved, and the man stared. He knocked again and pointed toward the door. The man remained motionless. Seriously rattled, Gavin moved on.

The next building was church-like, with a cross etched into the stone near its peak. The windows by the entrance were tall, but did not appear to be church windows. Both an OPEN and a GOING OUT OF BUSINESS sign hung on the door. The elderly couple behind the counter greeted him with eager smiles.

"Hi, I need toothpaste, soap, a few essentials ..."

"Of course. We kept, keep that sort of thing for tourists. Not that there ever were any, unfortunately." The woman led him to a row of shelves.

Gavin felt the awkward need to say something nice. "I'm sorry about your business."

"Well—businesses, even towns, have a life span. They die out when the people die out. The locals are dying at a rate we can't compete with. Even when we first opened few bothered to venture into town. A community of hermits and recluses, I'm afraid. Who knows how many are left out there? Why, I believe you're the first new resident in ages."

"How ..."

"That lawyer was in here, asking about the town. I told him living here only ten years made us foreigners. We used to have a successful business in New York, but we wanted to spend our last days somewhere more peaceful. A huge mistake I'm afraid. I told him if he wanted the real dirt he'd have to talk to a local, if he could find one. I guess he talked to Whitby, as useless as that was."

Gavin gathered more than he needed into a small basket. The husband provided him with a few business cards of people who would deliver groceries, haul things, clean, or perform other chores. "A dwindling selection, I'm afraid. Sometimes you call them and their number's been disconnected."

A tiny figure appeared to wave to him from a nearby shelf. It was fashioned from dried mud, tiny twisted branches, tads of trash into somewhat of a face, something of a body. He peered closer. It had a mouth of sorts, full of dirt.

"They're all like that—a mouth full of mud, like the rest of us in the end. You can have that. Used to be a local craft. Interesting work, but we've never sold any. They're so ugly. I think they give folks the creeps." Gavin smiled and pocketed it.

"You knew my father?"

The husband glanced at the wife before speaking. "He used to come in all the time to discuss the history of the house, the region. I think he asked the locals lots of questions. Then later, he didn't speak much. Alice thought he was depressed. That was around the time the town visits from locals fell to almost

nothing. There were some funerals for a while. I went to one —
your father was there. A sad affair. I didn't go to any more. Then
we stopped hearing about the funerals altogether. But we're
still strangers here — we don't hear everything."

"Oh … trash pickup? How do I arrange that?"

"They don't pick up the trash here. We're on our own. You
could drive the twenty-five miles to the dump, or pay
somebody. Most just find a place to bury it."

"Bury it? Isn't that … unsanitary?"

"Hah! Well, it do catch up to you I guess. Bugs and vermin
and such tunneling in and out. So much around here is in the
ground already. What's in the ground is a mystery until you dig
it up, and we don't excavate every inch now do we? Else, where
would we stand?" He laughed a bit too loudly.

All the talk of trash and vermin made Gavin eager to get
back to the house and clean. But on the way out he stopped.
"One more question. All these wonderful stone walls — do you
know anything about them?"

Both of them laughed. "You wouldn't think them so
wonderful," the man said, "if you had to maintain one, or tear
it down. Some take the walls to be fences, but they never were.
In the 1800s it was all farms around here. Before that it was
forest, part of that old forest that once covered everything. So
they cut it all down to make their farms, thinking they'd
civilized it.

"But the soil around here has rocks. Left from the glaciers I
hear. To clear a field you had to carry the rocks to the edge of
your property and stack them. Stack enough of them and you
had yourself a wall. They're about thigh-high because that's
about as far as an average man could lift one of them stones.

"Then come next spring you'd find even more big stones
because the frost heaves them up. It happened every year. Can
you imagine? Folks said the Devil put the stones in the field.

I've heard that the locals, they didn't exactly believe in the Devil, but in something quite like him, not from the bible, but from somewhere else.

"And after all that work the crops never thrived here, least not decent ones. This county has always been terrible for farming—whatever you plant dies quick no matter what you try. No wonder the locals quit farming and went to the cities to work in the factories. The forest came back in and swallowed up them fields, leaving the walls and the old foundations betwixt them."

Gavin began by sweeping up the debris covering the rugs, then vacuuming until their faded designs were plainly visible. He cleared surfaces, tossing out accumulated mail, loose reading material, papers, and any worthless bric-à-brac. He didn't think much about it—he didn't much care. It was his house now and what that dead man valued no longer mattered. He wiped off all the books and the shelves they were on. In the end he had over twenty bags of trash.

He left most of his father's wall décor in place, and the objects on the higher shelves, not because he liked any of it, but because he was reluctant to touch them: odd specimens of taxidermy—all teeth and eyes and matted fur; dozens of dried insects in various stages of development; dusty framed displays of flies, butterflies, and moths; worms and reptiles suspended in yellowing liquid; bones and wings and stretched skins; and jars full of unidentifiable organic materials—animal organs, perhaps, with disintegrated floating bits.

He wouldn't be able to live with such a collection. Was there a market for such sad things? He had no idea how to find out, and at the moment there wasn't time. For now anything he couldn't bear to look at, he draped in a sheet or newspaper.

He carried the trash bags out the back of the house and hid them there. If he did have neighbors he didn't want to offend them. It was his first good look at the backyard, a smooth field of grass leading to the gated wall and the thick woods beyond.

Now and then he thought he heard something. Whatever it was—a sound, or odd change in ear pressure—stopped him in his tracks each time. He never could figure out its nature or its origin.

Gavin worked in the kitchen the rest of the day, washing dish- and cookware, cleaning the floor and cabinets, filling several more bags of trash. When he carried them out back and set them down a vague unease crept in, queasiness in his stomach and chest. Something was different. He gazed at the large stone sitting on top of the grass—a foot high and at least two feet across. More boulder than stone, really. He hadn't noticed it before, but it was right in the line of sight between his back door and the iron Blackburn gate.

Frost heave, the storekeeper had called it. Surely it didn't happen this quickly. He walked over and put his hand on the rough surface—so warm he jerked his hand away. Gingerly he laid his hand back down on the rock and felt a subtle vibration. He looked around—there were no other stones. He pushed against it—it was immovable.

He walked up the slight incline to the gate. The lawyer had not exaggerated—he'd never seen trees so densely packed. Up close their trunks made a giant fence with narrow gaps between. These gaps drew the eye simply because of their scarcity. There was movement between them in several spots— browns and reds and blacks gliding and blurred, animals he supposed, but nothing identifiable.

He went to the gate—it was streaked with rust and slightly ajar, no key necessary. The hinges might be frozen. The wooden BLACKBURN'S FIELD sign was splitting and barely attached, the lettering broken and illegible.

When he touched the iron some distant sound leaked up into his body, making him clench his teeth as if electrified. Teeth bit into him, something raked his side, and he fell to the ground.

Sometime later Gavin climbed to his feet and shuffled gingerly back to the house. He looked at the stone again and was relieved to see there were no others. Back in the house he continued to clean, focusing on that single practical activity to the exclusion of everything else. He approached those filthy glass cabinets in the living room with less trepidation now, throwing them open and curiously examining the objects inside. Most of the items had been destroyed, their contents sprayed on the interior of the glass as if they'd exploded. A handful of pieces remained: tiny twisted figures of twigs and trash and mud like the one the shopkeepers had given him. Each of the figures was unique, the materials used and the twisting of them resulting in a variety of tortured poses. All had mouths of some sort, stained or filled with dark earth, straining to speak the inexpressible.

Gavin didn't retire to his upstairs bedroom until well after midnight. He opened the curtains for a final glimpse of the backyard. The clouds had blown away, leaving the grassy lot visible beneath the full moon. The stone was still there, as dark as the silhouettes of the trees. A light appeared deep within the woods, dancing and flickering, ragged like a burning torch, before going out.

Distant animal cries, growls, and a chorus of mania. Humming and panting and Gavin was awake, staring at the ceiling. Light so bright coming through the windows he imagined at first the house was on fire, and then realized it was simply the day.

Over the next few weeks he didn't venture out, concentrating on making the house more to his liking. Using his cell phone and the cards the shopkeeper gave him, he had groceries delivered and trash hauled away, a few things repaired. Most of the phone numbers were no longer valid, and one of the handymen stopped answering his phone. After some haggling, he found a man to tow away his old automobile at a ridiculous cost. This left him without transportation, but he had nowhere to go. He supposed at some point he would need to seek employment—he would find a car then. He should have been somewhat anxious about being unemployed, but was not.

He removed the coverings from the things he hadn't wanted to see. Most of these he carried from the house, stuffed into black bags for the next trash pickup. A couple he kept as curiosities: a stuffed squirrel either attacking or fleeing, and a Christ-on-the-cross wall hanging similar in style to the small figures, with twisted vines plastered with mud for limbs, a piece of red ceramic apple for a torso. Christ's head was almost entirely mouth, a cavity smeared with black earth and illusory deep.

He carried out several old pieces of decaying furniture and placed them by the bags. If his trash-hauler wouldn't take them perhaps he could make a bonfire. At one point he stopped and surveyed his collection of refuse. Several bags and some furniture appeared to be missing. He looked around and found no other signs of disturbance. He gazed at the stone in the back yard to make sure it was still there and no others had been added.

To the left of the woods was a vista of gentle hills, tall grass, more trees in the distance, what might or might not have been structures, which might or might not have been occupied. A succession of blurry dark figures crossed his field of vision. They might have been animals—perhaps some of them were—but the shapes appeared to be too vertical, so he assumed they were human, strolling across the fields, entering the distant forest, perhaps even passing into the far side of his own walled-in woods. He presumed these were locals, the scarce Disleigh natives, going about whatever business kept them away from the center of town.

Once things were cleaned and the furniture arranged in a manner suiting him, the trash and the discarded belongings hauled away—whether by haulers he'd hired or by folks stealing his refuse really didn't matter—Gavin was content to sit in his new home and read, or meditate, or whatever he supposed a modern day hermit must do.

In the mornings, with the yellow light coming through the vine-veiled windows, he'd find odd insect markings and worm trails in the dust over the floorboards. There shouldn't have been much dust—he cleaned nearly every day now—but still it reappeared with some frequency. Perhaps he wasn't doing it correctly.

He supposed a house could die—he'd seen several of those on his way in to town. And before they died they'd doubtless become sick. Was his house ill? He supposed so.

The next morning Gavin went out for the first time in weeks. He'd ask that nice elderly couple for advice. On the way he stood in front of the building where he'd seen the bald man working, filling his bottles with powder. Peering through the window he could see the place was now empty. Several of the empty bottles lay scattered on the floor.

The couple's shop was also dark, however, the door stripped of its GOING OUT OF BUSINESS sign. Of course—the shop had been close to closing, and Gavin hadn't been back in weeks.

He began to feel an uncontrollable anxiety rising up from his stomach. His hands began to flutter. He'd never experienced a panic attack—was this what one felt like? He walked to the next store front, and the one following, the houses in between, even the structures appearing near collapse, completing the tour of the circle he'd started his first days here and never completed. Why hadn't he checked this town out more thoroughly before moving? He knocked on doors, he shouted, he jerked on every doorknob and handle. The only sounds in Disleigh were the desperate ones he made himself.

Whitby came running around a corner, narrowly avoiding a collision. The man was wide-eyed, even crazier-looking without his hat. "Still here? Still?" he cried, jabbing Gavin's chest with his forefinger. "Sad fool! Sad fool! Sad fool!" he brayed.

Gavin thought it some bizarre rite of self-identification and stepped back to avoid the poking finger. "Where is everyone? Have they all left? Are we here alone?"

Whitby tilted his head. "Sad ... folks only come here to die." He grinned and leapt off the sidewalk onto the cobbled street.

The car was a gray blur which became physical when it punched Whitby just below the hips, tossing his broken shape over the hood and bouncing it messily a good twenty feet behind. Gavin recognized his old Toyota wagon from the missing left rear hubcap and the dents on the driver's side. He didn't get a good look at the driver. Several people were inside the automobile, the windows full of their pale mashed faces and withered hands.

Gavin heard himself wailing for help, but once again it was the only sound in that too-quiet town. Even the noise of his escaping vehicle had been unaccountably drowned.

Knowing there would be no response he still beat on the doors and shouted, yelling until he was too hoarse to make an intelligible word. He walked back to where Whitby had been thrown. A long smear of blood had darkened the stones, but the old man's body was nowhere to be found.

He hid in his house the rest of the day considering if there was any way he could walk out of the town. It was so far, and seemed much too dangerous, and in any case he was too frightened to try. That night Blackburn's Field—his field—was full of fire and distorted voices engaged in asynchronous song. Periodically he would see shadows entering and leaving the woods from its sides, and some through the gate, but the firelight created so much distortion he couldn't be sure. The dark itself appeared to have broken down into a variety of either celebrating or suffering shapes.

Gavin crawled out of bed the next morning with a crushing headache, the bitter stench of smoke permeating the house. He went around opening windows to let some fresh air in, avoiding looking outside, not ready to see what might be waiting.

He knew he should do something, call someone. He'd seen a man die right in front of him. But he had no body to show. He had convinced himself this was a dangerous place, but what real evidence did he have? Whitby's death—as terrible as it was—didn't mean he himself was in danger, but everything he felt told him he was. He had no friends he could ask to come get him. Besides, it seemed hysterical to run away from his home.

That thing Whitby said—folks only come here to die. Certainly Gavin hadn't come here for that. He had plenty of reasons to live—he just hadn't discovered all of them. Whenever he'd felt hopeless he'd always told himself if he died he might miss something wonderful.

After some time he went back into the bedroom and stared out the windows at his backyard, the path to the gate, the woods—Blackburn's Field—beyond.

Threads of dark smoke floated through the blackened trees, dissipating into a grayish cloud above. The iron-gate was wide open, the ground in front of it disturbed.

He lowered his eyes. The giant stone was gone. In its place several ragged cats furiously dug at the ground. One dropped a bit of bloody cadaver from its mouth as if to focus its efforts.

Without any sort of plan, Gavin bounded down the stairs and out the back door. The cats stepped aside as he marched toward the open gate. He paused to glance at where the stone had been—the ground there looked rusty and chewed. He stopped just inside the gate, this time careful not to touch any of its metal parts.

He peered into the first few feet of the woods. There were signs of fire, but nothing severe. If anything, it had reduced the amount of undergrowth to a manageable path. Or perhaps that passage had always been there and he hadn't examined the area enough to know. Smoke had darkened the lower trunks of the trees and blackened the ground, although again, it was possible this ground had always been black.

The wooden BLACKBURN'S FIELD sign lay in pieces. Now he might rename this Gavin's Field without too much consternation from the locals, assuming there were locals left to care.

The wind picked up and blew a fine black mist around him. With it came that odd music he'd been hearing since he'd arrived in Disleigh, like birdsong blended with fragmented human voice, animal grunts and cries, a mixture which somehow sounded both like lament and desperate pleasure. And though it seemed a terrible idea to follow it, it also seemed clearly the right thing to do. He had to know the boundaries of what he'd experienced here in Disleigh, on the possibility it still might be harmless. He focused on that blackened winding path through the dense trees, and followed it.

A scorch line lay low to the ground, but only a foot or so above the vegetation thrived. Lopsided, asymmetrical flowers crowned jagged, ferocious-looking ferns. Patches of a thick, sooty fog clung above the tree roots. A few yards in, a narrow trickle of spring appeared by the path. It moved slowly, thick with rust-colored and greenish debris, as if this area of forest were bleeding.

Gavin came to a tree that appeared to have been blown apart from the inside. Beside it lay some unidentifiable corpse, too small to be human—unless it were a child—mutilated and fed upon by a shimmering blue bird. The bird flew off and the desecrated body began to move. Then Gavin realized it was the insects inside. Beyond this point animal parts were strewn over twenty or so feet of the path. Some appeared to be relatively fresh.

Something crossed the path in front of him covered in insects so thoroughly there was no indication what it might be. The constant crawl of the insects was all that was visible.

A strong wind rose again, blowing a deeper reek of burn down the path. Around him the branches warped and cried. Bits of rubbish fell from the sky. He thought these might be leaves, or clusters of twigs and seeds, but when they landed they were mostly dead birds with the occasional broken bat or large moth.

He saw several odd-looking beetles—swollen and lopsided and of a slick green. Their legs were unusually long, more like spiders' legs than any beetle's he'd ever seen. They scurried around exposed tree roots as twisty as snakes. A long gray worm crawled out from under the roots and wrapped itself around a beetle like a tiny python. The beetle struggled to escape by climbing the tree with the worm stretched out and still attached. The bark suddenly peeled from the tree and flew away. Gavin fell onto his knees. One large piece of bark was still moving. It was a moth the size of a large bird. It started to fly, then fell onto Gavin's forearm. He cried out and jumped to his feet, trying to shake it off. It shed so many scales it appeared to completely disintegrate.

Something drifted in the air between the trees, finer than dust and yet somehow more substantial. Although he couldn't have described it, Gavin found it to be breathtakingly beautiful and attempted to follow it with his eyes. That's when he first saw the people in the woods, moving quietly among the trees in their animal heads and giant insect masks, their mottled skin paint, and attached strips of fur and feathers. They passed by without bothering him, heading in the same direction as he.

In the next spread of woods he found stone rubble scattered throughout, upright blocks isolated in rows like foundation pilings, others stacked or leaning against exposed roots. He thought it might be the remains of a house or other building. But reaching them he saw that they were worn headstones, most of the names faded to illegibility. He recognized the scattered outlines of sunken graves, but most of this ancient cemetery had been obliterated by decades of natural growth. It seemed outrageous so many deaths should leave such an insubstantial trace.

He heard them before he saw them: the grunts and the muted sufferings of human beings forced to do things against their will. At the center of the wood lay an irregular clearing of black, troubled earth. A dozen feet from its center several men and women had been forced to their knees, their hands tied behind them. At the back of each stood one of the figures in insect- or animal-garb.

It took a few moments to assimilate what Gavin was seeing. All of these people were naked, the figures in masks and partial costume naked below their chests, the men and women on the ground wearing nothing at all.

It embarrassed him that he could not look away. It embarrassed him to see his adolescent shame so thoroughly portrayed. He had never been close to a nude woman, had seen few naked men. Even when taking care of his failing mother he had had a female aid to handle the intimate chores.

He'd always felt this lack of experience made him something less than a functioning adult, but he never could imagine how he might repair it.

He recognized one of the bound figures as the lawyer Martinson, who apparently never made it away from Disleigh. The man looked so incongruous, that gray-haired, distinguished-looking face, pressing his legs tightly together to conceal the mortification of his genitalia.

Martinson gazed at him desperately. Something dark and crumbling filled his mouth. With a violent retch he expelled some of it—rich and drooly gobs of dusky mud. He spat furiously. "The locals did everything, but nothing would thrive here. And so, so they accepted it. They embraced it!"

A sudden, blinding pain erased whatever else the lawyer had to say.

From his final vantage-point on the ground, Gavin could see most of his still-living companions, and a few whose suffering had ended. The naked lawyer lay on his side, eyes distended and mouth leaking mud. Across the circle the elderly shopkeeper and his wife kneeled, eyes closed and throats struggling to exorcise the dirt that filled them. A pitiful corpse which might have been Whitby lay closer to the center of the circle, where the black earth churned and rose and fell.

Whitby's body descended into the ground and the ground brought up a large stone as if in replacement.

Gavin imagined this was where his father had ended, where he also soon would end. He wondered if his father's house had been a gift in atonement, or a hateful invitation to suffer a similar fate.

Gavin decided not to struggle when the man-sized insect began feeding the muck into his open mouth. It really wasn't that terrible if he let himself relax and accept what he was being offered. The taste—rich and dark and nourished with death— was not at all unfamiliar.

An Gorta Mór

Jerome turned off the TV having had his fill for the day. He wouldn't watch at all except to gauge the danger. People had become unbelievably cruel, or perhaps they'd always been, and he'd just failed to notice. He needed to secure the house better. No telling when someone might try to force their way inside. He doubted there was much he could do to stop them. He'd never been physically brave, and now a retired old man of seventy he could do little to protect himself.

The ache he felt was difficult to pinpoint. It might be hunger. It might be cancer. He knew sometimes dehydration was mistaken for hunger, so he drank glass after glass of water until he was afraid he might drown. But the ache was still there so maybe it was cancer. He knew sometimes loneliness was mistaken for cancer, but he had no remedy for that.

He should have gone to the doctor early on. Now he was afraid to go where most people went because they were sick.

Jerome picked up a can of "hearty" beef stew off the floor, thinking he might heat it up for dinner. Cans of food were stacked around the living room, stuffed into the corners, leaning against the walls. He'd started ordering extra groceries early, before any of the shortages. He'd filled his cabinets, his closets, and then started stacking cans on the floor.

The picture of the stew on the label didn't look realistic: too bright, too perfectly arranged, nothing like the brown goop he knew would pour out of this can. He wondered when everyone started lying about food and figured it must have been centuries ago. Neither the food on the label nor the food inside the can tempted him. He reminded himself that the food in cans was his emergency stash, to be eaten if the world took a terrible turn. Before that he had to eat all the food in the freezer, and before that he would empty the perishables out of his fridge.

However, none of this food, despite the pervasiveness of his ache, appealed to him. So much of the world had become poisonous. Poison permeated the air he breathed and the food he consumed. He wasn't sure when all this had occurred. He recalled when his mother baked cakes she always let him lick the spoon. Was he being poisoned even then?

A rhythmic noise pounded next door. It was the middle of July and he'd been forced to leave a few windows partly open for air. Along with the pulsing music there was splashing and barking laughter and the stench of burning meat on the outdoor grill, and a faint note of tanning oil on baking bodies underneath. His stomach flirted with an unwelcome sensation which fed an unreasonable anger.

He went to the thick sliding glass door leading to the back patio, but he didn't open it. The trees in his backyard looked thinner than last year, their pale branches stretching for something unobtainable. It was impossible for trees to lose girth, so maybe something was wrong with his eyes. The past few years he'd slipped in and out of Type 2 diabetes, and he hadn't checked his blood sugar in quite a while. So, add his vision to everything else that was deteriorating. He shouldn't drive, but he wasn't driving anyway.

The rest of the yard appeared malnourished, the grass yellowish with tall weeds scattered throughout, and dead vegetation in abundance. His garden shed in the corner was layered in gray vine. The base of the Japanese-style pergola was obscured by tangles of brown brush. Spring seemed late this year, but maybe the problem only existed in his yard. Jerome could see little of the neighbors' lawns from his windows.

He wasn't sure where all the dead plants came from—he had no memory of their green counterparts from previous years. He mused on the possibility of dead plants multiplying, spreading increasing deadness throughout the neighborhood.

Even through the thick glass he heard the party next door. He couldn't see over the fence but imagined all those people in their bathing suits oiled up and pressed together, laughing, talking, and maskless. He didn't understand—they'd had years of drought, but this man—Wingate, first name Jim or Tim, he couldn't remember—had a giant pool full of water. Pool parties during a pandemic. Pandemic soup, although perhaps the disease didn't work that way. He didn't know.

Jerome could do some yardwork: add or subtract plants, weed, trim, spray, whatever real gardeners do. But he'd always hired someone and now he was hesitant to venture outside. The newscasters assured him there was no risk by himself on his own property, but he no longer trusted assurances. No one had the whole picture; anything seemed possible. His life had ground to a halt. He craved transformation, even an awful one.

A scrawny rabbit came out of the high weeds along the back fence, then froze into a piece of taxidermy. Jerome wondered if it sensed some hidden danger. He lived close to a greenway reaching all the way into the foothills, and sometimes foxes, coyotes, racoons, and bears found their way into these tidy suburbs. Once he saw a deer on the front lawn but by the time he got his camera it was gone. He'd heard wild animals in the area became bolder during the lockdown. Perhaps some of them never left.

When one door closes another one opens, as his grandfather used to say. Jerome pretty much stopped eating when Angela left. He didn't know where she was. An old woman choosing to be alone—it made no sense. He started losing weight and the pounds were still coming off. Maybe it was the sadness, or the stress. Or maybe it was cancer. Whatever it was, he saw it as an opportunity for a new self. The pandemic made him want it more. He had nothing better to do.

He backtracked through the narrow pathway between his castles of cans to the stationary bike he'd set up in front of the living room window. Sometimes he opened the curtains in case people thought no one lived there and contemplated a break-in. Today he kept them closed, climbed up, and began furiously peddling. He couldn't remember if a warmup was recommended or not, but he preferred it this way, peddling as if chased, as fast as he was capable, as if all life depended on it. Periodically he took a break for water, and leaned on the handlebars to rest, then he started peddling again, driving through fatigue, driving through exhaustion, continued pumping the peddles even when his vision blurred and filled with dark shadow.

Jerome wasn't satisfied until he reached that sense of distortion at the end of every long ride: his arms elongating until they overlapped the grips in front, his legs thinning out to bone and hoof piercing the floor beneath him.

Once he was done, he rarely felt like eating. But every night he knew he had to try. He went to the refrigerator and surveyed its contents: wilted lettuce and green-spotted cheese, a variety of corrupted vegetables, discolored liquids in old bottles, faded containers he didn't care to open.

Sometimes Jerome clawed through the lettuce to find the unblackened bits and chew on those. Or pick part of the food discoloration hadn't reached. There was usually a jar of peanut butter to stick a finger in, protein bars or crackers in a cupboard, and sometimes Jell-O containers, or chunks of fruit in a clear tub. Jerome continued to lose weight but didn't starve. He wasn't suffering. He was hungry, but then he wasn't hungry, aching with an undefined rawness going deep as bone, and it did not stop no matter what he did. If things got bad enough, he'd start cooking the food in the freezer, and dip into the supply of canned goods. But life hadn't yet reached the apocalyptic stage. He was sure he'd know when it did.

He played with eating and not eating for an hour or so, and like most nights fell into bed exhausted, dreaming he was some desperate animal scavenging through people's back yards, looking for the thing that, once eaten, would heal him.

The next day was burning hot. Despite the heat he was cold most of the morning, finally changing into heavy sweats. Transformation was never easy. Ask any butterfly. He scoured the internet for inspiring images. The figures in James Ensor's *Banquet of the Starved*, feasting on insects and a raw onion. Egon Schiele's emaciated but provocative figures. And An Gorta Mór, The Great Hunger, and the Famine Memorial in Dublin. Years ago, he and Angela had seen that arrangement of emaciated statues staggering towards a new life. Angela had been appalled, but Jerome had seen such nobility in those faces.

It was grocery delivery day and he waited, fiercely pedaling, while staring out the window. He felt some dizziness and had no idea how long he'd been on the bike. Concentration had become an issue in recent weeks, but his fuzziness coupled with gazing outside did provide the illusion he was getting somewhere.

He couldn't remember what he'd ordered: more lettuce, an assortment of Jell-O and grapes, cuts of melon. He may have ordered more canned things. He hoped not. He didn't need more canned things.

When he saw the masked man on his porch, he momentarily panicked. What a perfect cover for a robbery, he thought. He saw the bags on the first step, and the man turning to leave, and Jerome climbed off the bike and headed for the door.

But opening the door he was shocked to find himself face to face with the delivery man, who'd returned with two jugs of purified drinking water. He didn't know what to say. He couldn't make himself nod and shut the door instead.

Embarrassed, Jerome retreated upstairs until he heard the man's car leave his driveway. He put on gloves, went down, and peered outside. Seeing no one he went out on the porch to retrieve the delivery. A sound came from his throat like that of an angry dog. He tried to swallow it but could not. He got the groceries inside and stuffed them into a nearby closet, intending to get to them later.

The music next door was blasting again, drowning out everything else. He wondered if it was meant to disguise the outrageous number of people Wingate had gathered there.

Jerome worked out on the bike until he was unable to move his legs anymore. The ache had spread from his belly into all four limbs. He didn't remember going to bed, but when the next day came, he was lying there in heavy sweats.

Changing into shorts he saw a cut on his leg from three weeks before hadn't healed. He'd fallen off the bike during a particularly vigorous ride, and the two-inch wound still oozed fresh scarlet beads. But he was so impressed by the thinness of his legs—his pale skin hanging off narrow blades of bone—he didn't care. He wrapped it with clean gauze and threw himself into cleaning the upstairs, using exaggerated movements as if performing calisthenics.

He'd disposed of Angela's abandoned belongings months before. Yet there still seemed to be so much of her in every room. They'd never communicated well. He needed space, and time for his reading and other personal activities. When she left, she told him, "Now you'll have all the privacy you want." Her statement had sounded cruel, yet accurate.

After he thought he'd successfully removed all her stuff more Angela debris continued to turn up, contact lens cases and bits of jewelry, buttons and photos and little notes. Once a desiccated flower she'd saved from one of their early dates, wrapped in pale pink tissue with a beautiful violet ribbon.

He'd intentionally kept one of her house plants. He had no idea what kind it was. Not wanting to see it every day, Jerome stuck it in a corner of the unused guest room. Occasionally he'd check its progress as it grew paler, stems elongating and leaves growing further apart as it reached for the window. He was curious how far it would reach, how much it might become unlike itself. Once on an impulse he snatched off a leaf and ate it. It was tasteless as paper.

At a certain time each night his neighbors howled, in celebration of the doctors and nurses, the essential workers, in celebration of themselves and their shared crisis. Jerome did not howl, for fear once he started, he wouldn't be able to stop.

He maintained this routine for weeks: riding the bike, listening to Wingate's parties, riding the bike, retrieving delivered food from his front porch, spotting strange new animals in his back yard, riding the bike, watching himself disappearing in the mirror, his body diminishing, joints expanding, gratefully receiving bone where there had been none before, listening, riding, finding more and more of what Angela left behind.

He did eat occasionally, although he wasn't sure what or when. The ache did not go away but spread and continued to find new forms. He eventually found the groceries he'd stashed in the closet weeks ago, ruined except for the jugs of water, and another can of that unappetizing-looking stew.

Now and then he fell into spells of agitation, tasting each of his shoes until he found the best one, chewing and consuming bits of his fingernails, biting his lips and the insides of his cheeks, calmed by the saltiness of his own blood.

Once he spent several days seeking out and calling old acquaintances, ostensibly to check on how they were doing during all this disruption, when in fact he was making a final attempt at reconnection. When Phyllis, a woman he'd worked with years ago, said "You sound as if you need a hug," he burst into tears, hung up, and blocked her calls.

At some point he stopped wearing shoes. He didn't remember making this decision, there just came a time when neither shoes or socks seemed useful to him. He also stopped cleaning the house for much the same reason. What was a house but a nest, a place of safety and rest, and as his house became more nest-like, a spreading pile of broken furniture, ripped apart floorboards, and unrecognizable wreckage, he eventually discarded clothes entirely.

Jerome still suffered from the cold, from an all-consuming ache and a fever that rendered his eyes into two, deep-burning pits. His body felt narrow, compact, and for the first time in years, containable.

In the meantime, Wingate continued his celebratory, negligent, partying ways. His neighbor was relatively young, and Jerome recalled the man had had some sort of job. At least he'd left every morning in a suit and tie carrying his briefcase. He must have lost his position during this calamity as had so many others. Certainly, this was the likely explanation. And now he was wasting all his remaining funds on these parties in a countdown to doomsday.

Today, however, the music had been soft and slow, almost mournful, and not unpleasant to hear. Had someone died? But of course, they had. These days someone was always dying, and most likely someone you knew.

Jerome began swaying to the music. He had made no decision to participate, but his body ruled things now, and wanted to sway. The raw points of his legs pierced what remained of the floor, bone sliding into planks then lifting, the wood splintering, and then the legs coming down with deliberation. He wrapped his arms around himself and continued this tortured ballet, unable to manage this only a few months ago—with a body too thick, and arms that wouldn't have reached. His hands began caressing his back. He'd seen a comedian on TV do this once as a joke. The audience thought it was hilarious. But it was comforting. He had a sense of how much weight he'd lost because of all the places his hands could now reach. They were phantoms fluttering across his back, fingers infiltrating the hair line and playing with the curls. Although long and thin on top, his hair felt strangely thick near the base, like a dog's coat, like fur. He gave himself a squeeze, and then another one. He couldn't remember the last time anyone else had held him.

But the soft music ended abruptly, the melody cruelly cut, and that rhythmic pounding he'd endured for months exploded into full volume. Jerome felt his enormous head fall back, the weight of it almost pulling him over. His mouth yawned open into a wounded animal's scream and he charged the patio door, knocking it shattered into the backyard.

He stopped, confused. How long had it been since he'd looked back here? The back fence was hidden by a wall of tall weeds and scraggly trash trees. One end of the pergola had collapsed, and gray moss had crept into the wrecked timbers. The corner garden shed was gone. In its place three coyotes peered from a swirl of shredded brush. Other creatures were semi-hidden under bushes and edging from shadows, but none brave enough to approach what he'd become.

Jerome heard Wingate's high, intoxicated laughter abruptly floating above the music. He snapped his head left, took two impossible steps, and soared to the top of the fence. He teetered there, sharp hooves dug into the fence's horizontal wooden supports, and glared down at the glistening, aromatic, semi-naked bodies. Wingate gawked up at his giant form and dropped his drink. Jerome couldn't remember the last time he'd spoken to his neighbor, didn't know if the man even knew his name. He hoped Wingate fully appreciated the breadth and the volume of Jerome's new head.

"Jerome?" So perhaps Wingate knew him after all.

When he made his great leap, he still wasn't sure if he was reaching for murder, or an embrace.

BLACK WINGS

Sheila was upset by the sudden arrival of a new bush in her backyard one late afternoon, an unidentifiable perennial apparently so deeply green it appeared black in the waning light. She had purchased no such bush. It did not fit into her landscaping design. Had some practical joker planted it in the middle of the night? She rarely understood other people's notions of humor. She had spent a great deal of her late husband's insurance benefit on landscaping and had no intention of seeing it spoiled.

But the bush shook off its bushiness and opened its wings. Now she gazed at a large black bird, perhaps the largest she had ever seen. Harry would have known the species, and no doubt could have recited a page full of boring facts concerning its anatomy, and passably charming anecdotes regarding its talents and peculiarities. She assumed it was too large to be a blackbird. She had no idea what the difference was between a crow and a raven, except ravens were a bit more important weren't they? Ravens were famously in residence at the Tower of London and figured prominently in that spooky poem by Poe, so she imagined them larger and more regal than crows.

Sheila wanted to say it was a raven, but this bird—she couldn't quite put her finger on it—had a stupid and clumsy look. This awkward-looking birdie did not project any sort of regality. So probably not a raven, but she'd always heard crows were clever. This bird didn't look clever at all. Perhaps she had discovered a new species? Wouldn't Harry have been so jealous? Discovering a new species would have been his dream.

Despite her late husband's obsession, Sheila knew almost nothing about the habits of birds. Class Aves, she did know that much, because it was a term Harry used all the time. She tried to pay no attention while he prattled on about his bird friends, but that tiny factoid had wormed its way in. Birds ate worms, disgusting creatures.

She watched the fowl as it hopped about the yard. She supposed it was approximately the size of a big chicken. Were there black chickens? Every time it paused it did its business and moved on, finding new spots to contaminate. This was only one of the ways birds spread contagion. She'd always been afraid Harry's specimens would someday give her some terrible disease. A few days after his death she hired a company to remove the filthy wings and heads and stuffed corpses from cabinets and drawers throughout the house and disinfect everything. They'd worn hazmat suits, which for her was absolute confirmation she'd been in danger living among Harry's collections all these years.

Unwilling to watch, she'd moved briefly into a hotel. As far as she could tell they'd done a thorough job, although tufts of feather still appeared among the balls of dust in corners and under furniture.

Now, after all the expense, she had an active source of more such contamination wandering her property. She'd witnessed birds pecking at dead animals (including their own kind) and scraping about among the spoiled and rotten. She wondered if she would ever feel safe in her own backyard again. She closed the curtains over the patio doors, wondering if the same company she hired before could also rid her of living creatures. If not, she wondered if a surprise blow from a fireplace poker might kill it.

With Harry's collections gone the house was slowly morphing into some semblance of what Sheila always imagined it could be. Where large wall displays of amputated birds' wings once hung were framed mountain landscapes and floral wall hangings. In the dining room, where she'd struggled to digest her food beneath a forbidding arrangement of beaked onlookers, she now dined in serenity within freshly painted walls.

She still imagined she smelled those feathered vermin, even though the professionals swore they'd removed every bit. Despite Harry's protestations there had always been a stench of death and decay and negligence. But she couldn't expect to have survived marriage to such a man without some lingering birdish stench.

She went to the calendar hanging on the new refrigerator. The previous model hadn't been more than a few years old, but despite her threats some of Harry's specimens always seemed to find their way inside. It was always safer to replace rather than clean. She had a hectic week planned, lunch with some of the girls tomorrow, a movie with Janice the day after, and the bridge club at her house on Friday. Company had been rare during her married years. She'd been too ashamed, not only because of the condition of her home, but also Harry's insistence on sharing endless avian lectures with their hapless guests. Now she welcomed visitors at every opportunity.

Sheila forgot about the bird for a time. Out of sight and all. She was far too busy. Life was to be enjoyed. She'd always told Harry that, but he was too distracted by his collections. They'd never gone anywhere together. They'd never done anything as a couple after the courtship was completed. Harry knew far more about the mating habits of birds than he did the romantic requirements of his own wife.

Friday she was setting up the house for her bridge club, vacuuming the rugs, dusting the surfaces, preparing plates of gorgeously composed mini sandwiches. Still self-conscious about the scent of things, she'd perhaps sprayed a bit too much room deodorizer. The air smelled of perfume. She opened the curtains thinking she'd crack the patio doors and let some of the perfumed air drift outside.

The black bird stared up at her from the other side of the glass. In such proximity it was even larger than she'd thought, more the size of a dog than a large chicken. It was difficult to say with all the plumage. Its feathers rose and fell as if it were a giant, beating black heart. She embarrassed herself by making a little squawk of panic. The bird itself said nothing and made a little hop.

It turned its head sideways as if to examine her from a different angle. The bird still projected an aura of ignorance, its small dark eyes too close together, its beak appearing broken and poorly repaired. Sheila was relieved she'd noticed it before sliding the door open. What a nightmare if it found its way inside.

She needed to rush to get the house ready in time. The bird hopped away in a disorganized fashion, and she couldn't stop herself from watching as it fell over and then righted itself, falling over again and then spreading its wings as if to take off from its recumbent position, but remaining flightless it appeared it could only lie there and flap its wings vigorously, spreading bits of feather and birdy dander all over her curated patio and yard. Sheila wondered if its body had grown too large for its brain to maneuver properly.

She shut the curtains and hoped none of the ladies asked to see the backyard. Her bridge friends arrived shortly thereafter. They all had nice things to say about what she'd done to the house, but Sheila understood from experience such compliments meant little. She watched their faces. Paula Hershfield kept wrinkling her nose. Either she was fighting off a sneeze or she smelled something unappealing. Sheila might have asked Janice if she smelled anything—in fact she probably would—but Janice was her best friend (or at least pretended to be) and couldn't be relied on for an honest answer.

"Sheila, I just wanted to, once again, extend my condolences. Has it been too hard? How long were you and Harry married? He was an engineer, wasn't he, good with his hands?"

Marie Willis knitted her eyebrows and smiled so aggressively it must have caused her considerable facial pain, clear evidence her sympathy was feigned. Sheila didn't want to answer the other questions, so she replied, "He taught science at the local high school." Embarrassing, but she had no desire to embellish Harry's few accomplishments.

"Oh. Well, I'm sure his students must miss him. I feel for you. I don't know what I'd do without my James." Rumor had it the Willises' marriage had been in trouble for years. Perhaps Sheila would mail Marie a sympathy card tomorrow.

None of the women were good at bridge. Half of them were borderline dreadful, but the purpose of these gatherings was primarily to share gossip, devour unhealthy snacks, and provide the host with an opportunity to impress. Due to Harry's failings this was Sheila's first time hosting. She cared about the day more than she wanted to.

There was a knocking sound on the sliding glass door. Janice looked at her but said nothing. Several minutes passed and then there was a rapid knock-knock-knock. The glass was thick and double-paned, but Sheila still feared it might break beneath the persistent blows.

"Sheila, I think someone's knocking on your back door." Marie looked at her with a forced smile. Sheila didn't know why—maybe it was the only way the woman knew how to express herself.

"Pay no attention, ladies. There's construction two houses behind us. Sometimes the vibrations feel as if they're right outside, hammering, or whatever it is they do."

The women looked doubtful. A few seemed too focused on their cards. Several minutes passed and then a succession of heavy impacts shook the glass door. "It sounds like—I don't know, Sheila. Is someone throwing things at your house?" Janice stood up and ran to the curtain. Marie tittered. Sheila stood up to stop Janice, but she was too late. The curtains slid open with an obnoxious scraping noise.

No bird was in evidence. But a small oval on the outside of the glass appeared caked in tomato purée, the multiple red blotches beneath imprinted with feather-like patterns.

Sheila refused any help cleaning up after the gathering, although Janice was the only one who offered. Sheila insisted nothing was wrong but ushered the women out as quickly as possible. Janice gave her a fierce goodbye hug. This made Sheila intensely uncomfortable, but she appreciated the gesture.

She had not slept well the night before, and the afternoon's excitement took its toll. Further cleanup could wait until the next day. She went to bed almost, but not quite, feeling sorry for herself. She had made great improvements to her home, and yet something felt vaguely incorrect. She might have to hire a consultant to tell her what it was.

Sheila was outside spraying water on the glass doors when she heard the commotion behind her. She turned around, the hose still in her hand. Momentarily distracted from the frenetic activity just beyond her gaze, she watched the water slip over the patio stones, ridding them of any trace of debris. The activity was both wasteful and gratifying.

She dropped the hose. Her backyard was full of birds. More black ones, much smaller than the one she'd come to think of, proprietarily, as her own, but what they lacked in size they made up for in numbers. Also, gray ones, pigeons, she supposed. Also, blue ones and red ones. She didn't know the names. She was no Harry. She supposed there were cardinals, blue jays, grackles—those were names she recognized as being common to this area, not that she could be sure they were among the specific ones pecking and eating and making dirty everywhere.

She spied her bird in the middle, the dumb one. Some of the others appeared to avoid it, but there was some bullying, with birds pecking at its feet or squawking at it, stealing food right out of its mouth. It didn't make a sound. Today it wore a small dark-red, almost brownish cap. She couldn't tell how the cap was attached, then realized it was the caked-on blood from the day before.

Harry once told her crows could make tools like hooks and poky things for grabbing food. So, her bird could not possibly be a crow. Her bird did not defend itself, but at least it didn't cower. Being a pitiful creature was bad enough, but to see it cowering would have been unbearable.

"Go on, Mister Bird, fight back," she said, raising her voice almost to a shout. "Stand up for yourself. Don't let these small minds defeat you! They're beneath you!"

There was no response, not from her bird or from any of the others. She picked up the hose and without thinking began spraying all those other birds, avoiding her own. They disappeared as if washed away. If only all life's problems were so quickly solved. Her bird sat there, unmoving. She turned off the hose and went back inside.

Sheila spent the rest of the day getting the house back to its pre-bridge club condition. Her friends had left a mess. Crumbs on the floor were already attracting ants. They appeared as fast as she could vacuum them up. Clearly having guests over wasn't going to work for her.

She was coming around the kitchen island, broom in hand, when she encountered the bird. Her bird.

She glanced at the patio door off the living room. It was still closed. She was sure no other windows or doors were open. Dark muddy drips spread from the bird across the surrounding pale pink linoleum. It made her furious, although she was the one who had created the mud with her hose. The mud was her doing.

"Shoo!" She approached the bird with the broom in a shoveling motion. "Shoo!" She came up right to it. It was looking at her. She could see its dark shiny eyes. But it did not budge.

Where did she want to shoo it to anyway? It was oozing mud. Her bird and her mud. She couldn't bear the thought of either getting onto her nice things.

"So, what do you want from me?" she asked. "What is it you want me to do?"

The bird stared at the floor, no longer looking at her. She backed away and left the kitchen, closing the door firmly behind her. She would go to her bedroom and lie down, and then call Animal Control, or that cleaning company. Or maybe she'd call them before lying down. She could leave the front door unlocked, and they could just come in while she was sleeping. She would leave a note. By the time she woke up the bird would be gone.

She trotted up the stairs and hurried down the long open gallery toward her bedroom. Harry had kept many of his display cabinets full of his butchered birds up here in the gallery. Not content to use up all the wall space, he'd arranged them on the other side as well, blocking the balustrade and the view below. That thing he called himself, a "cabinet naturalist," he said it was on old term. He loved his old terms, his old jokes, his old dead birds. He could have loved his old wife more.

She wanted to put up some nice pictures on the walls but had not yet decided which ones. Creating the right ambiance was essential. She opened the bedroom door. Her dirty bird was perched on her best bedspread, waiting.

Harry would have known what to do in such a situation. Harry was a fool who had no idea how to be a husband, but he understood his birds.

She turned around and headed back toward the stairs. She felt ill, so she stopped and held onto the railing. Below her she could see the top of the chandelier. It was filthy—how was she supposed to clean such a thing? Keeping this house presentable seemed impossible. Below the chandelier was the bright and shiny entrance way, and the front door. Perhaps it was time to check into a hotel again and let someone else solve her problems while she was away. That's what civilized people did. Civilized people with money, which she probably wasn't anymore.

She made her way to the top of the stairs. Harry had been too old to manage the repairs to this big house, or even to maintain the vast collection he loved so much. Too old and too weak. That day he decided to bring a cabinet up from downstairs and into their bedroom. "It'll be lovely," he'd said. "These are all birds in flight, my best specimens. Can you imagine waking up every morning to birds in flight? How beautiful that would be!"

The cabinet had been a gorgeous cherry. At least that much had been true. But it had been so large and unwieldly. He should have hired someone. He never allowed anyone to help.

He'd struggled up the stairs, the weight of it pushing him back. He'd reached the second tread from the top when the cabinet began to tip. "Help," he said, with no force at all, as if he'd realized his mistake and already given up.

She'd been so disgusted by the whole affair. He hadn't even asked her opinion or what she wanted. She'd laid her magazine aside and gotten up from her chair where she'd been watching from outside the bedroom—she never did finish that article— and walked to the stairs facing him. "What do you want me to do?" she'd asked, but instead of waiting for an answer she'd placed her hand on the lovely cabinet. She'd had no intention of making things more difficult for either of them, but gravity took over, and gravity cannot be bargained with.

The way he'd tumbled, she did not know a human being could move like that, and the image of him on the floor below, crash landed with broken glass, shattered wood, and disintegrated birds—she'd laughed at the sight of him. It embarrassed her terribly. There was surprise in it, and grief, yes, grief. And she hadn't laughed in years.

Sheila took a step down, and her bird—all hers, it was too late to get rid of it now, and too late to stop—was right beneath her shoe. When gravity came for her, she was thinking how stubborn the dirty thing was—it still refused to make a sound, even as its black wings beat about her face and neck.

As she lay there on the floor thinking about the mess she'd made something unexpected came over her, and she heard herself making this awful sound with notes of both despair and defiance while she flapped her broken arms.

BAGS

Hank's father insisted he take the waste out after dark because he was embarrassed. That's what he called it: the garbage and the trash and the miscellanea, everything he'd kept too long and now was keen to dispose of. The man had lived life poorly and this was the visible evidence. But it made no difference. In the morning, the bags and the boxes would be sitting in the alley for the entire world to witness.

Hank hated carrying these discards out at night. Their floodlight had shorted out years ago, so he only had the moon and the arc lamp above a distant street corner to guide him. Deep shadow made him uneasy. Anyone might be watching.

He was halfway through the back yard with the last bloated bags when he stopped, thinking he heard his father call him. A weather front was coming in. It sounded like distant applause.

He turned and stared at the back of the house. He'd hauled a wealth of junk from this small, unimpressive mid-thirties bungalow. You buy, you throw away, and then you buy some more. The "regurgitating economy," Dad called it. Dad was as bad as everyone else in this regard, but at least he recognized the problem. Hank heard him coughing in the dining room. He waited for any choking sounds but hearing none decided he needn't rush.

The dark squares of window screen bulged, the porch stuffed with Dad's belongings staged for disposal or donation, the old man didn't care which. Dad said he wanted to throw away everything before he died so Hank might have a fresh start. This might have been true, and Hank didn't want Dad's shabby things, but the mania with which he'd purged himself of possessions this past year was scary.

The silhouette of the house was humped, the roof altered during his grandfather's time to add an attic room. The amateur remodel resulted in leaks, which had been causing damage for decades. How could he get a fresh start in something so ruined?

His arms began to tremble. One bag dripped as if perspiring. It felt awful brushing against his bare legs. He reeled off balance toward the alley. The area along their fence was already crowded with bags and spoiled bedding, junk-filled cartons and a few pieces of furniture in such poor shape the thrift stores wouldn't take them. A scavenger would grab what the trash service didn't haul away.

His father wanted all this material expunged, he didn't care how, but he didn't want to hear any details about thrift stores or junk men or pickers or recyclers. More than once, he'd referred to them as ghouls.

The front was cold and punishing when it arrived. The plastic bags made a rapid snapping sound in the wind. Dad never bought good bags. He never bought good anything. Hank was ashamed—it was an uncharitable thought about a dying old man who loved him.

Their neighbors' unsecured trash cans rolled down the sloping alley and gathered in the street below. They'd be blocks away by morning. Hank would have gone after them, but he couldn't leave his dad alone for long. He noticed an unfamiliar black pickup truck tucked away beneath the trees near the street. It was an aged model, so battered he couldn't be positive about the brand.

An unusually lean figure slipped from the shadows by the truck and entered the street, picked up each trash can with ease and peered inside, tossing them away as if they weighed nothing.

The sight disturbed him but he could not look away. Trash pickers had always worked this neighborhood, scavenging items they could use, repair, or sell, but they came early in the morning before the garbage trucks ran. Hank knew many, and sometimes waited with coffee and an offer to help load their trucks. He had never seen one working the alley at night.

The dark figure picked up another can, hovered over it, then paused, and Hank could have sworn it grew taller, and broader, its head expanding to fill the opening. It tilted its head back and lifted the can, upending it as if to drink the contents. All at once the slim silhouette grew fuller, its torso swelling so quickly it drunkenly staggered back.

The murky apparition twirled around and shuffled toward the truck. Hank's insides went liquid.

Hank's perceptions were unreliable. It was dark and he was stressed—Dad was dying. Yet he couldn't bear the thought of this creature looking at him. The wind intensified, pulling at his clothes. A nearby tree bent over crazily. He grabbed the stretchy cords attached to the chain link fence and tried to secure the bags he'd just brought out beside the others. He didn't know what was in them—his father had filled them a few months ago before this last illness. The older bags were more gray than black, layered in dust and the openings secured with those old-fashioned wire twisty ties. One bag split under the cord and something sour dribbled from the wound and down the taut skin. Dad would hate that, but he would never know.

The moment Hank entered the house he heard his dad talking. "Did you get all the bags of smelly garbage? Make sure you got them all!" His father's voice turned harsh and wheezy when he was anxious. These days he was anxious most of the time. That was okay. It showed he was still engaged.

"It's okay Dad! I got them all!" Hank hated raising his voice.

"Then why does the house still smell like garbage?"

He didn't want to tell him he was smelling his own recurring stink. He hurried down the hall, dodging wobbly stacks of boxes overflowing with mess. There was something deeply unpleasant about brushing against dry cardboard. He had no time to process the disturbing whispers which resulted. "You've got to give it some time, Dad," said loudly to drown out the unidentifiable muttering. "I just now took them out."

Our bodies are three-fourths water, our slipcases of skin little better than leaking bags. This was painfully true in his father's case. The elderly man, lying shirtless on a rented hospital bed in the dining room, dripped, oozed, and sweated. Hank had moved in a TV for him, a bedside table full of books and magazines which had so far been ignored, framed photos of family members which his father also ignored, but insisted they be where he could see them just the same.

No eating took place in this dining room. Food smells made his father ill. His dad derived nourishment from a creamy liquid in a hanging bag via a tube plunged into his chest. Another tube delivered medicine into the back of his hand. Chemo had rendered him mostly bald, leaving a few thin strokes, a dream of hair. Pale lids capped sunken eyes. If they hadn't just been talking, Hank would have thought him asleep.

They'd sold the dining room furnishings: the good dining set, a couple of antique sideboards. Their absence left a large, tattered hole in the faded rug showing extensive floor damage. Dark spots speckled the boards, mildew, or black mold he supposed, but he didn't know the difference, nor did he want to. He could cover it with another rug.

His father opened his eyes. They moved around, pale and filmy. Hank wondered how much he could see. Dad refused to wear glasses anymore.

The darkness outside the window changed. Hank stared, waiting for movement, looking for a face or figure, something, but could not find them.

"What took you so long anyway?"

"It's dark. I was trying to be careful. Remember, there's no light out there."

Dad grunted. "How's the bag?"

Hank glanced at the feeding bag on the pole. "At least a third full. You're not feeling hungry, are you?"

His father snorted. "If I were hungry, I wouldn't need that thing. The piss bag, Hank."

Hank lifted the sheet hanging off the side of the bed and examined the drainage bag attached to the frame. "I'll need to empty it in a while."

"Is Sue coming over tonight?"

"Not tonight." Hank paused. "I think she has other plans."

"You don't know for sure? Call her. Invite her over. But make sure you dump the bag before she gets here. Remember to pull my sheet up too. She seems to think she has to say hello every time she comes over, and I don't want to scare her away with this big gross belly."

"I don't think she cares, Dad. But I will, if she comes over, but I really don't think she is." The abdomen looked painful, swollen like a tick, decorated with stretched and distorted surgical scars. His dad had spread thick cream all over it with his free hand, partly for comfort, but mainly because he was afraid of insect bites. He'd developed a terror of insects crawling or landing on him. A half-dozen nasty yellow sticky fly strips hung from the dining room ceiling, each jeweled with insect carcasses. Whenever the nurses visited, they complained about these strips, and how the cream got all over the IV tubing and the bandages, but Dad refused any changes to his self-prescribed precautions.

I will not end up this way, Hank thought, and immediately felt disrespectful. He'd die before he reached Dad's age. He wasn't that healthy.

"You make the appointment for the belly tap?"

"It's Thursday afternoon."

"You couldn't get me in sooner? I feel like I'm going to burst."

"I know it's uncomfortable, but that's the soonest I could get an appointment."

His father grunted and closed his eyes again. Ever since his last stay in the hospital he kept his eyes closed most of the time, in embarrassment, or so he couldn't see what was happening to him, answering the doctors' or the nurses' intimate questions with mumbles and head movements.

"You two should get married you know," Dad said, eyes still closed. "Don't make my mistake."

"Maybe Mom was always going to leave. People do that."

"I didn't pay her enough attention. I was too busy with my own projects. Now those projects are in trash bags, and I haven't seen her in years. I'm sorry I did that to you."

"She could have called me or written. I'm her only child. She didn't. I know nothing about her. You stayed, Dad."

"Don't wait until I'm gone. Don't screw this up." Hank knew he was a disappointment. The fact he'd become Dad's caretaker was proof Hank had nothing better to do.

His dad raised his head and stared as if he'd been struck. "You have to lock down this relationship now, while you still look halfway decent. Trust me, you don't want to grow old alone." He fell back onto the pillow and closed his eyes. "Make sure the doors are locked," he whispered. "If somebody tries to break in—"

"Nobody's breaking in, Dad." But Hank was no longer sure.

"I said if. I can't stop them. People see stuff coming out of here, they might think we have something worth taking. How's it going with the back room?"

The back room was the biggest room in the house, packed wall-to-wall with furniture, trunks overflowing with his mother's belongings, projects his dad abandoned. Hank had no idea what most of it was, just that it had filled the room thirty years or more with an inaccessible, impenetrable accumulation.

"I think I found a junk dealer who'll take it all, maybe even pay you a little for it."

"I don't want to know the details. I don't want to watch— have them come through the back door. I can't be thinking about strangers pawing over my stuff. But that's good. It'll make a nice size bedroom for you two. Sue will have an empty house to make her own. She won't say no to marriage if you can offer her this house without me in it."

Hank didn't reply. There was no point. He watched a mayfly land on his dad's belly and struggle in the ointment, stuck fast. He grabbed a tissue and snatched the bug, leaning over and kissing Dad on the forehead to disguise what he was doing. His dad's eyes sprang open in confusion.

"Goodnight, Dad." The eyes moved around as if searching for something, then closed again.

At some point he would have to tell him that he and Sue broke up weeks ago. If his dad died before then it would save them both a painful conversation, but he wanted his dad to live as long as possible. Hank just didn't want to see the disappointment in his face.

With surprising strength Dad grabbed him by the back of the neck and pulled him within inches of his mouth. "Keep the ones you love close," he whispered hoarsely. "They're all you have in the end. To the rest of the world, you're food."

Trips to the hospital meant unhooking everything and getting him into sweatpants and a shirt, sitting him up on the edge of the bed, and a short but difficult transfer into the wheelchair. Dad struggled to help but he had little strength left.

He was slippery. His dad was always wet. The massive belly made a sloshing sound and the shift in gravity made the move tough to control. Hank hadn't dropped him yet, but he was afraid every time.

The hospital admitted them through the emergency entrance and provided a bed in an alcove some distance from the other patients. Dad wasn't happy about it. He said going through those Emergency doors made him feel like he was dying. Hank did not remind him that he was.

Hank didn't want to watch, but Dad said he needed him there. They sat Hank in a heavy steel chair a couple of yards from the plastic paracentesis canisters. The clinicians needed at least five for his dad, but several more were ready if needed. Hank always turned away as the large needle went into his dad's belly but felt a morbid fascination as he witnessed canister after canister fill with the straw-colored liquid. This fluid would be analyzed but they already knew it was full of cancer cells.

It was called ascites fluid, and despite the fancy containers it was biomedical waste and had to be eliminated. Hank had no idea how they did it; he assumed they couldn't put it out with the regular garbage.

He was surprised the belly didn't shrink more given the amount they drained. Dad contained an endless supply. With each visit Hank felt a little sorrier for the old man.

An observation window stretched behind the surgical table, with doors opening and closing as workers moved carts and gurneys around, removing canisters and other materials and bringing in fresh supplies. Hank didn't pay much attention until a towering figure in dingy, stained scrubs wheeled in a filthy metal cart. He was alarmed such an unclean presence might be permitted in a hospital. The individual wore a voluminous surgical cap and a duckbill mask so Hank couldn't see the face. This masked worker bent awkwardly as if its waistline were misplaced. It slinked around the room examining the equipment as if unfamiliar with the environment.

The figure lifted a canister full of ascites fluid, sniffed it, and held it up to the overhead lights. Hank was so convinced it was going to take a sip he turned away and shuddered. He stood up to warn the clinicians. One turned and said, "Sir! You need to sit down!" Hank pointed at the window, but the area behind the window was empty.

Trips to the hospital exhausted Dad and he slept for hours afterwards. Hank took advantage and made arrangements in advance with a local junk dealer, who arrived with two trucks and a crew. Hank closed the multi-paned French doors to the dining room and the workers carried bags, boxes, and loose items from the back room out both the front and back doors. Some were curious and stared through the glass doors at his dad and the festooned tubing. Some neighbors gathered outside to watch. Hank paid attention to what was coming from the back room; much he couldn't remember having seen before. He supposed the day provided entertainment for everyone.

Some big men worked on the junk man's crew, broad men, and tall men, one so incredibly tall and of such unlikely strength Hank felt compelled to follow him around. They all wore dust masks. Maybe Hank should have been wearing a mask every day while living in this house.

He supposed he should ask them to slow down and let him peek into those containers. There might be some valuable objects leaving their home. But the goal was to get rid of it all, and his dad wasn't going to sleep forever. Besides, downsizing and making space felt as if Hank were accomplishing something.

He vaguely recognized his mother's hats and dresses, a favorite painting, a jewelry box, a vase. There were cartons full of correspondence—some might be letters from his mother—he didn't know. Heavy furniture requiring four men to carry, water-damaged antiques good for nothing but firewood. Bags of art supplies from when his dad wanted to be a painter. But if there had been paintings Hank never saw them. Bags of jottings and notebooks from when his dad wanted to be a writer, but as far as Hank knew he'd never finished anything. He felt some regret, but he wasn't going to stop them. Better to be done with the job and have all this gone.

When they finished the junk man gave him a small check. Hank didn't feel cheated. Clearing the room had been the goal. It was what his dad wanted. The junk man said, angrily it seemed, "There's something I want to show you," and walked back into the room. Hank followed.

With the room emptied he was alarmed by the scars and cracks in walls and woodwork. He knew something was odd the moment he walked in. He felt a slope in the floor, and it bewildered him, as if he'd strolled into a funhouse. A shuddering sensation passed through his feet as he tried to find some balance.

"You can feel the instability, right?" the man said. "Look over here at the baseboard." At least a three-inch gap yawned between the baseboard and the floor along one wall. The junk man walked toward the far corner but stopped well short. "It's worse over here. I came close to pulling my people out. Do you have a wet basement by any chance?"

"Sometimes." Seepage had ruined everything in the basement more than a few times over the years. He rarely went down there due to the stench.

"I'm guessing you have a few rotted posts. You need to get an engineer in here; this house might not even be safe to live in. I've seen it before—the skin of the house is intact, but the bones are gone. The hoard filling this room might have been the only thing holding the house up."

Hank wouldn't be calling anyone. There was no money for it. It was hard to believe in upcoming catastrophes beyond the disaster which was already here. He couldn't see the point in worrying his dad further, who still slept soundly. He should check on him, he thought, but what could he do if there was something wrong? Things were already as wrong as possible for his father. Hank retreated to his own bedroom to lie down and think.

Unlike the rest of the house, Hank's room was a study in minimalism, open and clutter free. Forced to live with the tangle of his father's possessions made him intolerant of mess in his own space. The ability to stretch out and roll around on the floor like a child, staring at the ceiling and imagining stars, was priceless.

Today he could see the cracks spreading through that firmament, and where the corners and door and window frames misaligned. He'd stared at those surfaces countless times before, seeing what he'd wanted to see.

He heard footsteps in the hall and for a brief, impossible moment thought Dad might be up and looking for him. He opened the door and saw through the French doors a towering figure in faded scrubs leaning over Dad's bed. Visiting nurses sent by the care service had come into the house unannounced before, but Hank still considered it unacceptable. The nurse turned, but due to some distortion in the glass panes she or he had no profile. "I'll be right with you," Hank said. He went back into the bedroom to change clothes.

Slipping into fresh jeans he kicked over the pillowcase holding some clothing and other things Sue had left behind, spilling them everywhere. He didn't know if she wanted them, but he couldn't bring himself to throw them out with the trash. He scrambled to gather them back into the case.

He'd never seen a person as tall as today's nurse. He or she was new. These services had a tough time keeping personnel. He hoped this one had been properly vetted.

Hank rushed from the bedroom. The nurse was no longer in view. He jerked open the doors and ran to his father, who lay crumpled to one side, small and deflated within his over-abundant skin.

As strange as his father's last moments had been, Hank found it even stranger how quickly a life is wrapped up, packaged neatly, and the process of erasure begins. Everything had been prepaid. As per Dad's instructions he called the funeral home and two young men looking uncomfortable in their old-fashioned black suits came to pick up the body. Another phone call to the medical supplier resulted in the removal of all rented medical equipment within the day. A week later a man delivered the ashes in a burgundy-colored plastic container slightly bigger than a cigar box. Everything his father had been weighed less than five pounds in Hank's hands. The awkward gentleman unhelpfully explained the cremains were bone fragments processed down to resemble ashes.

Hank had no idea what to do with these ashes or bones or whatever they were. He had an unreasonable fear of accidentally throwing them away with the remaining trash.

He spent the next week hauling everything left out to the alley and the fence. The city service wouldn't take it all and he wondered if he might be fined. The pickers would be grateful for the bonanza. He worked all day every day with short breaks, stopping in early evening because he didn't want to be out there at night. Without his father to goad him the timetable was his own.

On what he planned to be the final cleanout day he ran late. It was past twilight, and the shadows flowed in. He kept thinking how relieved he would be when the job was finished. He had the last items in the back yard, boxes of housewares, and bag after bag of miscellanea, mostly those bags Dad filled ages ago.

He could barely distinguish one rough shape from another. The backyard was almost full, and he couldn't imagine how he was going to manage it all.

A tumult erupted from the alley, cats screeching and dogs barking, heavy movements in the gravel between the alley pavement and their yard. He was hesitant to walk out there, but eager to be done with this final chore.

It began to rain. The soft beginnings of it, landing on the bags, sounded like beating moth wings, of which he'd seen many when dragging stuff from the rooms. A rapid metallic tapping began, and Hank turned around and looked at the house, the rain hitting the metal flashing and the gutters, pouring off the sides because they hadn't been cleaned out in years, leaves and twigs and fragmented roof shingles clogging the openings into the downspouts. He glanced up at the roof itself, saw the gaps where shingles had been torn away, and couldn't understand why he'd never noticed this damage before. He felt irresponsible, like a neglectful parent.

Waterfalls began to pour here and there from the cracks between the board siding, tearing away bits and pieces of the house. Hank knew little about construction, but assumed water was getting in from the damaged roof and down behind the sheathing. He looked around, finding fallen plaster and crumbling brick. Cracks spread through the limestone foundation stones. There appeared to be a definite lean to the back porch, the lines no longer true, the entire structure beginning to separate from the rest of the house.

He heard a muffled groan and a cracking noise. A portion of the roof line suddenly complicated itself, breaking into several additional angles.

Hank held his place in the thundering downpour until it stopped, the world gone quiet again except for the gentle dripping of the bags. He shivered within his soggy clothes.

Furious with himself and with his father, he grabbed bags and carried them to the alley, threw them on the others and went back for more. He made several such trips before pausing to rest, collapsing against the fence.

The storm advanced the night prematurely. Streetlights came on. He heard distant traffic, but no cars moved on the nearby streets. He heard a damp shifting noise, and a bag moved. He assumed it was the contents settling, when one side stretched out, and the entire bag began to distort. The plastic near the top ripped, and something climbed out of the bag, but it was too dark to tell what it was. After a moment of stillness, it scampered away. Perhaps a squirrel or some other varmint had gotten inside while the bags sat in the yard. Hank approached the piles and nudged each bag with his foot, waited for some movement, and went on to the next. None of the other bags responded.

Something crawled across his arm, and he shook it off. He probed deeper into the layers of bags, their stench rising around him now the rain had ended. He wasn't sure what he was looking for, but he couldn't stop.

A few insects scrambled from the small openings where the bags were tied, then a larger number, and then a flood. Soon the dark plastic skins were thick with them, the bugs pouring off the bags and into the alley as if frantic to escape.

Hank heard scraping trash cans, and gazing down the alley saw the angular silhouette progressing brokenly from can to can, leaning over the dark mouths then standing up larger, swollen head and swollen chest, swollen belly then thin again, rapidly processing everything it had eaten.

It turned its body and shambled toward him, to the next garbage can, close enough that Hank could see the vague rot along its profile, its edges deteriorating from all the waste consumed.

Hank was faint with dread, legs too weak to support him. He'd been holding himself together so well, but he was so tired. The house was empty, and Dad was gone.

He felt himself settle into his skin and dropped to the ground between the high black plastic walls, as if he were hiding inside a large bag of his own making.

When it came his turn and the creature peered inside, its small eyes seemed impossibly far away, and yet its immense mouth so very close.

LATE SLEEPERS

Ted woke up in the dark with a dull headache, deciding to sneak out before the rest of the family got up. Going home for Thanksgiving was a terrible idea. He'd have to find some excuse to stay on campus for Christmas. Maybe he'd come home New Year's Day, if he wasn't too hung over. He'd slept in the same clothes he wore at dinner. He didn't know why he hadn't changed; he didn't remember going to bed. His dad worked all day on their ancient furnace, banging a hammer and making dinner late. Mom was furious, and that started the first argument. Then his brother got into it, followed by his brother's wife. There'd been something about Ted's major, the wasted college fees, his low grades, and other upsets he couldn't remember at all. Politics maybe. Or a neighbor's careless and tragic end. So much he couldn't quite point to. For once his dad hadn't participated. He just sat there staring at them. Ted remembered leaving the table mad at everybody, but nothing after.

The meal might have gone better if Emily had come. They might have tried harder with a stranger present, but Emily was amazed Ted had even invited her. "We don't have that kind of relationship." His confusion and embarrassment over her answer made him feel stupid. He'd promised them his girlfriend was coming for Thanksgiving.

Just once Ted wanted to be the one who got the girl. In the movies, the loser sometimes got what he wanted. That was supposed to encourage guys like him.

He carried his coat and bag out to the staircase landing. The inside of the house appeared unfocused, layered in shades of gray. He couldn't have said what about that bothered him. He strained to see more detail, making his headache worse.

He crept down the staircase gripping the railing and watching each step. He walked into the dark dining room. The table should have been empty, but he could see a spread of silhouettes. He flipped on the light. Dirty plates were still around the table, greasy glasses and silverware, a fork under his sister-in-law's chair, debris from the great bird and bits of lettuce and bread scattered across Mom's best tablecloth, a bowl almost empty of mashed potatoes, an unserved pumpkin pie. His father's plate was still full, surprisingly untouched.

His mother hadn't cleared or cleaned anything, yet she was such a neat freak. Had she been that angry? Or maybe she'd gotten sick. He'd call in a few days and apologize, make sure she was okay.

He paused at the front door. The stillness troubled him. He didn't hear anything, but it seemed the noise of nothing was pounding in his head. He breathed in deeply, smelling only the stale air. Maybe all would be forgotten by his next visit.

No one was up in their small town. The downtown Christmas lights were hung, a glitter of brilliant white with the occasional splash of red. Everything else lay dark.

A half hour outside town, Ted saw the Paradise Cinemas sign, the only building visible for miles. The vertical theater name and the rectangular marquee below were outlined with a triple row of blinking blue and red bulbs. He'd gone there all the time when he was a kid. It was the first twin cinema in this part of the state. Showtimes were staggered so you could see a movie in one theater and then move to the next. By his high school years, most people had taken their business to the eight screens at the new multiplex.

The Paradise used to run movies all Thanksgiving night for those with no better way to spend the holiday. He slammed on his brakes to make the turn onto the access road, the rear end of his Celica fishtailing on the icy pavement. He felt suddenly ill. He stopped the car, opened the door, and threw up onto the road.

There were six or seven cars in the gravel parking lot. The marquee said, "Late Sleepers & S*l*cted Horror Clips." A hand-lettered cardboard sign on the art deco door stated, "Final Day / Thank you for 50 great years!" The theater's front door made a soft scraping noise as he stepped into the ice-cold lobby.

The interior had the same décor Ted remembered from childhood. The carpet bore a complex pattern of Asian temples and jungle animals in several colors. Badly worn when he was a kid, it was far worse now. Dark floorboards peeked through in spots. The wallpaper was pinkish-red and flocked with a felt pattern a few shades darker. The main figures resembled giant upside-down roaches. The chandelier overhead was missing numerous prisms and other glass trim.

A huge man in a pale-yellow suit and a fur cap stood up from a chair wedged behind the heavily scratched glass counter. His forced smile looked painful. His "Manager" tag was pinned to a ratty-looking red sweater beneath his suit jacket. "Hello sir, welcome to Paradise," he uttered in a monotone. His lips were wet and his eyes red and tiny.

"Hi, the movies still playing?"

"Right until dawn."

"How much?"

The manager pouted. "Usually five bucks, but this is the last night. Let's call it free. Besides, the main feature, *Late Sleepers*, is a weird independent film out of Atlanta. But it's all we got."

"I can't argue with free. What are the clips on the marquee all about?"

"Just a bunch of scenes the owner put together from stuff that's played here. I don't know where he got it all. Some of it he's had for years. Sometimes a reel falls apart on you, you know? Sometimes part of that reel doesn't get put back." It sounded dubious, but what did he care? "Can I sell you some refreshments?"

"A medium Coke, I guess."

"Popcorn? Candy?"

Ted looked at the popcorn maker, half full of yellowish, stiff-looking popped kernels. The butter appeared discolored. The candy bars sat neatly arranged in the glass case but they all had faded wrappers. As he surveyed the offerings, he was pretty sure most hadn't been made in years—Marathon, Reggie, Starbar, PowerHouse, and Texan.

The manager had the drink ready on the counter, two thick fingers tapping the lid. "The Coke will be enough. It's kind of late," Ted said.

"Three bucks then. Find yourself a seat in theater two. Movie's on a loop. You're about forty-five minutes from the end before it all starts up again. Stay as long as you like, until dawn at least. That's when I kick everybody out and the Paradise is done. Next month they're turning us into a parking lot." He made a hoarse, gurgling laugh.

Ted had no idea what he was talking about. "What's playing in theater one?"

"We shut that one down years ago. Projector went bad. Couldn't afford to replace it. I like them old projectors. They make a little rattling noise that tells you you're in a theater and not watching TV."

Ted nodded and walked to the gold curtain with the black numeral "2" above it. A small paper sign by the opening said NO SLEEPING ALLOWED. "Are you serious about 'no sleeping'?"

"I am. People snore—it disturbs the other customers. Almost worse than talking."

"But people fall asleep during movies all the time."

"Not in my movie theater. They get one warning. After that, they're gone."

"I see..." Ted paused. The manager's face became angry. "I've never heard of this before."

"It's like church. You're not supposed to sleep in church. You let the screen do your dreaming—that's what it's there for. Did you know in the Thirties they called movie theaters dream palaces? They understood back then. We've just forgotten."

"Well, thank you. I didn't know." Ted pushed apart the curtain and stood inside until his eyes adjusted. He hoped he wouldn't fall asleep. It was pretty late.

More of the old carpet ran down the aisle. The rows of seats looked uneven as some seat backs had collapsed and some were missing corners. He could see very little of the walls in the dark, but he remembered huge water stains descending in some sections, and even bigger ones flowering across the ceiling. He doubted they had been fixed.

The screen was watchable, despite several vertical splits and puckers near the edges that distorted the image. It was framed by two halves of a giant red velvet curtain. He wondered if they still closed the curtain between shows. Even in its shabby state it suggested the possibility of something grand.

His tennis shoes stuck to the carpet with each step, making a soft kissing noise when he lifted his feet. All those decades of dripping butter and pop, he thought. He looked for the seats that appeared less worn, less sunken. Pickings were slim. He tried several before finding one somewhat bearable. He had to squeeze past a few patrons as collapsed-looking as the upholstery. His apologies were met with silence.

He assumed the scene playing on the screen was from *Late Sleepers*, but he couldn't figure out what was going on. He was looking at a vaguely familiar living room in a modest home somewhat like his parents', so dark it might have been black and white but for a few visible glimmers of blue and green. The soundtrack had a discordant metallic hum, the rhythm of which shifted unexpectedly, increasing in volume gradually until he found himself wiggling around in discomfort.

The scene went on with no actors, and no other sound except for that loud mechanical noise. Ted began to wonder if there might be something wrong with the projector. He twisted around and checked out the rest of the audience, looking for impatience or confusion or alarm, anything indicating they might be seeing it the same way he was.

There were eight or nine forms slumped into their seats, heads tilted back, motionless. Ted couldn't see any of their eyes, but from their attitude and their stillness, it seemed some of them must have been asleep. Maybe all of them. They were breaking the special rule of the Paradise, so why hadn't they been removed? They were completely silent—no snoring that he could hear. He couldn't even hear them breathe. Perhaps making noise was the major concern.

He returned his attention to the screen just as the machine noise faded and the scene ended. The words "End of Part 4" appeared.

There was some scratchy black leader and then the first clip began, or at least the first clip Ted had seen. A hand-written title appeared in black ink over white stock. *Possession.* He'd seen it, if it was the one he was thinking of. Isabelle Adjani appeared walking through a heavily shadowed subway passage and he knew immediately it was that movie. Suddenly she was convulsing, throwing herself around as if an outside force controlled her body. Ted clutched the armrests, knowing what was coming. Isabelle fell to the dirty pavement in agony, hemorrhaging copiously as she had a miscarriage. They'd picked the most terrible scene from the film.

The "clips" appeared to be a compilation of scenes from Seventies and Eighties horror flicks, many Ted recognized and many more he did not. They ran without interruption, separated only by dark or bloody or plain nasty-looking leaders, each introduced with a hastily scrawled identifying title, one after the other like a feverish, disjointed nightmare.

Next came Jason's rotting body pulling the girl under the lake in *Friday the 13th*. Then there was Chucky coming alive in the mother's hands in *Child's Play*, followed by an illegibly labeled clip in which a baby ate its own fingers in a jittering black-and-white soundless sequence so badly scratched Ted wondered if maybe he just imagined it.

The music behind many of the scenes was loud to the point of distortion, the colors so bright and garish they appeared to burn through the screen. His head ached again. Then came that awful ending to *Sleepaway Camp* in all its politically incorrect glory, the shattered looking face he had never been able to get out of his head. Ted felt ill again so he climbed out of his seat and ran for the bathroom off the lobby.

The manager wasn't behind the counter. The men's room was under the staircase leading to the closed balcony. As far back as Ted could remember, the balcony had always been closed. He squeezed through the narrow doorway and down a crooked hall. At some point the three toilets and sinks had been painted bright-red, but the paint was mostly chipped off, leaving a haphazard blood-spatter effect. He went to his knees before the first bowl and vomited, almost passing out. He put his head against the cold floor, vaguely aware of how filthy it was. He got his head above the bowl before vomiting again.

He had no idea how long he was in there, and he felt no urgency to return to his seat. He rubbed water onto his face and into his hair and staggered out. Still no sign of the manager.

As he walked past theater one, he thought he heard a noise from inside. Like the sound of a projector motor. He pulled the curtain back and peered inside. The projector clattered above his head. A bright-white nothingness flickered on the screen. The dark outlines of all the seats appeared swollen and misshapen, as if occupied by a sold-out audience. Suddenly a heavy hand on his shoulder pulled him back into the lobby.

"I told you that theater ain't open to the public!" The manager's face was livid and dangerously close. That hadn't exactly been what he'd told him but Ted wasn't about to argue.

"I'm sorry. It won't happen again." Startled, he squirmed away from the manager and ducked back into theater two. He felt sick with embarrassment, like some stupid kid.

Late Sleepers was apparently in the midst of another chapter. Still no actors in evidence, but the camera was taking the audience up a staircase and down a hall, presumably to the bedrooms. The hall was so dark Ted could make out very few details. It all looked terribly familiar, but then many houses built during that time had similar layouts. Then "End of Part 7" flashed on the screen. He had no idea he'd been gone that long.

There seemed little point in staying—he hadn't seen any characters yet and had no idea of the plot—but another round of clips began and he was reluctant to leave.

Several odd characters scrolled across the screen, followed by some quick cuts of an old lady being ripped apart by giant demonic crickets in some nameless, sickeningly-lit Asian film. This was followed by the exploding head scene in *Scanners*. Apparently, the owner, who Ted strongly suspected was also the manager, liked this so much he repeated it twice.

After a pause and random streams of color, he was treated to the incredibly visceral transformation scene Rick Baker delivered in *An American Werewolf in London*, one of Ted's favorites. A couple of friends once claimed it was a comedy but he couldn't remember ever laughing.

The next clip began but almost immediately bubbled and burned. The house lights came up abruptly and Ted could hear cursing—or was it screaming?—coming from the projection booth behind him. He saw an irregular patch of shadow flowing down the center aisle and realized it was a mass of roaches fleeing the light. They disappeared into a rip in the carpet. He turned around wondering if anyone else caught a glimpse. Some people must have left because now he could only count four besides himself. Three of them had their eyes closed, heads tilted sideways. The remaining pallid elderly man stared at him, unblinking. He slowly caressed the curved handle of a thick wooden cane he had clutched to his chest. Ted turned away.

It was his first chance to get a good look at the theater's walls and ceiling. The stains were still there, but multiplied. In some places, the wallpaper had disintegrated completely to show separating sections of plaster, their edges gleaming with moisture.

The lights went out again and the clips continued to roll. The tree outside the boy's window in *Poltergeist* warped into footage of the overactive hand in *Evil Dead 2*. The clip ended abruptly and went directly into Jeff Goldblum's final transformation in *The Fly*.

The deep suggestion of filth in that movie made Ted feel profoundly uncomfortable. He shouldn't have left his parents' house so abruptly. He should have stayed and made amends, helped them clean up the dreadful mess the next morning.

The nasty kitchen in Tobe Hooper's *Texas Chainsaw Massacre* appeared on the screen. It was an unstable clip, which only fueled the electric anxiety of the characters. Layers of flesh and bone debris, greasy plates and silverware, dried regions of blood. Ted began to sweat, and a burning sensation moved across his chest. He wanted to scratch himself, but the itch spread everywhere, and once he started scratching, he couldn't imagine stopping. Things moved in the far corners of the scene, a suggestion of insects wandering across the table and touching the scattered bits of food, something crawling in and out of a small carcass, a suggestion of a rodent.

"End of Part 3" flashed on the screen, followed by some scratchy leader, then more footage from *Late Sleepers*. The pieces must have been out of order, not that it mattered as far as he could tell. Still no actors. The camera moved slowly into the dark dining room when a small spotlight, like a flashlight— presumably attached to the camera—went on and off to illuminate individual plates, serving platters, wine glasses tipped over and staining the lovely tablecloth with splotches of deep red. Grease gleamed off the fine holiday china and close-ups zeroed in on forks, knives, and spoons smeared with animal and vegetable remains.

Ted grew increasingly anxious as each new detail was revealed. With the camera so close to the table this could have been anyone's dining room, and holiday meals had a certain uniformity across the country, but some angles and perspectives appearing at such size across the theater screen shook him with unsettling recognition. The burning and itching returned and were more intense, like armies of filthy insects marching around his torso. Soon it was almost unbearable. He jumped out of his seat again and raced for the bathroom.

Once under the mirror's bare bulbs, Ted shed his coat and peeled off his shirt and stared at himself. Large cherry-red blotches covered his pecs and belly. Even brighter red islands had risen on his forearms, like the flocked patterns of the lobby wallpaper. These continued onto his hands, blistering one of his knuckles. He probed the tender spots, searching every inch of skin to map the spread of his symptoms.

Maybe he was allergic to something on the seats, and the blotches would be gone by the time he got to campus. But this place was so filthy, it could be anything. God, he should never have drunk that Coke! It was probably contaminated. He might have to go to the infirmary once he was back on campus. Not that they could help him. He wondered if they were even real doctors. He locked eyes with his mirror image. It was like watching a movie of himself. This damn Thanksgiving. His damn family. He'd heard that sometimes people got rashes just from being upset. Well, he was plenty upset. Every time he came home he was upset. He should have left right then, but he wanted to see how it all ended. He put his clothes back on and went into the lobby.

The manager had the elderly man Ted saw earlier in theater two trapped in his arms, dragging him away. The old man's cane fell to the floor. The manager glanced at Ted and growled just as the man went slack. "Go back to your seat!" the manager barked as he hauled the poor man into theater one. Ted could hear that projector clacking and whirring so loudly, it must have been flying apart.

He wanted to help the fellow, and started after them, then stopped. This wasn't a movie, and he was no match for a behemoth like the manager. He went to the front door and struggled to open it. It was locked. He looked around frantically, expecting the manager to burst through the curtains. A payphone hung from the wall by the restroom door, but the handset had been removed, colored wires splaying from the armored cable, He picked up the cane, and ran back into theater two looking for help.

Ted scanned the seats. The theater was completely empty. A snippet from John Carpenter's *The Thing* was playing—that hideous upside-down head growing segmented legs and trucking rapidly across the floor.

He ran to the front of the theater and used the cane to pull back the curtains on both sides of the screen. The two emergency exits were boarded up. He walked back up the aisle trying to figure out what to do. He avoided touching the seats. He turned and gazed at the screen.

"Heeeeere's Johnny!" as Jack Nicholson's head protruded from a jagged hole in *The Shining*.

Late Sleepers started playing again. The camera glided along the upstairs hall of that too-familiar home. Ted needed to leave, but there appeared to be nowhere to go. He gripped the cane tightly, getting ready to use it as a club. Up on the screen of his dream palace an unseen hand opened each door along the hallway and the camera, and Ted, floated inside. In the first bedroom his parents lay on the floor, dead eyes staring at the ceiling, their cheeks bright red. In another room the bodies of his brother and sister-in-law lay contorted in bed, tangled in the covers. The rising sun peeked through the window.

The film ended, fading to black before it got to Ted's room. He ran out to the lobby, cane raised. The manager was nowhere to be seen. Ted waited, looking around, listening carefully, hearing no sound. Then he noticed that the front door was cracked an inch or so, just enough to let in the dawn. He slammed it open with his shoulder, turning and swinging at nothing until convinced he was alone.

Ted drove back to his parents' house, understanding he would not be returning to school, a surrender more than a decision. The filth and chaos of the dining room looked worse in the light of morning. He thought back to the beginning of that terrible day, and how it all seemed to begin with his father's frustrations with the furnace. He breathed in deeply, seeking some kind of smell, but there wasn't one. He quietly climbed the stairs even though he knew he risked disturbing no one. He thought about peeking into the other bedrooms but didn't have the heart. He took off his shoes and climbed into bed with his clothes on. He might have taken the time to slip into pajamas, but he knew it wouldn't be that kind of sleep.

A THIN SILVER LINE

For Harlan Ellison

A thin silver line: color of moonlight, or morning fog, the highlight on your grandmother's lips. The fading borders of the dream just before you discover it is morning. It's a separation keeping you from the dream, the day from the night, and the fantasy from nightmare. The division is less substantial than mist; you can cross it and not even know.

When Bobby came downstairs that morning Linda was cleaning the kitchen. Her hair was tied back, her face red and glowing with perspiration. Her smock's yellow color was almost startling, appearing to draw all available light to itself. The air smelled of ammonia. He watched her, thinking how pretty she looked, how settled. He'd never felt at home anywhere his entire life, until now, here, with her. In this home that seemed far more conventional than any he would have imagined: dark wainscoting, old-fashioned wallpaper, wooden floors, wrap-around porch, gables like half-a-dozen raised eyebrows. And comforting for all that.

"Don't wear yourself out, woman," he said softly. He laughed and went to kiss her frown away, stroking the prematurely gray cleft in her black hair. She held on longer than he expected, and he stepped back. "Something wrong?"

"I just ... *worry* all the time. I don't know what's wrong with me these days."

"You're pregnant."

She punched him playfully in the stomach. "You always say that. *Everything* isn't natural just because I'm *pregnant!*"

"The baby's becoming real to you, to us, for the first time. That's scary. If we lose the baby now it'll feel like our child has died. And it didn't feel that way before."

He thought she was crying against him but he couldn't be sure. It was a painful reminder of his general inability to comfort her, but he sensed he should just let her cry. It pleased him he could know that.

The dog was barking on the back porch.

He felt the hairs rise on his neck, an odd puckering sensation along the skin covering his spine. A tooth prodded his inner lip. He was suddenly frightened, and felt a passing, oddly animal-like sensation.

The dog was pawing at the door, frantic.

"What is it?" Linda whispered.

Bobby walked to the door and opened it. First there was the white dog's wagging tail, and then his back—oddly tensed—then something underneath his muzzle.

"Bobby?"

"Wait here."

He shut the door behind him. There was a sharp, metallic odor in the air. Their cat, Miranda, recently pregnant herself, sat on the clothes hamper, staring at the dog. And beneath the dog's paws, gasping, its neck and legs at odd angles, was one of her kittens—Feather, the blonde one, Linda's favorite—the dog licking at the long line of scraped fur on the kitten's belly.

He picked Miranda up quickly in one hand and dragged the dog back into the kitchen.

"What's wrong?" Linda was so scared it made him look away.

"The kitten, it must have gotten in his food." He gestured vaguely at the dog. "He must have grabbed its neck and slung it; it looks all broken up, tortured."

"Feather?"

He nodded, disturbed Linda knew which kitten it was without being told. "It's still breathing. The way it's suffering — I … need to drown it." Linda shook her hands nervously. "Better keep the other animals in here."

"Do you need my help?"

He knew she didn't want to, could not do it, but she must have felt she had to ask for all the times he'd disposed of dead animals: birds the dog and cats dragged in, a rotting squirrel Linda found in the bedroom after a vacation. "I'll do it."

He didn't look at the kitten as he poured water into a plastic bucket. He was angry, angry at the dog, the cat for having kittens, the kitten for bothering the dog's food, himself for not knowing anything better to do, and for allowing so many animals in the house—too many, the closeness putting everybody on edge, making things like this more likely to happen. But most of all he was angry at Linda for once again forcing him to handle a death in the family. Leaving it to him to pick up the battered body, bury it or toss it unceremoniously into the trash. He knew that was unfair to her, but he couldn't help it. He had become a deathwatch, a garbage man.

He set the bucket beside the kitten and looked for something to hold her down. He picked up the dog's orange plastic dish and an old towel. Then he let himself look at Feather.

Her body convulsed, the mouth opening and closing, the throat jumping in a frightening way, as if a current were passing through. She must have been in agony—he was moving too slowly. Crying, he used the towel to grab her legs, then lifted her—the torso not moving, her spine not bending—and dropped her into the water. She was so small. He held her down and sobbed. He couldn't help it. He hoped Linda couldn't hear him.

The furious splashing scared him. She was almost dead; how could she struggle like that? Had he made a terrible mistake? He didn't know what else to do so he pushed harder and the struggling increased, the bucket rocking back and forth, water splashing over his arms, his knees, all over the porch. He was sickened. Now it felt as if there were a child in the bucket, filling the bucket with a child's strength, a child's struggle to survive. Again he was horrified by what he was doing, hesitated, and eased up.

The kitten's head popped out to one side of the bright-orange dish. One foreleg slid out and rested tentatively against the back of his hand. As if to say stop. *Please. Enough.* Bobby looked into the kitten's wide, gray eyes.

Eyes rimmed in silver, the silver burning brighter even as he watched.

He pushed the kitten back in, pushing down as hard as he could. Maybe the bones weren't as broken as they'd seemed … maybe it hadn't been in that much pain … maybe he should have called the vet … it might have recovered. The struggle was strong, but brief. Blonde hair floated up around the dish.

When he removed the dog's dish the kitten's body turned over in the water. Eyes wide, teeth and jaws open and extended. A silver line gleamed on one of the teeth, and then passed into the water, reflected off into his face. He fell back and had to swallow a whimper. It turned to bile in his mouth. When he looked back the water was dull gray, with no reflected highlights.

Instead he could see his own face, the long pale lines of it, the dark shaggy hair, a sharp grin. But the grin was impossible. He rubbed at his face, disgusted. He heard a low moaning, and then realized it was coming from him.

They were having a baby; he should be happy. He was uneasy.

A chrome line, a thin silver line crawling over his legs like a snake. A reflection, a faint silvered shadow, creeping across his chest. Linda's eyes gleaming as the silver enters them, and then turning up in her head, turning white…

He sputtered from sleep, as if he had been drowning. He swam his hands into the dim light, and then realized he was in bed, his wife Linda asleep beside him, asleep with their baby curled inside her. He touched her, felt her rib cage rising, and was reassured by the shallow sounds of her breath. Then he knew she was awake, staring at him.

"Linda?"

"I haven't slept all night." He couldn't see her lips move, and it unnerved him. Her eyes were fixed, as if they were painted on. "I'm scared, Bobby." The bed seemed too close around him, her breath too warm.

He touched her stomach. "You're getting big. About time you were buying maternity clothes."

"I want to wait a little while more, make sure nothing happens." She said that every time he brought it up.

She moved her head closer to him. "What's the matter?" he asked.

"I don't want to lose the baby." Her voice broke, and he touched her face.

"It's okay. There's no reason to think anything's going to go wrong." She pressed closer and he stroked that gray patch of hair that suddenly seemed larger than before.

And felt like a liar. He was terrified.

Linda had tried to convince him he should tell his mother about her pregnancy.

"No … let's wait," he said. "Something might … go wrong. Let's tell her when you're just a little further along."

"But you keep saying that, Bobby, and it's already five months."

"Just a little while longer, okay? When you're a little further along, then we'll tell her."

The truth was he didn't want to tell his mother at all. He couldn't explain that to Linda, because he didn't understand it himself. Since his father died and he left home he'd had little contact with his mother. He tried to write a few times, call her, but he just couldn't do it. He liked to pretend he never had a family in the first place.

Something had gone awry with his father's side of the family. His great uncle went crazy and shot his wife and two kids before turning the gun on himself. And a great-great-grandfather had taken his family out into the woods one day, hauling along everything they owned, and set up housekeeping in a cave. They lived there for years, waylaying hikers and hunters, robbing and killing them. The old man killed three of his own children with his bare hands. Other, less dramatic incidents involving male members of the family had left Bobby reticent about maintaining those family connections.

"Aren't you happy about the baby, Bobby?"

He looked down at her, wondering how long she'd been talking to him. She looked hurt. "Of course I'm happy. Happiest thing that ever happened to me ... really. I'm just scared, that's all."

"Because you might lose it, that maybe you don't deserve it."

"Yeah ... of course." *But something even scarier than that.*

"You'll be a wonderful father, Bobby."

He squeezed her so tightly he thought he must be hurting her. He wished she wouldn't say that. He wanted to shout at her to stop saying that.

Her pelvis seemed much too small. He wondered if the birth would be caesarian.

Over the next few weeks Linda broke down and bought maternity clothes. She was beautiful in them, radiant, but Bobby would look at her—the bright-orange and -red and -blue tops with the small birds and animals on the sleeves, the pants with the elastic panels sewn in—and think about the cat, its one paw reaching out to stop his hand.

Everyone asked about names and so they came up with some: Alan, Richard. Bobby resented all this; Linda grew sullen. They were due to begin natural childbirth classes within a couple of months, and Bobby had no idea how he could stand it. He wouldn't even fill out the form.

Since he'd been an adult he'd never imagined himself with a family. He held Linda to him so they were like nesting spoons at night, and in that act alone he realized how different it must have been for his parents; he could not imagine them doing the same. He and Linda hugged each other frequently. The house was comfortable and full of growing plants, picture albums, and contented animals. It smelled of lilacs, and browning roast beef, and lemon polish. But now things were changing.

He'd been lying in bed, Linda asleep beside him. Occasionally he would touch her just to be sure she was there. The reality of the child-to-be was coming to him in a quick succession of images now: holding the sleeping baby against his stomach; watching him—Alan—squeal over a stuffed tiger; helping him—Richard—try out the smell of a bright-red flower. Holding him up to his cheek, giving him a kitten to play with.

Thinking about the cat with silver-rimmed eyes, convulsive throat...

He wondered if his father had ever done those things with him, ever held him like that, looked at him that way.

Then he heard the beating against the bedroom window, and saw the shadows of the leaves twisting and turning in the wind, flapping like birds tied to strings, trying to escape the tree and break the window. Silver highlights at the edges of the leaves, the streetlight reflected on the ghostly stems ...

He watched as the thin line, silver in the window, crept across the pane like a sliver of moonrise. But he knew it wasn't moonrise. It floated across the foot of the bed, rippled along the folds of the covers, and entered the gray sheet on Linda's side of the bed, disappearing above her belly.

He tried to remember what a fetus looks like at five months. Linda had the book and he had skimmed it when she wasn't in the room. And he could see the picture superimposed over her sheeted form: large head, definable features, definable fingers and toes, already resembling a human child.

And saw the child dead in her womb, a silver line wrapped around his neck.

He used to stare at pictures of his father for hours at a time, particularly when something was bothering him. He sensed a secret knowledge in those pictures, in the old man's face. He never did find any answers, but it had become a ritual.

On his dresser Bobby kept a picture of his father holding him up to pick a dogwood bloom from the tree in front of their old house. The man in the yellowed photograph is young, blond, wearing a loose windbreaker. Smiling and looking directly at the camera while the young Bobby concentrates on the flower.

There's a speck of silver at the corner of the young man's mouth.

Bobby had always been disturbed by that bit of silver, even as a boy. He'd examine it by the hour, thinking at times it was a bit of saliva catching the light just so, a food particle, or maybe even the end of a cigarette holder. But it didn't look like any of those things. It was too bright. For a few years he had himself convinced it was merely a flaw in the film.

When he'd asked his father about it, the man was silent a long time. Then he'd said, "I don't know," in a cold and weary voice, a voice denying Bobby permission ever to ask again.

Another picture on the wall in Bobby's study: an older version of his father sitting in the shadows of the front porch watching Bobby play ball out in the yard. Grandpa is also on the porch, a little further back in the shadows. He'd always been scared of his grandfather: a sullen old man who seldom spoke, who looked at people as if they were something dead in the street. There had always been this frightening intensity between his father and grandfather, although few words were ever spoken. In the picture his father and grandfather—not looking at each other, in fact their chairs turned away from each other— their fingertips seem to glow in the shadows. Twenty fingertips glowing like birthday candles. With silver flames. It had to be a trick of the lighting.

A picture stuck inside an old book, hidden away because Bobby found it so hard to look at: his father out in the backyard, underneath the willow, drinking. He's staring at the camera sullenly—Bobby took the picture. His father's eyes shining, as if burning with a white heat.

And the picture that frightened Bobby the most, even though at first glance it always seemed innocuous. A day didn't go by that Bobby didn't stare into it. He was too afraid of that picture to hide it. It is the day of their last hunting trip together. Close-up of his father in a hunting cap, checkered jacket. Thin, hard lips. Pale wrinkled skin and frosted hair. And mirrored sunglasses that make his eyes look enormous, and completely gone to silver.

"We're going hunting."

Bobby was fifteen, and he'd had other plans. He hated hunting, but he'd given up arguing with the old man. His father was already waiting by the door with a pile of gear. Silently he handed the boy a couple of packs, then started out to the car. After a moment Bobby followed him—something bad was going on here, something new.

As soon as they got into the car his father turned the radio to the country music station and turned up the volume. They rode that way into the mountains, past fields of snow and over ice-encrusted gravel roads, and pulled into the wooded lot before his grandfather's old cabin around sunset. That night Bobby's father went to sleep by the door, fully clothed and with his rifle in his arms.

For the next two days they did nothing but walk around the snow fields.

"Walk in front, boy! Don't get behind me! Get your rifle ready!" But they never shot anything. "I'll tell you when to shoot, boy." But although they saw game everywhere, the old man didn't give the word.

"Dad ..." Bobby started to ask him what was going on. But looking into the old man's sunglasses, the shocks of white hair stiff with frost, snow which should have melted or blown off but did not, he could not speak. Bobby turned and continued to plod through the knee-high white.

Every night his father slept by the door, fully clothed, the rifle in his arms.

On the third day of the hunting trip Bobby found a dead fox on the trail. He started to tell his father but he stopped himself. He pulled his scarf up around cheeks aching with cold. The old man was out of sight, around the bend or behind the trees. The corpse's fur was matted, hide torn here and there, neck broken. He was thinking about what he should do with the thing, if he should try to break the frozen ground and bury it.

Light was flashing on his jacket sleeve. He could almost feel the heat.

He turned. All he could see was the blinding, silvery light, creating painful haloes. He was looking directly into his father's mirrored sunglasses. He moved, trying to escape the bright reflection. And saw the dull tube of the upraised rifle, his father's finger poised on the trigger.

His father's dark form burned into Bobby's eyes. He began to shake. Silver played with the rims of his father's sunglasses, glinted off the clenched teeth, and rose up the barrel of the rifle.

It could have been sun coming out from behind the clouds, but later, after years of observing reflections off all kinds of surfaces, Bobby would know that light never flowed as that silver sheen did across his father's body.

Bobby closed his eyes. And heard his father howling.

He opened his eyes as his father fell forward, knees splayed and digging into the snow, his mouth thrown back like a wolf's. A silver film coated the inside of his father's mouth—or was it mucous? And silver fragments tore at the corners of his father's eyes—or were those tears glistening on his lined face?

"Get it ... out... of me!" his father screamed. "It's eating me ... alive!"

Bobby listened carefully, but without comprehension.

His father drove them home as if nothing had happened. But he didn't turn the radio on this time. When they got into the house he went into the garage alone.

That night his father used the rifle on himself. Bobby was in bed, and thought the moonrise had awakened him, for his bedroom wall danced with the silver reflections. The gyration of abstract patterns had almost lulled him back to sleep when he heard his mother scream.

Linda had spent the day cleaning out the storage room for a nursery. Bobby thought to stop her a half-dozen times, wanting to tell her she was overexerting herself, but the doctor had said exercise would be fine, and Bobby felt uncomfortable talking about the baby in any form.

Linda was happy; he had never seen her so happy. She'd apparently decided to ignore his standoffishness and enjoy the pregnancy on her own. He couldn't help loving her for it.

He woke up in the middle of the night, shivering, stray images from his dreams intruding: *mirrored sunglasses, thin lips of ice, the cat's eyes turning into enormous disks of silver as it dies ...*

Linda stirred beside him, then bolted upright. "No ... No!"

"Linda?"

"No ..." She looked at him wide-eyed. "I dreamed the baby died. I dreamed the moon took him."

He put his arm around her. "It's okay ... everything's okay."

He went downstairs into the darkened kitchen to get her a drink of water. He was careful to get it the right temperature. He tested it, poured it out, ran the tap and tested it again. He was entranced by the task, and afraid to look too closely at the shadows in the kitchen. The water in the glass was rippled in silver. The moon was high, and it was snowing. He thought he could hear animals scurrying across the snow-packed roof. He thought he could hear small animals lost and crying in the cold, cats crying like lost souls.

"Bobby."

He shivered and continued to run the water.

"Bobby." He didn't want to turn but he didn't know what else to do. She was standing in the doorway, her hair mussed into a shadow surrounding her head, her face dark.

"You should be in bed; I'll be right up," he said.

"Bobby, I'm scared. The bed, it's all wet. It doesn't smell like urine."

He led her upstairs and checked the dampness of the bed. The moon reflected off the wet sheet made it difficult to go near at first. But he had to; he knew there were a lot of things he was going to have to do.

He had her call the doctor. He felt bad about that, but he just couldn't do it.

His voice shook when he asked her.

"He says I need to go to the hospital, Bobby. He says I must be leaking fluid."

Furiously he began to get dressed, panic-stricken when he couldn't find a belt.

She asked him to get her a pair of panties out of the drawer and he fumbled through her things, shouting when he couldn't find it.

"It's okay, Bobby. Slow down. I don't think there's any hurry." She was infuriatingly calm, speaking much more slowly than normal. But then as she walked to the steps a heavy stream of liquid dropped, splattering the carpet. Bobby looked on with mounting horror. He couldn't think; he imagined her entire body leaking away. She turned and her face broke. "Bobby! Our baby's dying!"

A young intern came out to tell him his wife was miscarrying. Her amniotic sac had broken prematurely. It was rare; they weren't even sure what caused it—perhaps some subtle infection. There was no reason to believe it would happen a second time, she assured him. He nodded mutely. The corridors were long, and dim, silver haloes along the gray walls.

They had a choice. They could let nature take its course, with the small possibility the baby could go to term. But with the loss of amniotic fluid the baby's head would be subject to such pressures there was virtually no chance it would be normal. And the chances of debilitating infection to both Linda and the baby because of the now-unprotected birth passage were great.

Or they could induce an abortion.

"You know, you couldn't have had an induced abortion in this hospital a few years ago, even in this case," the doctor said. "It's a Catholic hospital." He said that several times.

Over the next several hours Linda attempted to sleep. Attached to an IV, she couldn't get up, and Bobby had to bring her the emesis basin. He walked around the hospital, wishing they hadn't thought about names. Both of them had called the baby "him." Alan—that was the name Bobby had in mind. Bobby tried to think of it as a fetus, that its time just hadn't come yet, that Alan's selfness would go back into some vast ethereal pool until it was his time again.

Bobby looked for silver haloes in the hospital corridors, bright reflections in the patients' eyes. He studied the hospital as he had studied the photographs of his father.

Get it... out... of me! It's eating me ... alive!

Why had his father committed suicide instead of shooting him that day?

Get it ... out... of me!

Why had his father stopped holding him when he was so little?

It's eating me ... alive!

They moved Linda into a labor room in the maternity ward. Sterile except for patterned green wallpaper, a lacy lampshade. Every time the nurse opened the door he could hear women in other labor rooms in the final physical struggles preceding birth, and occasionally, farther down the corridor, the cries of the newborn. It would take place there.

Linda was in labor. The nurse kept telling her it really wasn't labor. There was no more indication of a heartbeat; when they'd come into the hospital it had still been going strong. She was giving birth to a corpse. His anger was rising steadily. The nurse came into the room periodically, always efficient, always officious, examining Linda as if she were studying a boil.

He was alone with her when the baby's head came: a dark, blood-stained mass between her legs. It was so sudden he found himself staring in shock, not knowing what it was, panicked that something had gone wrong. He started shouting for the nurse, and then Linda touched his arm, whispering to him, calming him.

It happened quickly after the nurse and resident came in. He sat down on a chair by the bed, trying not to see.

He felt his hand pushing at the back of Linda's hand, pushing as if to make her stop, pushing like the drowning cat's paw on the back of his own hand.

Light glinted off the bright fixtures overhead, reflected off the chrome instruments on the table, caught on the stethoscope around the nurse's neck.

"It's perfect," the resident whispered. Bobby looked up at the man and saw the clinical eyes, the casual slump of the shoulders.

Linda was groggy, almost out, but she managed to whisper, "Please ... I don't want to know." The resident nodded.

A few minutes later the nurse moved the baby between Linda's legs. "It's male."

"I said I didn't want to know." Linda whispered harshly.

The nurse paused a beat and said, "We have to put it in our records."

Enraged, Bobby could not say anything, and he hated himself for it. Instead he stood up to look at his son, briefly, because he knew if he didn't he would always wonder.

The baby was a dark beet color, almost ten inches long. Not what Bobby would ever expect of something called a fetus. Perfectly formed fingers, toes, ears, and nose. But the face appeared closed, molded like a doll's.

Silver rested in baby Alan's mouth, then slipped out and across the bed like a serpent of bright light.

They took her into the delivery room to scrape out the rest of the placenta. When she came back she had tubes in her nostrils, and didn't move. Bobby had never seen anyone sleep so soundly, skin as still as plaster.

He felt he'd been okay up until then. And he knew Linda was fine—he was just sleeping. But it was such an unnatural sleep everything seemed wrong, as if she might never be the same again. As if she was dead.

"I love you, Linda," he whispered. And when she didn't move he left the room, walking faster and faster, afraid he might cry and knowing if he did he might not stop for hours.

Out on the streets the snow had melted, leaving the city black and glistening. The moon was lying melted on the sidewalk, and when he moved it followed him.

The air smelled heavily of damp leaves and oil. The dark seemed to have matted it all down into a slimy layer covering the parked cars, the grass, and the street. And in the process smothered the city into an uneasy silence. Bobby couldn't hear a thing. He quickened his pace, looking side to side for some place to run, stumbling around a street sign, ducking beneath a tree, crossing the dark street to another sidewalk, his knuckles brushing the wall of wet brick. He looked back and the silver moon peered from a stop sign. He turned the corner and ran, turned another corner and glanced over his shoulder.

The silver moon flowed in slow motion across an empty display window.

He ran two more blocks thinking about his great uncle's, his grandfather's, his father's eyes turned to silver, the bright metallic teeth.

Get it … out … of me! It's eating me … alive!

He turned and stared at the thin silver sheen creeping over the sidewalk behind him. "Leave me alone!" he cried. "Leave us all alone!"

Then he saw the drunk lying in the doorway, and watched in fascination as the silver sheen flowed there, slipping under the drunk's shabby clothes.

A beat later Bobby saw the drunk stepping out of the doorway and turning to face him with silver glinting in his eyes.

Silver sparkling in his ragged beard. A thin silver line dribbling out of the corner of the shadowed mouth.

And as the man approached him, slumping slightly, his legs taking on an animal tension, his face contorting with rage, Bobby walked toward him, his arms open, his footsteps steady and direct. *Enough.*

The drunk crouched and raised his head.

It has to stop.

The drunk raised his head into the light and the specks of silver—in his eyes, his beard, gleaming in his throat—danced hungrily.

Get it ... out ... of me!

And as the drunk leapt and the silver exploded Bobby opened his mouth wide, screaming his own rage.

It's eating me ... alive!

And something dark and silver, something old and foul entered Bobby. When he opened his eyes again the drunk was lying at his feet in a stupor. The night was dark, with no hints of silver.

He held Linda's hand tightly, afraid to let go.

"I'm okay ... really," she whispered. He squirmed uncomfortably on the edge of the narrow hospital bed.

"I know."

"But you look so *worried*! Really, I'm fine." She stroked his arm. "It was hard, but I'm fine. And I heard you say you loved me, even as out as I was." She squeezed his hand, smiling. She was beautiful, but he couldn't react as strongly as he would like. He saw her from a great distance, and the distance was widening. "We'll have another ... we'll try again," she said sleepily. He didn't answer.

He stood and stared out the window, at the thousands of lights beginning to blink out across the city, as light crept over the mountains in the east. Day had already come to the mountain towns, dots of silver being swallowed by a greater light.

He didn't even notice the young intern walk in behind him. She didn't speak; he turned when he heard her shuffling. "The baby," she said. "I thought it was impossible ... your baby is *alive*."

He was vaguely aware of Linda laughing, Linda crying in the bed behind him, the intern chattering away about ... something. He'd turned back to the window.

The silver in his father's eyes, silver death in his mouth. His father's struggles to contain it. To keep that away from his son. Like the most cannibalistic of beasts, protecting the offspring it might someday devour.

But then he'd killed himself, and the silver escaped.

During the last moments of darkness, when it was just slightly darker outside the hospital room than within, Bobby stared at his reflection in the window. He tried to stop the smile that came, but he couldn't help himself.

One tooth glowing silver, a shiny speck in the corner of his mouth.

INAPPETENCE

They slipped from the shadows to monitor his decline. Impatient, they moved forward to taste the light. All the world was hungry it seemed, except for him. Even the thought of food repelled him.

Guy stared at the spoon his daughter Ann had shoved up to his face. The yellow glop sitting there glistened with a pre-digested sheen. "I can't." He turned his head away.

"He's just like Princess was," a small voice said. One of his grandchildren, he wasn't sure which. One of the girls maybe. "She didn't eat anything for over a week. And then she—The vet took her away and we never saw her again."

"Inappetence. That's what the vet called it. She couldn't eat. They look at the food but they can't eat the food. They're just not interested. It was because of her teeth. Are Grandad's teeth okay? I know he doesn't have them all, but he has some. But how are the rest of them? Maybe his mouth hurts and that's why he won't eat."

That was Tony, who'd just started college. Tony was a bright kid, and Guy loved him, but the boy always had an explanation for everything. Young people needed to learn how to listen. You can't listen if you're always talking. Guy didn't talk much anymore. But he was listening all the time.

Guy turned his head and looked forward again, but kept his mouth clamped shut in case his daughter tried something sneaky with the spoon. His vision was blurry. They were all standing there, he thought, at the foot of his bed and around the side, so many of them. He and Cassie had raised a huge brood. Their bodies were far brighter than anything else in the room, except their faces which were shadowed or blurred – he wasn't sure – at least out of sync with the rest of them. He couldn't make out individual facial features, so he was unable to tell them apart.

"Let Ann help you, Dad." That was Robert's voice, his oldest. Jimmy was somewhere in that bunch as well, and Jimmy's wife. They all let Ann take the lead. Ann was like her mother, always taking charge when someone was sick.

He loved his children and grandchildren, all of them. But he had no appetite for them right now, or anyone else. He had to figure out what was going on with him, with his world, and it seemed he didn't have much time. He might not understand a lot of things, but he recognized when time was running out.

He felt an itch somewhere on his right leg, but he couldn't pin it down. Even if he knew its exact location, he had no way to scratch it. He imagined his skin was breaking down, little bits of it falling off everywhere. It was the sort of thing you normally didn't think about. But at this stage of his life most of the things he thought about were entirely new to him.

Ann held his hand. "Dad, if you can't eat your doctor will put you back in the hospital. I know you don't want that. None of us do."

He shook his head. "Water. Please."

A straw poked at his mouth. He grabbed it with his lips and sucked the cool liquid in. So delicious. When he was done, he pushed the straw away with his tongue. His eyes cleared momentarily, and he saw it was one of the boys, Jude, who was holding the glass. "Good boy." He smiled and Jude smiled back. Such a handsome boy. Guy didn't think he had ever been that handsome, even for one day. Why Cassie agreed to marry him he had no idea.

He began to choke. He couldn't catch his breath. Things went flying out of his mouth and he felt intensely dizzy. He heard a couple of the children crying and a rush of activity. Someone propped him up and held a cloth under his chin. Something came out of his mouth, mostly phlegm, but maybe something else. He wondered if he'd lost a piece of tongue, some bit of throat lining, a tonsil perhaps, or something deeper. Did he still have his tonsils? Probably not. At the moment he couldn't remember exactly what tonsils were.

The sudden trauma cleared both his head and his vision, and apparently the room, as only his daughter and Tony remained. "What? Did somebody die?"

"Dad!" Ann leaned forward in the chair by the bed, her cheeks damp and her eyes shadowed with exhaustion. Beside her was the table stacked with his vast repertoire of pills and other medicines.

Tony's face looked stricken. Guy felt terrible. "Oh, I'm sorry kiddo. That was just a stupid joke. I meant no harm."

"S-okay," Tony said. He was trying to smile but failing. Guy imagined the boy didn't want to be there, but he was sticking to his guns, acting like an adult. Good for him.

Guy shifted his head and gazed at his daughter. "Could I rest a while, honey? Try again at dinner? Some Jell-O maybe?"

"Dad, that *was* Jell-O."

"Maybe a different color then, if we have it."

"Sure. We've got all the colors of the rainbow down there." She kissed him on the cheek and they left the room.

He wasn't sleepy. He wanted to be by himself for a while. He couldn't look at their eager faces wanting him to be better. He couldn't tell them he was done.

He had a big house and didn't mind they'd moved in downstairs. In fact, he wished they'd done it sooner when he'd been healthy enough to enjoy their company. Most days he could barely hear them. The murmur of their conversations might as well have come from next door or even down the street. Sometimes there were gentle vibrations emanating from below. He liked to imagine they were from children joyfully playing. Sometimes cooking smells drifted up the three flights of stairs and into his room. These were not welcome as they triggered nausea almost instantly. Guy couldn't even think of food. Everything meant for consumption seemed poisonous now.

This room at the top of the house had windows all around. It was octangular and clung to the corner of the structure, hanging slightly above the third floor. When he and Cassie bought this place, they called this room the lighthouse. Sometimes when they took walks at night they'd come back and see its windows from a block away, all lit up and showing them the way home. "It looks so full of life," Cassie would say. "I bet some very happy people live in that house."

She'd used this room as her art studio. That was her painting hanging high on the wall above the foot of the bed: a natural bower of trees by a stream rendered in layers of olive green and umber and russet shadow. Every day Guy stared at the painting and thought he saw something different arriving in the gloom beneath the trees. This disturbed him, and yet he often thought about lying down in such a place and waiting for whatever was to come. Something stealing out of the shadows. Something rising out of the water along the bank. It unsettled him to think this way, but he couldn't help himself.

Several of the windows were open to facilitate a nice cross breeze. Cassie had liked it this way and Guy wanted to recreate at least some of the ambiance. He had plenty of blankets on the bed, but his daughter complained he would get too cold. He let her close most of the windows at night rather than argue.

He heard a car door slam. Probably Ann's husband Mark coming home from work. He was a good man and treated them all well. He told Guy tales of the progress he'd made with various household repairs and remodeling, because he recognized this was news Guy would appreciate hearing. But death embarrassed Mark, and of that they did not speak.

He could hear the kids playing outside, the crisp sounds they made as they stepped on the first fallen leaves, the random exchanges between neighbors he hadn't talked to in months. He might have been able to get himself up with the walker and use it to get over to the window and look out, maybe even call down a word or two, but he might fall, and ruin the evening for everyone. Besides, he didn't want to see how the colors had changed, how activities were still taking place without him, how life still maintained its same, inevitable pace. The world outside was still hungry. People were still starving to do things, to eat their time away. But Guy had no more appetite.

Late afternoon shadow slipped into the room and spread across the floor. Despite its placement high on the house, this room went dark first due to the placement of the nearby trees. But it was the beginning of autumn, and once the leaves were off the trees and spread across the ground, he'd see bare limbs and the steel clarity of winter light again, assuming he lived that long.

He wouldn't mind getting to hear the crunch of all those leaves again, the kids kicking them swish swish swish as they came home from school. He'd always enjoyed that particular sound, and the explosive crush when one of them dived into a thick pile.

Ann came up with a plate as it turned dark. He saw the shiny green of the lime Jell-O, and at least his stomach didn't react. She sat next to him and asked if he wanted to feed himself. He sat up, but his hand was too weak to securely hold the spoon. He hadn't expected that and didn't know how to feel about it. She fed him a few spoonfuls, and he relished the slight tang of flavor, but then his stomach clenched. She pushed the emesis basin under his chin just in time.

After she'd cleaned him up and he could speak, he said, "We'll try it again in the morning." He tried to smile but didn't know if he had actually succeeded at creating one.

She kissed him on the forehead. "Light on or off?"

"On for now. But could you check on me later? I mean, if I should fall asleep, you could switch the light off. I hate wasting electricity. The planet, you know?" He didn't want her to know he was scared, but perhaps she already did.

"Of course, Dad." The sounds of her descending steps went on for a long time.

He thought about the creamy white stuff they fed you in the hospital, when you couldn't or wouldn't eat. They filled a thick plastic bag with the stuff and hung it from a pole. They inserted a line directly into your chest, and the white stuff ran down the tube and fed you through there. He didn't want that. He tried to imagine eating without tasting or smelling, without using his mouth or nose at all. He wanted to talk to Ann about Hospice, but he didn't know how to bring up the subject. Ever since she was a little girl, he'd always hated disappointing her. The look on her face broke him every time.

The wind picked up. Cassie's painting rattled against the wall. He thought he saw movement inside the bower, something coming out to the stream to drink, or going back into the shadows to hide. But the painting was shaking, the wind trying to lift it off the wall, so possibly that was all.

He could hear the trees creaking and bending, the branches shaking, the sharp crackle of dead leaves as more began to fall. The yard must have been swimming with them. Both the open and the closed windows were clattering within their frames.

He began to smell the corruption. He was sure it wasn't him. He'd worried a great deal about his personal hygiene during his illness, whether they could help him stay clean enough so he wouldn't stink. He didn't want his grandkids to remember him as a smelly old man. He didn't know exactly what the odor was but it wasn't any smell he knew a human body made. The stench was somewhere outside the window.

He heard them moving through the leaves. He thought he might have been hearing them for several minutes but he'd been focused on the wind and Cassie's painting. He had no idea how many of them there were. The crunching leaves made it sound like an army.

Guy couldn't understand why they were so impatient. Perhaps he wasn't meant to understand. But they could have waited until he stopped breathing. Maybe people who were dying gave off a particular scent or emanation that drew them. Maybe they couldn't help themselves. That was what he wondered when he first saw one, the one bony shoulder and the side of its pale unformed face in the open window a few weeks ago.

He'd had a suspicion, so he asked Tony to read to him from a couple of books in his lawyer's bookcases. They would be Tony's eventually, along with everything else in the cramped office space which had been his retreat for decades. He'd made that clear to Ann even though she struggled as much as possible not to talk to him about the *after*. "He can use some of the supplies at the university, and maybe later he'll want to dig into my library, maybe even build one of his own," he'd told her. "I know he likes to read. He's a smart kid. I'm proud of him, tell him that. Tell him he can have anything in my office he wants. It's all his."

Tony was not the most patient lad, but he seemed to enjoy reading to Guy. He'd read well, with no stumbles. "From Arabic mythology. Ghoul or Ghul. Ghouls feed on human flesh, drink blood, rob graves, prey on corpses, etc. It also refers to a person who revels in the loathsome and revolting. I think I know some people like that."

"I think we all do. What does the other book say?"

"There are some pictures, but they're all over the place in terms of conception and approach. Your basic hideous creature, I guess, whatever that means to you."

"That's okay. I can use my imagination. Anything else?"

"Um. Drinks blood, we already knew that. Steals coins. Wait. 'Shape-shifts into an ostrich.'"

"You're making that up!"

"No Grandad – it's right here." He started to hand the book over.

"I'll take your word for it. I'm not seeing that well these days. Go on."

Tony skimmed the page with his finger. "Sometimes preys on lonely travelers or children."

"What does it say about that?"

"That's all. It's the last line of the article. Maybe if it can't find a corpse it eats whatever's handy. If you like I can see if I can find out more on the internet. Why are you interested in this Dungeons and Dragons stuff anyway?"

"I remember hearing the word, and Halloween's coming up. Have you picked out a costume yet? You could go as a ghoul or whatever."

"Grandad, the last time I dressed up for Halloween I was twelve, and even then I was embarrassed."

Guy remembered smiling at that bright and lovely boy. There was probably nothing to worry about. When the body was stuck in bed the mind had nothing better to do than to imagine the worst things possible. In any case, that was folklore. Even if he had seen something to worry about, the reality was likely far different than the human interpretation.

He heard scrambling on the brick outside. He began sweating profusely. He was being ridiculous. He knew prolonged bed rest sometimes resulted in psychological stresses besides the usual physical complications. Decreased concentration, orientation, and intellectual skills. Anxiety, depression, irritability – he'd experienced all those. Occasional hallucinations.

Then there was the smell again, originating from some rotten mouth, a corrupted gut. He hated to think Cassie might have experienced any of this during her final days. With all his being he hoped not. She'd been unconscious most of her last two weeks. Of course, he didn't know what she'd dreamed about during that time. He liked to think it was of a peaceful afternoon under the trees beside a stream, with nothing hiding in the shadows except more green.

The light went out. Had Ann come up and flipped the switch? Had he dozed off? He listened for footsteps on the stairs but heard none. From the spirited sounds of the wind, possibly they'd lost power. He wondered if she would try to check on him.

A shush of sound, and maybe something sliding over the windowsill. He felt an anxious itching in his extremities with no apparent location, a vague sort of nibbling.

A scramble and a crawl and he thought he would scream. He stared at the foot of the bed. The painting hanging above was swallowed in shadow. He had no taste for this. He wasn't cut out for it.

They stood up with all their blank faces, hairless bodies emaciated and vaguely doglike, their long fingers ending in sizable claws. He listened again for footsteps on the stairs and hoped not to hear them. He needed his family most of all to stay away.

For a moment his brain skipped, and he was back in the hospital bed with no appetite left for anything, the doctors towering above him, discussing his case as if he weren't there. He'd wanted to shout and tell them he could hear every word.

Then back in his own bed, in the lighthouse at the top of his world, the blank faces looming closer, then as if to tease him, the faces becoming his own, except with the hunger returned.

"Just do it!" he shouted. "Do your damn job!"

And they did.

THE WINTER CLOSET

It was a summer of painful colors and the hottest days on record. He could not remember the last time he'd felt happy, or safe. Most days he feigned hope because he'd heard people found despair unattractive. For months he slept with all the windows open even though the air was full of smoke. He woke up each morning with lungs like crumpling plastic. Many nights his sleep was interrupted by the distant sounds of gunfire and explosion. Whether actual or dreamed he did not know.

He counted himself fortunate he'd lived a few golden moments, but it wasn't worth the grim probabilities. Still, he couldn't see himself as a suicide. He was possessed of too much morbid curiosity. Although he feared it, he wanted to know what happened tomorrow.

An occasional glimpse of his future self in the mirror filled him with dread. He was the author of his own history. What people called progress seemed an accretion of inept decisions. Even those who once knew everything had lost control. The powerless could only hope to avoid the maximum amount of pain.

Despite his claustrophobia he refused to venture outside. He could not tolerate that effusive stench of grief.

The sudden drop in temperature should have brought relief but it made him fearful of his lack of preparations. The change in seasons wasn't unexpected—in fact, it was long overdue—but it had lost its comforting predictability. Although he welcomed the cold, its abrupt arrival still felt unnecessarily cruel.

The house was plagued by myriad drafts. He'd put off necessary repairs for years. Now he spent hours each day tracking down leaks, filling cracks with plaster or putty and holes with wadded up rags, but some he never found, and these multiplied, small pockets of intense cold running across his feet, up his legs, and around his neck, their bites turning his flesh numb.

Desperate for some protection, a warm coat, a heavy sweater, a simple, fuzzy scarf, he made his annual trek to the back of the house, where the winter closet lay sleeping, behind its heavy door.

There was no direct passage. Whoever designed this archaic residence must have believed advancement needed to be earned. He maneuvered his way around crowded rooms and edged along shabby galleries, negotiated stairs both up and down, past staggered photo arrays of the dead and the missing, navigated around the piles of thoughtless accumulation assembled at frequent points along the way, gathered over a lifetime, because he'd always been afraid to travel into the future with too little. He'd cultivated a bad habit of clinging to what was meant to be temporary but purchasing a quantity of ephemera at least provided a way to fill the time.

Several rooms he could not enter because they were overly full. Others featured goat trails bleeding between towering, precarious geometries. He could not manage these narrow paths without triggering frequent collapse, generating movements which rippled throughout the house for hours.

By the time he reached the massive closet door he barely had the strength to open it. His arthritic fingers could scarcely grip the knob. His arms shook as he dragged the heavy wood against the gritty floor. The shriek it made recalled someone's final, humbling pain.

The initial smell carried a hint of grave. Coats, sweaters, and jackets hung on both sides with a narrow aisle in between. Stacked high on shelves were the scarves and hats, with gloves and muffs piled beneath dust and cobwebs so thick he was loath to touch them. On the floor the extensive collection of old boots lay scattered like the remains of some careless slaughter.

Few of the garments had been his. They were the hand-me-downs of generations, of children, adults, dead, misplaced, or estranged, all that was left of a family he could not let go, but which had drifted away from him anyway.

The winter closet was so deep he could not see its end. There was no interior light. He had to rely on the dim bulb hanging in the hall.

The first few feet consisted of children's snow suits: vivid swollen torsos and arms with extraneous padding. His children who'd worn them had resembled dyed snowballs. He couldn't remember who had owned what, not that it mattered. He imagined they would tell him if they visited.

His late wife's coats were soft and woolly or shiny like her, and two or three, improbably, still held her fragrance from back when she was well and they all took better care. He resisted the urge to try them on. He understood the dangers of lingering here, and plunged forward, back into the years when he was a boy, and all the years before.

He'd expected it to be warm in here, a cozy adventure surrounded by furs and flannels, leathers and fleece, the intense fabrics of the departed. What he discovered instead was a deeper concentration of cold.

Stuck between the outfits and shoved to the walls were the not-clothes, the antique skis, the mops and brooms, the broken toys, the lopsided stacks of tattered books printed in languages he did not recognize. The closet walls themselves were papered with stained and yellowing maps, a tangle of routes highlighted, annotated, or crossed out.

Subsequent outer garments were greasy, and bits of fiber and lining and glue came off and stuck to his hands. The next strata smelled so intensely of smoke and fire he fought to breathe.

The last few coats still had arms inside their sleeves. He struggled to push his way past hanging carcasses, shrouded in stylish winter fashions and the stench of meat, their collegiate scarves wrapped around missing heads.

He kept pushing, even though he worried what he might discover on the other side. His bones had turned brittle, and his skin had become painful to touch. He was terrified of the possibility of frostbite and needed something warm to force himself into. Anything remaining would have to do.

As his hand punctured the final thinness of wall, a carbon black film tearing and disintegrating, he fell the rest of the way through, and realized he'd pushed his endeavor too far. Everything dropped and curled into nothing, and he stood alone on the ash-covered, tortured ground.

Here was a landscape evading recognition, and yet he knew every inch. Upheavals of concrete and earth adorned with the abstract markings of soot and rust, asphalt vomitus and a spray of metal renderings, plastic dust, and drifts of toxic vapor. In the distance, remnants of blackened trees sprawled as if executed.

So many people lived hoping for the good that might someday come. Religions and governments had been built using this hope as currency.

Random drips of movement made him blink. He blinked again as these accidental gestures resolved into animated shapes of annealed flesh poking from the wreckage, their humanity recognizable, although he suspected these empathetic faces had been baked, or painted on, and in fact they were too self-involved with their own hopeless solitude to notice him.

At least they could not communicate, so he didn't have to listen to their pain. He tried to examine his own flesh, but his brain would not allow it. Everything he'd ever cared for lay somewhere beyond his reach.

All good intentions were no longer relevant. Here even his skin did not fit.

It was a winter of painful colors and the coldest days on record.

PRIVACY

He had no idea who hired the surveyors, or what their ultimate purpose might be. One week they appeared in their orange jumpsuits, hard helmets, tinted goggles, gloves, and breathing gear. They came in twos and threes with cameras and laser equipment and went around taking pictures and measuring his property, the road, the trees, every rock and bush, whatever was visible, it seemed. Then they were gone. He should have gone out and asked what their business was and why they felt they had the right to disturb his privacy, but he did not. He was so troubled he couldn't see their faces that he'd remained inside, hiding.

It had been a quiet house for twenty years. He no longer had a family, and although he loved animals, he was reluctant to take responsibility for the life of another living creature. He had no houseplants for the same reason. He had become absentminded. He no longer knew how to prioritize. He could not be trusted.

He got rid of his landline years ago. He owned a cell phone for emergencies, but he kept it locked in a drawer. He took pleasure in the fact phone solicitors could no longer call him pretending to have his best interests at heart.

He had an old laptop computer, and sometimes he took it out to type notes into a diary. The entries were often months apart. He had no internet because he'd discovered people were at their absolute worst when they weren't face to face.

He owned a television, but he couldn't remember the last time he turned it on. He saw no reason to keep up with the news unless one wanted to feel worse. He owned a car, but he rarely used it. He had become unreliable behind the wheel. He had everything delivered.

Sometimes he believed people were trying to break into his home. He had no proof. He checked the exterior of the house every day, and although he discovered things he could not explain—a small tear in a screen, a scrape beneath a window, a dent in the door, a dead rabbit on his welcome mat—he failed to find conclusive proof of tampering.

The house itself rested bunker-like, half-buried at the top of a grassy lot surrounded by a cast-iron fence. It had been built in the late Fifties and showed its Frank Lloyd Wright influences with concrete and glass bricks, floor-to-ceiling windows, a simple unadorned interior, and custom-made lighting fixtures and tiles. It was a little on the cold side, in terms of both temperature and style. He didn't love the house, but he felt adequately contained within its walls.

The interior was painted various shades of white and gray, creating shadows which weren't really shadows, and as the sun went down, the walls seemed to move. This phenomenon had become a substitute for company. And like company, he sometimes found it worrisome.

He'd come to understand that in solitude was the way people lived, even if they imagined otherwise. They pretended a knowledge of others they did not have. Now that he was elderly, the anxiety from loneliness had become palpable. He had to lie in bed with fists clenched until it passed. If a manual existed for old age, he would certainly read it.

Sleep never came easily. He felt under threat the moment he lay down. If he heard a noise outside, he had to devise an explanation for it. He'd always been a troubled sleeper, even when he was still married. He'd lie in bed and listen to the house. Sometimes he'd hear sounds suggesting someone was trying to open the front door, bumping into furniture, coming up the stairs. Or he'd smell an odor, something burning, something dead. He didn't understand how she could sleep through all that. It was always up to him to get up and investigate.

Lately he'd become aware of flashes of light outside and a whispering too soft to interpret. He couldn't remember the last time he'd been close enough to someone to share a whisper. He wondered if this might be evidence the surveyors had returned, or perhaps some new threat he hadn't yet considered.

It wasn't that he wanted to be a hermit. All he wanted was some control over people's access to his life. It wasn't that he disliked people. He simply believed they lied about everything.

He avoided going outside except to search for signs of interference. He could see his front yard through the living room window, the sidewalk and the street, the empty field on the other side, and the line of trees in the distance. Beyond the trees he knew there were tall apartment buildings (on a clear day he could see their upper stories), a few warehouses, and a large outdoor shopping center.

If he opened a window a few inches to let in air, he heard traffic noises. Those noises had decreased significantly in recent days. Some days he heard no traffic sounds at all and wondered if something had happened to discourage people from driving. The last time the grocer delivered, he'd asked the young man if some big event had occurred, but the lad feigned ignorance. He told the boy he'd pay him to stay and chat, but the fellow would not be persuaded.

On low-traffic days, the whisperings returned. On heavy-traffic days, these conversations had been easy to miss, embedded within so much background noise. Once he perceived them, he could no longer ignore them. At times they sounded like the laments of the suffering.

He began hearing the noise of distant machinery at night. This was nothing like the traffic noises he'd heard before. These were poundings and scrapings and grindings, with the occasional beeping, and now and then the harsh bleat of a horn. Much like road construction sounds, he supposed, but they were so loud and so close, yet he was unaware of any such project happening nearby. These sounds normally started late, right after he went to bed, but sometimes he'd hear them earlier, just after dinner, or right after dark.

A few times he went out into the yard with a pair of binoculars to see if he could see anything. The sounds were much softer outside the house than they had been inside. He couldn't tell which direction the noises were coming from. Some evenings they seemed to be coming from everywhere, surrounding him. The binoculars were useless, revealing only the faintest glow beyond the trees.

His closest neighbor was an eight-story apartment building across a side street. It wasn't an expensive building. The wooden trim was heavily weathered, the pale stucco grayed. Each apartment had a balcony facing his house, where the residents kept small grills, chairs, or hung laundry. Some balconies were used for storage.

He'd never seen any people on those balconies, but he knew they lived there. Sometimes the contents of the balconies changed, and in the summer, he smelled their barbecues. He found that oddly comforting.

The machinery noises went away during the winter. He should have slept better consequently, but he was too agitated waiting for their return. With warmer weather they came back a few notes at a time, until by summer there was quite the symphony. He heard it early in the evening, and just before bed, and was frequently awakened when this concert periodically amped up in volume during the night. Sometimes this was accompanied by various lighting effects, red strobes alternating with broad beams of white light, blasting through even the thick curtains he'd hung over his bedroom windows to protect himself.

With the summer heat he began spending more time outside, sitting on a lawn chair in front of his house. No one bothered him. No one walked on the sidewalk below or even drove by. No one appeared on the balconies of the apartment building. When he used his binoculars to examine those balconies more closely, he saw they were thick with dust and debris.

Some afternoons he saw plumes of smoke rising above the distant trees, and sometimes there were lights, alarms, and beeping, not as intense as what he'd experienced at night, but still evident and distracting.

He ended these lawn chair observations following a series of "weather" events, although they were nothing like conventional meteorological occurrences.

Things had been quiet for an hour or so, and he had been thinking of going inside to take a bath or read. Anything, really, seemed more productive than sitting in the lawn chair staring at an uneventful horizon. But then he felt the hairs rising off his arms and legs, and then the hair on his head began to lift, followed by an unpleasant rippling sensation across his skin. He abandoned the chair and retreated inside, where the sensation disappeared.

A few days later, he was back in his chair, staring at the horizon, listening to the discordance of machinery, when it all stopped. Not just the machinery, he thought. He had a notion things had stopped everywhere to take a breath.

A cloud of dust appeared above the distant line of trees. Within seconds, it had reached the road in front of his property. Once again, he ran inside and watched behind the glass as dust blasted his house for the next two days, leaving his windows scratched and grimy.

When he was finally able to get outside to examine the damage, he discovered clouds of dust obscured those distant trees. He heard the crank and rattle of machinery somewhere inside the dust, and sometimes the flashing colored lights bled through.

Over the next few days, the air began to smell and taste of metal. Copper and iron. He realized he hadn't had a food delivery in weeks, but he hadn't been all that hungry, and was satisfied to rely on the canned goods remaining in his cabinets. There had also been no mail delivery, but that was not unusual.

A week later he smelled the burning, and the ashes fell everywhere. The world fell silent under drifts of gray. He used the opportunity to take to his bed. He'd read there was no real catching up on lost sleep, but he was determined to test the theory.

When he did wake up, it was again because of the noise of machinery, so loud this time it sounded as if it were coming from his own yard. The lights turned the interior of his house a deep red, and then a blinding white. He imagined he'd arrived in an unpleasantly clamorous heaven.

He went out the next morning to find everything gone, disintegrated, plowed under to within a few feet of his house. The apartment building had vanished, as had the street, the fence, the walk, the field, the trees. His house sat alone on a plain of thoroughly turned ground. Clouds of dust obscured the horizon in all directions. He carried the lawn chair out to the front of the house again and sat down, waiting, and watching.

When he spied the earliest signs of movement, he wasn't sure what they were. They could have been cars, or animals, anything. They were too far away to tell.

When he realized they were people, not running, but walking at a steady pace, he folded up his chair and went back inside. He sat at his kitchen table. The windows were too dusty to see with any confidence what was out there. Perhaps he should have cleaned them, not that he wanted to impress anyone. He waited a while, but not as long as he expected. There was a polite knock at the door. He could have pretended no one was at home. He got up to answer.

They had gathered shoulder to shoulder at the door, and he could see six or more deep behind them. Men and women, a few carrying children, and a few children standing and clinging to the adults as best they could. He knew there were many more he could not see, but he decided not to delve into the implications.

He cleared his throat. He couldn't remember the last time he spoke out loud. "May I help you?"

Apparently, it was all the permission they required. The people streamed into his house. It wasn't as if they forced their way in. He supposed for them it was a continuation of the journey. But he had to stand back against the wall just the same.

He was alarmed to see some were partially dressed, and a few naked, both men and women. The fact that they seemed inured to embarrassment told him how awful and lengthy their experience had been. He felt awkward about his own secret body. Hidden by his clothes, it was like slabs of pale flesh applied by a poor sculptor to a failing armature.

He wanted to find clothes for them, or at least some kind of drapery, but there was no space left to move.

He had no idea how many there were—maybe a hundred, or maybe many more. They filled his home, some having to lie down because they were injured, their loved ones hovering over, the rest pressed together so tightly he couldn't imagine how they could bear it. He worried most for the children. This couldn't be a safe situation for them. At least the open door allowed them to breathe. The entranceway was so crowded he couldn't have closed the door even if he wanted to.

His new houseguests remained silent for a time. They looked stunned. Most avoided eye contact, but a few did the opposite, staring at him until he felt compelled to turn away. He didn't know what he was supposed to do with all these traumatized refugees. He was ill equipped, to say the least, to handle such a circumstance.

A murmuring began from somewhere near the back of the house, around his kitchen area, he thought, or perhaps from one of the bedrooms. It was reminiscent of the late-night vocalizations he used to hear while attempting to fall asleep, a litany of lamentations and complaints, a cataloguing of suffering.

Once started, this murmuring spread through the house, differentiating into anger, indignation, and weeping. When it reached the living room, and people were talking over one another and shouting into each other's faces, he couldn't take it anymore, and walked outside. Several people squeezed past him to take his place. He couldn't have gone back inside even if he wanted to.

A few dozen of the evacuees waited outside. Most were sitting or lying down. A thin old fellow sat propped up against the wall by the front door, staring off into the distance, his hair disheveled, clothes torn, stinking of sweat.

He crouched by the old man and put his hand on his shoulder, thinking this was what empathy looked like. "I'd bring you water, but I'm afraid I can't get back inside. Could you tell me what caused all this?"

The man raised his arm and pointed. In the distance were the shimmering images of three large, orange-colored objects. He couldn't make out any details. From here they vaguely resembled beetles.

He began walking toward these beetle-like objects. He knew it was a foolish thing to do. He was old and out of shape, unused to exercise of any sort, and those things appeared to be a fair distance away. He might collapse or have a heart attack from the exertion. And if they had caused all this destruction, he had no business being near them. Still, he felt this was what he was meant to do. In any case, there was no more room in his house. He had nowhere else to go.

There was a consistency to the disturbed ground, the totality of the destruction, which was almost admirable. All he saw was fine dirt strewn through with pill-sized bits of color. He picked up a handful of the colored bits. They looked to be plastic, glass, concrete, metal, wood, a variety of materials all reduced to roughly the same size and shape. If nothing else, it was a remarkable technological achievement.

It seemed he arrived at the orange objects sooner than he should have, given the distance. It was evident the three large objects were machines, and as he drew closer, it became apparent how enormous they were, as massive as four- or five-story buildings.

He struggled for a comparison. They were unlike anything he had ever seen before. They appeared swollen, their armored coverings curved to give them that beetle-like appearance, although this close he thought they looked more like gigantic robotic ticks. Below the armor, a series of sharp metal gears connected to a complex configuration of great curved blades. Anything they ran over would be reduced to bits, and then further reduced by the redundant ranks of gears and blades behind.

The machine in front of him had a vertical cage attached that ran all the way to the top, with a ladder inside. He could barely see the cab up top, the beetle's head. He leaned back and shouted, "Hello! Is anyone there?" He tried twice more, but no one replied.

It would be quite a climb for someone of his age and limited physical abilities, but he could always grab onto a segment of the cage if he fell. He could even let the cage support him if he needed to rest. It would seem pointless to turn back now. What would he tell the others?

As he began to climb, he was struck by the machine's pronounced electrical smell. It was still quite warm. He was okay handling the rungs but if he let his hands stray too close to the body of the machine, he had to jerk them away to avoid a burn.

The dome-shaped cab was empty and felt welcoming. The soft chair in front of the dashboard hugged him as he settled in. The dome was see-through—he imagined it was a variety of plastic—and remarkably clear. From this height he could see for miles. It was all pretty much the same, as far as he could tell: plowed ground seeded with colorful bits of what used to be, and the scattered humpback shapes of these giant orange machines. He could see into the cabs of the two machines closest to him. They, too, appeared to be empty. He saw no people other than the tiny figures lounging outside his home, which seemed small and insignificant now.

The dashboard was packed with gauges and dials. He thought of the cockpit of an airplane, although he'd never been inside one. He had always struggled to learn new technologies, so just the dashboard's appearance was daunting. But there was a large red button, a large green button, a button with the icon of a horn beside it, and a joystick at the bottom of the board. He decided everything else must be optional. Human beings loved their options.

He pressed the green button. The machine hummed beneath him. He barely touched the joystick and the machine spun around. There was more noise this time, as wheels turned and things engaged underneath him, but it was relatively quiet for equipment of such size.

He played around a bit, backing up and moving forward, circling the other machines. He had to be careful; if he turned too quickly, it made him dizzy. It seemed he could change direction with only slight pressure applied to the stick. He couldn't remember the last time he'd *played*. He hadn't felt such freedom of movement in years.

He was too far away to see his house in any detail. But more people had come outside, and all the fluttering he saw might be waving. From here they looked like toys, like action figures satisfied with wherever he placed them or how he decided they should move. They shouldn't at all be surprised if he decided to kill them off. As a child, he'd killed his toy soldiers all the time.

At least he didn't have to walk back. Now he could drive.

He headed in that direction, much too swiftly it seemed, because some of the people were running away. He didn't want to scare anyone, so he pulled back on the stick a bit to slow it down. Still, people were running away, as they should, he supposed.

His house looked out of place, a bit of an eyesore, the more he thought about it.

He didn't know why he was doing it. It wasn't as if he wanted to hurt anyone. He knew this was what he needed to do. Maybe because he couldn't bear to be the only one whose world had been spared.

He honked the horn. It was much louder than he'd expected. It shook everything. But it had the desired effect. People were pouring out of his house and running away.

He kept blasting the horn. He didn't want to hurt anyone, especially the children, but he didn't want to be responsible for anyone's harm.

He paused a few yards away, triggering the horn repeatedly, until it appeared everyone had left, running scattered across the empty plain. So he'd done his due diligence. No one could ever say he hadn't.

He pushed the joystick forward, and plowed through his home, backing up and circling, running over the area again and again. The machine sounded different, even satisfying, as it ground and scraped and eradicated, until every bit of his world was gone.

MONKEYS

All of a sudden it were morning, and Maude couldn't hear herself think what with all the rattling carriages going about. She swore some days all that metal on stone shook the nerves right out of her, and she had to scream inside her head to rid herself of the sound. Most mornings she weren't up to dick. She needed breakfast and a drink, but mostly a drink. Drink enough and you didn't think too much about the state of your belly.

Polly offered her some bow wow mutton and the little she had left from her pint. Maude thought she'd have to spit that foul mutton out but knew she shouldn't, less she pass out in the street. Besides, Polly were her chuckaboo, and Maude didn't want to be rude. Polly'd talk your ear off, a real church bell, but if Maude weren't too drunk she liked to listen. She didn't have nobody else to talk to these days, and Polly was kind. Yesterday she give Maude a bag o' mystery right from her pocket and Maude was grateful to eat it. She learned a lot about goings on in the Chapel from dear sweet Polly. And she trusted what Polly told her. She knew Polly wouldn't sell her no dog.

"You best watch yourself, Sweetie," Polly said after their eating was done. "The Ripper got another Judy last night. Mary Kelly, member her? We used to see her at the Queen's Head. They say he butchered her like a pig. Tore up every sweet piece."

"Oh, Polly. Folks is always throwing the hatchet. You shouldn't believe everything you hear." But even as she spoke, Maude believed ever last word.

Maude needed fortification, so she searched the place till she found Old Charlie, who always seemed to have a bottle on him by whatever means. It didn't take much cuddling to get him to give it up. That, and a quick peek at her crinkum-crankum. Still, she didn't want to cheat him, so she give him a little of her quail-pipe. Then he played some with her kettle drums till he passed out again.

By the time Maude got outside the doss she was surely half-rats, and on her way to being tight as a boiled owl. It were a fine start to her day. There was a small crowd a few steps down. One of them foreigners had his self an ape. No, a monkey. Maude seen one before, not that long ago. Oh, he'd done all manner of tricks, that one. He wore a little red military hat—he was quite the gentleman, bowing to all the whores. Then later she reckoned he'd had too much to drink, and went after their faces. Now the coppers muscled them out, if they saw them, them and all them other animal acts. Most of them foreigners with their singing dogs and dancing monkeys and painted pigs. Some mores had canaries doing clever things, some mores had mice.

She didn't blame the monkey because of the drink. Only a put would give an animal a drink, not to mention it were a sad waste of liquor. But she knew the feeling—more than once she'd felt like tearing a face off after a drink or three. Not that it stopped her from drinking. She reckoned it wouldn't a monkey neither, once it got a proper taste.

But she liked them monkey acts well enough. This one here didn't have no liquor—she reckoned the word got around that it weren't the best idea. But the way it eyed her bottle—she tried to keep it hid. This one's clothes was plain, no better'n one of them street arabs, really. Course she still didn't get too close because of them big yellow teeth, but also because both the monkey and the foreigner handling him stank like shite. But oh how that little monkey could dance, and he'd play fight with you with his little wooden sword!

Shame the way the coppers would chase them out. He weren't out to cause no trouble—he was like an artist or something. He could make her smile, and that was no common feat these days. You'd think the coppers would have better things to do with their efforts, what with the Ripper about and all.

They got all kinds of entertainers coming through the Chapel, men what would dress up and do some foolishness for a coin or two. Most of them weren't no real acts, not like you'd get in the music hall if you could afford it, but good enough for a minute or two she reckoned, just to distract you from whatever vile circumstance you was in.

Yesterday on the corner she saw a Billy Barrow in his cocked hat and red feather, wearing some kind of a soldier's coat. The day before there was this old gent in a painted face in three or four ladies' dresses (she reckoned because of the cold). He sang songs in a high-pitched geezer's voice, and in one or two he weren't too bad.

Not that all them performers was welcome, as far as she was concerned. Last month there were a feller in a devil's suit dancing and following her around, sniffing at her. No joke— whenever he got close enough to her she'd hear him sniffing and smelling her so hard it was like he wanted to suck her right inside. Of course she'd been drinking so maybe the poor feller was just sick with the crud and couldn't help his sniffing. Or maybe—him dressed up like a devil and all—he weren't there at all. Or maybe, it being the Chapel, he were the real Devil his self, there to give her a personal invite to Hell.

The shouting came at her like a bunch of broken church bells. Here come them raggedy boys again, them street arabs. They was more of a bother than the flies or the rats, and almost as many, buzzing in her ear, running over her shoes. They was like a whole tribe of monkeys, them boys, but worse. And the ones that was sick or lame, or been beat too bad, they'd just lie around in the corners of the alleys all day, touching on each other for comfort. It were a sad thing to watch.

"Hey you old dollymop!" one of them little cheeky bastards shouted as he came running by, and slapped her on the nancy. She swung around and tried to kick the ape, and nigh near dropped her bottle. You couldn't feel sad for them monkeys long, now could you, what with the pranks they pulled. "I ain't exactly amateur!" she shouted. It were the only thing she could think of to say. She didn't follow. That bunch looked eager for mafficking, so she stayed clear.

Not that it were their fault, she reminded herself. Anywhere you got lots of whoring, you got lots of them street arabs as a result. One begets the other—the ones what got no wheres else to go, homeless and barefoot. Half of them died before they were old enough to stand proper. And those were the lucky ones.

And they weren't all that scared of Jack, not that she could tell. "Watch out! I be the Ripper!" one of them shouted, and the rest went running away giggling like hens.

She looked sadly at her empty bottle. She didn't remember finishing it. After a while drinking was like breathing. Whoever thought about how much air they breathed? Whoever made it their business to count? Maude knew she oughtna drink so much. It got her into some terrible scrapes sometimes. That was how she met her last husband, weren't it? Ran into him in the pub. He could be right handsome, had a door-knocker of a beard. A bit of a gal-sneaker and too much of a tot-hunter, but he could say some awful pretty words. Said he couldn't help his self, he were a man who loved a bit o' jam. He always wore a nice coat, and a pair of gas-pipes showing off what he had to offer a gal. But sometimes he'd hit Maude in the sauce box or up on the face and she'd cop a mouse, and that would hurt her earning for a time, although most of her customers weren't that particular, long as she showed them a good backside.

She heard a shout and looked down the lane, saw them monkeys go batty-fang on an old man. She wanted to be bricky about it but she was too scared about what they might do to her. She didn't stay around to watch.

The rest of the day she went walking and scrounging, more walking than scrounging because times was hard and the competition were fierce. She'd never been good at either begging or thieving. What she was good at was best done in the dark, without folks looking on. Even in the Chapel folks could be modest at times.

She guessed that was one thing she had in common with the Ripper. Plying her trade in the dark. She still had a little bit of shame in her. Did he?

She knew that Mary Nichols. She got hers late August, or maybe September. Annie Chapman was September for sure— Maude seen her walking around the day afore. It happened that fast, like the Ripper was the Lord's very judgment. That slapped her a bit. There was always clergymen around, ministering to unfortunates such as herself. Could one of them holy men be the Ripper, delivering God's own last judgment?

Last winter they lost Annie Millwood and Ada Wilson. Course nobody knew about the Ripper then. Maybe he done them, too. Maybe he'd been doing whores long as she'd been alive, and before. She'd never trusted them churchmen—never would. She'd heard tales from other whores about the things they liked to do in the dark what weren't no joke. The question was, why wasn't God doing something about it, unless like everybody else in London he'd given up on them poor Chapel folk.

She cut through a court and stumbled over a couple of them street arabs, lying together on the side of the lane. They looked like nothing but a pile of rags until they started moving and panting. She hated to see it, children shouldn't be up to such doings, but times being what they were children was doing everything adults did, including all manner of crimes and evilness, including murder. So what's a little adult comfort when the young ones were suffering, long as it was for each other and not for some nonce? Where was the harm? Maude would have to let God sort that one out.

A bunch of them monkeys come running down the lane then and near knocked her down. She couldn't see their faces but she reckoned they was just more of that same bunch. They was everywheres today, and either their faces was too dirty to see what they looked like, or they had them rags wrapped round their heads like foreigners. It were spooky to look at, like somebody's sorry bit of laundry decided to run off by itself.

Some lucky soul was cooking fish somewheres. It made her mouth water so bad she had to walk away from there otherwise she might start bawling. She was hungry almost always, but it got far worse when there was cooking nearby. But sometimes just looking at a bit of shoe leather reminded her of what meat used to taste like.

She ran into another of them street monkeys all wrapped up in his rags and trying to sleep. She kicked at it as she walked by, and it groaned. She felt ashamed about it later, but them arabs had scared her right enough, and she'd been drinking.

She reckoned for most of them that street life seemed better than working the factories making match boxes, or sweeping the way for the rich to cross the road. Sometimes them folk would pay you, sometimes not, but it were always humiliating weren't it? Least she thought so.

There was always kids dying in the Chapel. Some deserving it more than others, she reckoned, just like adults. She couldn't do nothing about it anyways. It was hard enough keeping herself alive, much less some youngster.

At least she'd never shite one out herself. She was proud of that. Course maybe she had no choice in the business. Maybe God wouldn't allow it. Still, some whores she'd known turned their babies out at night so they could conduct business in the room. Let them children wander alone into all kinds of darkness. Least she'd never done that. She'd rather be a sack maker than do that to her own flesh and blood.

Especially what with the Ripper about. He cut that Eddowes woman up like a cow hanging in the market they said. She supposed any little boy'd be safe, but them girls, some of them girls looked older than they ought to. Some of them young girls might be just to Jack's tastes.

Them children in the Chapel—they didn't have no chance.

Still, nothing Maude could do about it. Any soul living up in a doss on Flower and Dean Street had their own troubles to worry about. 4p got you a coffin to sleep in, but most nights she ended up leaning on a rope. It were a blessing she was tired all the time. She reckoned she could sleep just about anywheres if she could just shut her eyes. If she had a walnut in her pocket least she'd have something to eat, but most nights she had nothing. Maybe some night she'd sleep so well they couldn't wake her up in the morning, and wouldn't that be a blessing?

It were getting dim now, the world closing its eyes cause it didn't want to see too clear the goings on down in the Chapel. Time to make her rounds, stand outside the pubs till some gent showed some interest.

She run her identical routine ever night, so she hoped the Ripper weren't watching her, cause if he did he'd know exactly where she'd be. She'd go through most of them ever night: the Queen's Head, the Ten Bells, the Horn of Plenty, the Britannia, the Alma, and the King Stores. Then a quick walk around Saint Botolph's Church to throw off the coppers afore trying another. They was whores making that round trip of Saint Botolph's all night ever night. What did the coppers think they was all doing, praying?

The bell at Christ Church rang, and she heard one of them criers in the distance selling whatever—she couldn't afford nothing anyway. Other than them few sounds the world suddenly looked empty and heartless, and quiet as death. Maybe she'd died. She could only hope. What was sure though was she'd lost some time. That's what come of drinking all day. You lost pieces. Which tweren't so bad.

She'd go stand outside the Queen's Head. Some gent would set her up good and proper—all she could drink, if she picked him right, and yet she'd still make sure she was up for walking away. She'd make sure he was very arf'arf'an'arf himself, cause he wouldn't be up for doing much. Later maybe she'd tell him they'd been up to all kinds of nasty business—she'd rub up against him plenty so he wouldn't know the difference. Not that she particularly wanted to cheat a customer, but some nights her lady bits was just all wore out from plying the trade. Some nights she just had to let them things rest.

She didn't like them shadows over there, or them over there neither. The dangerous thing about the drink were that it made her skittish, and kicked up her imaginings. Some nights she saw the Ripper everywhere, in many a gent's face, or in the shadows where probably no one be at all. Nobody really knew what he looked like, but you'd hear descriptions of him just the same. Some said he was pale, but then there was those who swore he was swarthy. Some said he had hair all over his face, more like an animal than any kind of proper human being. But others said he just had a slight moustache, or none. Lots of folk said he wore this long black coat, but more than a few said it were red (which she doubted, less that was because of all the blood he'd spilled). A lot of folk claimed he was a foreigner, but anything going bad in the Chapel they most always blamed them foreigners. He could a been a right famous gentleman, maybe even a banker. Maybe even a royal. No one knew. But ever moving shadow seemed like it might be him, or ever bloke leaving a pub, was that a knife he was hiding? Or she'd see some gent acting right skilamalink, and she'd think he must be the Ripper for sure.

Maude figured it were twixt four and five, and she couldn't see nothing much cept shapes and shadows and a little bit of yellow cast by the lamps, the sky being so black and the shadows blacker still. She'd pass a lamp and she'd see the black bits floating in the air, and she didn't like to think about it, but course that's what they all breathed—a little bit of air, a little bit of sky, and a whole lot of black bits floating down into you and gumming up your lungs. Good thing most died young, she reckoned, otherwise they'd grow old enough to fill up with black bits, burying them from the inside out.

At least the Chapel looked better in the dark, cause it couldn't look no worse now could it? She couldn't understand what held some of them buildings up, less it were the filth caked on them bricks. Tens and hundreds of years probably, with never a good wash. Course you couldn't keep clean in a city like this, less you was one of the rich folk what could afford a hot bath and new clothes.

A couple of them raggedy boys come screeching past, stinking of monkey. Scared the piss out of her. She'd shout at them but she could force nary a sound out of her mouth. She wished she had Polly here with her. That old gal would tell them monkeys a thing or three.

She'd had too much to drink that day, she reckoned. Or maybe she hadn't had enough. Maybe she was just about due. She felt all wobbly.

They was a big pile of rags in the middle of the lane. She kicked at it, but this time the rags didn't move, and made nary a sound, so either they was rags, or they was dead. But she didn't feel much like checking.

That brick wall in front of her was crumbling, and all drippy. She stumbled then, and fell against it. And found that weren't no brick crumbling off, but somebody's innards stuck to it and peeling off, and them dark coppery drips must be redder than red. She turned and barked up some sick, and looked at them rags again, cept now she knew they weren't no rags, or at least they didn't use to be. Used to be some poor whore, but all she was now was some ripped up rags.

The stench was something awful, which was saying something, given she'd lived in a slaughterhouse and a sewer most of her sorry unnatural life.

She heard him running on the stones, or maybe it was them children. There were too many steps. Too many sounds. She heard a child's pitiful crying, then realized it was herself making them sounds.

Maybe she'd just start running. Maybe she'd run down to Aldgate and Leman—she knew a few folks there. But it were dark, and what if there was nobody about she could trust?

Maude started running anyway. She could think of nothing else to do. But she kept running into them piles of rags. There was stinking piles of rags just about everywhere in the dark lane.

She went up to one, and she didn't kick it. She just nudged it ever so carefully with her shoe.

That's when them skinny monkeys leapt up, climbing over each other, climbing up to the height of a very tall man. And she couldn't tell amid their stink and their screaming if they was the real trained monkeys or them half-starved poor street arab babes she sometimes felt sorry for.

But what surprised her was how they had them tiny knives hidden in their scrawny little hands. And how they knew just how to cut, and where.

WHEN THEY FALL

Is someone there? Asking the question aloud would have been unbearable.

They bought the house because of the view: perched beyond the summit of a steep hill, the Cape Cod boasted expansive windows overlooking the center of town. Towering oaks on each side protected it from the worst of winter. It was a promising home for raising two children.

The only defect in its unadorned aesthetic was a tiny gable with an oval window protruding from the steep roof several feet from the central chimney: an odd, asymmetrical detail which made Ralph think of a giant's damaged eyeball. It was the house's tiny attic, hot and dusty, which their daughter Robin claimed as her playhouse.

His wife Emma never liked the drab colors: gray shingle siding and black shutters, an ashen roof, a few strokes of white trim. She said it was like living inside an old black-and-white film. They talked often of repainting, but they never did.

It was only after living there a few seasons did they grasp the property's difficulties. The steep road iced over most winters necessitating a detour of several miles to ensure a safe commute. The local children loved this road for sledding (they called it "suicide hill") and despite the posted warnings, serious injuries and near-misses accumulated each year. Ralph and Emma struggled to keep their small son John away from this particular danger. Mostly they succeeded.

For Ralph, however, the worst thing about the house had been those damn oak trees. Beautiful and stately as they might be, every fall they released acorns, twigs, and leaves a half foot long across the yard. The acorns sounded like small bombs hitting the roof and chipping the shingles. The fallen nuts attracted scores of squirrels and field mice who fought over them and drug them into corners where they rotted in musty, sour-smelling piles.

As they aged, the oaks dropped limbs, some of them tree-sized. A decade ago, Ralph wanted to have the oaks cut down, but Emma refused. "You'd be begging for more trouble. Hasn't this family seen enough sorrow?"

Now he could do whatever he wanted, but Ralph didn't want to do much of anything.

Is it her? Is it him?

The afternoon of Halloween the leaves lay thick over Ralph's lawn. He'd stopped raking years back. It was too hard. He could have hired someone, but he never did. He knew letting them accumulate wasn't good for the grass, but he couldn't remember why. He supposed it wasn't healthy for any living thing to lie beneath a layer of dead matter. He rarely looked at his yard anymore, but where dull leaves had blown away, he could see a paler, sparser version of the lawn they had when Emma was still alive.

The night before, he'd roused to a succession of soft bangs, like a series of doors closing. It wasn't the first time he'd been awakened that way. He suspected it wouldn't be the last.

He carried the rake out front thinking he'd scrape the flagstone path clean. It probably wasn't necessary, but he was feeling neglectful. Emma had loved her flagstones. The leaves were firmly compacted onto the stones due to frequent deliveries. He never went out, and no one ever visited. Smaller leaves, blown from some neighbor's yard and disintegrated to transparency, ornamented the larger ones. They resembled huge, irregular flakes of skin.

Something moved through the leaves on his left. He turned his head quickly but missed it. His vision wasn't what it used to be. A swift paleness intruded on his right side, and he jerked his head around again. Still nothing. It was aggravating. It might be a floater in his eye, or something worse, his retina detaching. More than once he'd glimpsed a fragment of memory in the borders of his visual field. He didn't know if that was normal and was afraid to ask his doctor.

A squirrel boldly approached, stopping within a couple of feet. The animal wore a child's face. Not his son's, he didn't think. But the creature was so jittery it was difficult to tell.

Ralph turned away and slammed the rake's metal teeth onto a flagstone and began to scrape. Leaves slid aside exposing a layer of tarry black. Disgusted, he tried kicking the leaves over to hide it.

The last few autumns had been strange, warmer than normal, the summers refusing to let go. Then when the seasons finally changed, they did so abruptly. The strip of ground in front of the windows had always been rich with fall flowers: mums and pansies, asters, violas, black-eyed Susans. Emma curated them for years. All he did was weed now and then.

An irregular flake of black shutter peeled away, turning into a butterfly which lit from one flower to the next. Surely it was a trick of the light, and it was about time for those flowers to turn anyway, but each flower the butterfly touched appeared to fade, curl, and wither.

A nearby bird whistled itself down to silence. The sky, the air, turned silver. Ralph felt on the verge of falling. A wind came up, and the sudden breeze brought flies, a narrow cloud of them like a dagger. There was a terrible stench, something far worse than rotting acorns, and for a moment he imagined he smelled his own death.

Ralph went back inside. Trick-or-treaters rarely came to his house anyway. The first Halloween after Emma died, he bought a silly clown mask and sat by the door with a bowl of candy. Less than a dozen children came. The next day he devoured the leftover sweets as if his life depended on it and made himself sick. Even fewer children came the following year. He gave the few that did come great handfuls of candy. Every time he made himself smile at a child he felt as if he were wearing a mask.

The house always smelled odd when he came in from outside. Today it was stale, warm sweat with hints of shampoo. Like a little boy's hair after playing.

The dim outline of a figure shimmered in the doorway to the dining room. He avoided looking too closely. He heard a wisp of sound so vague he couldn't tell if it was a voice or not. His big empty house felt too small for him.

Ralph dodged the dining room and went into the kitchen. The gunmetal counters were clean and uncluttered, the kitchen in general pristine enough for a house showing. He could tell immediately if anything had been moved.

This year he hadn't bothered purchasing candy, although he hated disappointing children, especially the smaller ones. He didn't know why the kids never came anymore. Maybe they thought the house unoccupied. The light above his front steps burned out years ago, he wasn't sure when.

He sat down at his laptop on one end of the kitchen table. There was an email from his daughter Robin, pictures of his three small grandsons costumed as superheroes. It had been a couple of years since they moved across the country, and lately she'd been sending emails instead of answering her phone. He responded with how much he loved their outfits and how he'd love to hear all their voices. Anytime. He was home all the time. He hoped she would call.

He wanted to tell her to be careful letting them cross the street. This was unnecessary advice. She was a grown woman and a good mother. But he wanted to tell her anyway. He wanted to tell her to hold their hands. Then he thought, with three kids, how could she grab all three, protect all three? He wanted to tell her to make Jack get off work early and go with them trick-or-treating. Ralph never thought Jack was the most responsible person, but he could at least hold on to a child's hand.

Ralph watched as the shadows of the leaves drifted down outside the curtained windows, a few at a time, then a sudden torrent. Maybe it would storm, and the children would stay away, and he could spend the night in peace, assured of their safety.

He closed his eyes and put his head down on the table. He could hear the hum of the house conveyed through the wood, tabletop to table legs to floor to beams to studs and whatever else was connected. He didn't know the physics involved but believed sounds traveled quite far if some sort of contact was maintained. But maintaining contact was always a challenge.

An old house generated so many noises which could not be explained. Many of those noises sounded like conversation. The refrigerator, the water pipes, the furnace, they all had a voice and those voices spoke to him because no one else was here to listen. Maybe he shouldn't have stopped drinking coffee, but it scared him the way caffeine made his heart race.

What do they want? What do they want him to say?

The afternoon light was waning. He needed to find a place where he could hide for the evening, so he could turn out the lights so no one would think he was at home. It felt mean, disingenuous, but if they thought no one was at home those hopeful children walking around with their empty treat bags wouldn't have their feelings hurt.

He heard a light knocking on the door, so soft he wasn't sure he'd actually heard it, then it came again, a hesitant, shy knock. He peeked through the curtains. He didn't see anything, then he heard the child's voice through the door—he couldn't tell if it was male or female—*Trick or Treat.*

It was too early. Even the parents of the smallest children in this neighborhood waited until four thirty or five, if they went trick-or-treating at all. These days the parents of small kids took them to neighborhood parties where they could control things, where it was safer.

Ralph sat in a chair by the door—the same spot where he had waited for the children years before—waiting for this child to give up and go away. But every few minutes came the light knock, and the announcement, barely above a whisper—*Trick or Treat.* Finally, the knocking and the entreaty ceased, and Ralph got up to make himself a sandwich before retiring upstairs, when he saw the small shadow appear in the lower portion of the front window, growing larger as it leaned in closer until the head hit the windowpane once, then twice. *Trick or Treat.*

Of course, it was just a child, but none had ever been this bold before. *He intends a trick*, Ralph thought. Well, Ralph thought he deserved one, a trick, some awful trick.

The shadow disappeared, then reappeared in the side window, the one off the dining room. Knock, knock, as the nodding head struck the glass. *Trick or Treat.*

Ralph moved toward the stairs, intending to go up to his bedroom, where he would hide and read until the night was over, but then the shadow reappeared in his kitchen window, which was too far off the ground for any child to reach, and yet there was the nodding, and the knocking head, and the louder, insistent, *Trick or Treat...Trick or Treat.*

"Go away! I'm calling the police!" he shouted, feeling foolish, because how could he call the police on a child?

The shadow suddenly ballooned, filling the window, then disappeared.

Was it his rage or theirs?

He was an adult. He knew life was ephemeral. Each person was given the slimmest shard of time. But children had no idea. They dwelled in the forever now.

Ralph and Emma always shared the Halloween duties. Emma spent hours preparing treat bags. The kids helped at first, but soon lost interest, preferring to carve pumpkins or watch some scary movie before going out to trick or treat themselves. Ralph helped with the pumpkin carving, but he hated the feel of the pumpkins' guts on his hands and between his fingers.

They used to put out elaborate Halloween displays in front of the house. Now those decorations gathered dust in the basement.

Emma would take one child out to make the Halloween rounds while Ralph stayed home with the other doling out candy, then after an hour or so they'd switch. They made sure both of their competitive children received equal attention and participation.

Emma was good at this. She had a knack for giving their kids what they needed at any given time. For Ralph, Halloween was a chaotic storm of worry and distraction. There were always too many kids dressed similarly in whatever TV- or movie-inspired garb was popular at the time, crowding each other on the sidewalks, pouring over the lawns. It would be too easy to misplace a child, or God forbid lose one to some costumed predator (although Emma insisted such things almost never occurred).

Robin insisted she was too old to hold his hand. John didn't verbally object, but the holiday made him overexcited, and his sweaty, squirmy hands difficult to hold. They tried to control his consumption of candy, but every year he managed to devour enough sweets to make himself agitated, weepy, and ill.

They were running behind. It had become obvious the sheet John was wearing with its misaligned eyeholes, turning him into a small, stumbling ghost, was too long. Every few houses they had to stop and readjust, tucking some of the sheet under John's belt which he insisted spoiled the look. Ralph was trying to get John home after his last turn so Robin and Emma could go out again. He could imagine his daughter's growing annoyance even as they turned the corner. But John was distracted, needing to explore every decorated yard, wanting to greet the wearer of every unique costume, oblivious to time.

It was a struggle of push and pull all the way home, Ralph practically dragging his son, who in his upset was spilling candy from his plastic pumpkin bucket, stooping to retrieve what he spilled, yanking his hand away.

They were crossing the street just past the top of the hill, less than twenty feet from their yard, when the push and pull between them broke, and John fell back just as a car topped the road, unable to see the little boy lying there.

Emma and Robin saw it all from their front door. The sound of Emma screaming, as if she'd been broken, was something Ralph still heard. He remembered little of the funeral itself: unable to let go of his wife's and daughter's hands, the stillness around them, all those others watching from a safe distance.

Are we ghosts hiding within our costumes of flesh?

Their house, Ralph's house, was now thought haunted by the neighborhood kids. Of course—that's why they stayed away. His life had become too sad and scary even for Halloween. He felt it as an insult, but he couldn't blame them. The past few years the days after Halloween were spent removing the bits of rotten pumpkin people threw into his yard.

Emma noticed the changes in their house, experienced those unexplainable events, before he did. Ralph largely checked out, but Emma went to therapy, joined grief groups, started a diary chronicling her bereavement. She never blamed him, at least not directly, but she must have thought—he didn't know what she thought. She never said anything about his part in it, and he never asked.

She used to ask him if he had moved things in the kitchen, in their bedroom. He had no idea what she was talking about. Eventually she moved out of their bedroom, but the disruptions—chairs moved, cosmetics disappearing, sheets torn from the bed—followed. He didn't hear the late-night rapping which drove her awake. Or the early morning weeping of something, or someone, lost.

They tried repurposing his room. For a while it was her sewing room, but she was never comfortable there. They changed the wall colors several times. But whatever paint they applied discolored into muddy and unpleasant shades. John's old room became the guest room no one ever used.

Robin lost her attic space to John's toys and other select possessions neither Ralph nor Emma felt able to throw away. They asked her, and she gave them her permission, but Ralph knew it was a terrible mistake.

The days fall away quickly, and disintegration cannot be stopped. What happened to the kisses they once exchanged, all those kind words? Ralph had no idea how to preserve them.

A month after Robin left for college Emma tripped on the staircase and fell halfway down, shattering her hip. She was never the same again. After another year she went into a care home. Three more years and she, too, was gone.

What was he more afraid of? That these presences were real, or they were not?

Ralph sat halfway up the staircase eating a sandwich, a glass of pale apple juice on the step beside him. It was five o'clock and he could hear children out on the sidewalk with their parents, and someone kicking through the leaves, but no one knocked, or rang the bell, or yelled *Trick or Treat!* He was fine with that.

The staircase walls were crowded with pictures, most of them Robin and her kids, and early portraits of John prominently placed. Ralph had some photos of Emma in his bedroom upstairs. The only photos of himself were tucked away in albums somewhere. He never looked at them.

Most of the older photos on these walls were ones Emma had hung of her own family—father and mother, uncles and aunts, numerous cousins, and unidentifiable extended relatives. He didn't know any of them, but it would have felt disrespectful to take them down. They were all ghosts now, or at least ghosts to him, the photos taken before they knew how they would end.

Ralph heard more kicking through the leaves, laughter and talking, distant doorbell rings, knocks on other doors. Most seemed to understand what his home's darkness implied and continued on their way. It was time for him to go upstairs.

He went up to his bedroom but couldn't bring himself to go inside. He felt rather than heard the footsteps behind him. He opened the door to the gritty old staircase and ascended into the attic, shutting the door firmly behind him. He fumbled for the light switch. The bulb was dim but burned.

He was surprised by how clearly he could hear the noises outside, the shrill voices of many children, shoes on the pavement, in the leaves, the rustlings of dozens of treat bags, cars on the road, the occasional explosive horn. Ralph went to the head-sized oval window and peered out.

He had an unobstructed view of the wide, slate-colored sky hanging over the center of town, the smoky clouds drifting in, and below, the armies of costumed children swarming the streets, the lawns and porches, everywhere Ralph looked, their impossible numbers flickering in and out of the shadows, doubling and tripling at times, anonymous, their mysteries hidden behind their masks.

Closer in, just below, his yard was full of more teeming figures, this year their outfits looking primarily homemade: pirates and princesses and ghosts, bizarre creatures in their antique Victorian clothes and rotting paper bag masks, hundreds of spirits hiding under a variety of sheets, brilliant white and softly beige, all the shades of smoke and gray, heavy and stiff, diaphanous and virtually transparent, although Ralph caught no glimpse of the children inside.

If he had known, he might have bought candy and prepared for a real Halloween this year. But he couldn't possibly have bought enough.

His son's toys lay nearby. He glanced at the boxes laden in thick layers of dust and felt ashamed.

He couldn't help feeling observed and judged. The stars were eyes in the darkness gazing down. They witnessed every bit of neglect, every careless deed.

The children continued to flood his lawn, the leaves disappearing beneath their feet. They seeped out into the street and beyond. They pushed out to the edge of the steep hill and the road leading dizzily down, and spilled over, hundreds of costumed children falling into the dark and nothing.

Ralph's eyes grew weary of staring. He heard the slippage on the roof, the groan of shifting timbers, and felt a gravity changing everything. Two dark holes appeared side by side in the night sky in front of him, depths so black no light could pass through. The vast shrouded face spread beyond the edges of the roof, obscuring the stars. It was all he could see or think about.

THE THINGS WE DO NOT SEE

One evening he became aware of a great shift in gravitation, as if something massive had suddenly entered this world. He could not see it, but he knew it was there.

Clarity was difficult to achieve. There was so much he could not see. He wondered if he had been lonely, before. Did he have friends? Did they enjoy his company? He considered whether he might have lived his life in a state of despair. He had no way of knowing, his prior existence a dream he'd forgotten.

Working all night in the print shop, Cooper compulsively checked the view from the front window: a sliver of sidewalk bathed in halogen glare, the asphalt road damp despite weeks without rain, the shambling gray figures of the dispossessed backgrounded by the stark silhouettes of the warehouses, rising above them the outlines of water tanks, transmission towers, and slender smokestacks. Beyond that he could only imagine, which all too often was an activity fraught with risk.

He heard whispering, talking, the occasional growl or moan. He could not be sure if these communications were exterior, perhaps from the abandoned parking garage next door, or interior. If he distracted himself sufficiently, they went away.

The stench was back, an oily fragrance with notes of salt and vinegar. He noticed it his first night at the *Print & Copy*, and since then it waxed and waned with no discernable pattern. Some nights he thought he'd suffocate. Even when he couldn't smell it, he knew it was present, enmeshed in the fabric of the neighborhood. Sometimes he wondered if he was the only one aware of the reek. His boss never mentioned it, and Cooper was hesitant to ask.

He proofread the flyer upside-down before calling the customer to the counter. His boss once asked how he learned to read like that. But Cooper couldn't answer. As far as he knew he'd always had this useless talent, a poor trade for a lifetime erased.

"Sir, your job is ready."

The small man in the long gray coat rose unsteadily from the bench. He shuffled to the counter and glanced at the top sheet. "Very…nice. You were correct about the paper."

"The heavier stock holds up better on bulletin boards, utility poles, or wherever you want to put it. Take your time. Make sure everything's to your satisfaction."

While his customer examined the flyer Cooper glanced outside. A scruffy vagrant stood rubbing his forehead back and forth against the window, leaving a greasy smear. It wasn't the first time. There was a cleaning solution and cloth under the counter for such occurrences. The man's face looked distorted through the thick glass, feverish and unwell, the skin inflamed, forehead wrinkles and laugh lines receding as he appeared to de-age. Then the derelict peeled his face away, and the way it momentarily adhered to the pane, Cooper was afraid he'd leave some of it behind.

"Perfect. Simply perfect," his customer said.

Cooper focused on the task of wrapping up the flyers. "This seminar, are you the instructor?"

The fellow looked up with watery eyes. "Guide. We learn from each other. You find your own path. I can only help you launch your voyage."

"*Creating Your New Story.* I thought it was a creative writing class. But it's more than that, am I correct?"

"Oh yes. It is a journey toward self-definition, personal growth, but most of all increased connection. Loneliness has become a fundamental problem in our world. Human beings are natural story makers. Their most important story is the one they make up about themselves and their relation to others. If you are unhappy with your life, it is time for a new story."

"That idea is quite...appealing." Cooper gazed at the flyer the guide held in his hand. He watched as the words rearranged themselves, letters reversing, turning sideways, expanding across the sheet, some shrinking into a series of dots or nothing. Others gathered at the middle of the page, sending tendrils trawling to the paper's edge.

"Perhaps you'd like to come. I accept drop-ins. You pay at the door." The little man placed the flyer, still busy with changing typography, into Cooper's hands.

Cooper's fingers tingled as the ink appeared to enter his skin. He tried not to react, but he felt his face burn. "Thank you."

He tried to occupy himself with busywork until the next customer came in. A moist sigh issued from somewhere outside. He opened the front door a few inches and listened. He heard nothing definable, a few of the older buildings creaking and bending in the wind. Something in the distance swayed, but it was impossible to tell what it might be—a tree, surely, or a loose panel, a sign. It never paid to speculate.

Months before, Cooper found himself traveling through this district on foot. He had no idea who he was beyond the name on his ID: Stefano Cooper, with a faded photo, a birth date, and an address for an apartment which might or might not have been current, but he had a vague notion the address wasn't far away. He had a wallet full of cash but somehow knew this was the last of his funds. He needed a job. For reasons unknown to him he required a job in this neighborhood.

The area was unpromising. Sad-looking, raggedy-dressed men and women wandered the crumbling streets and alleys. His own clothing seemed presentable. Cooper felt his face and hair. He'd recently washed and shaved, apparently in preparation for the job search.

The neighborhood was a complex of warehouses and abandoned rail spurs. Warehouses needed workers, so he searched for HELP WANTED signs on every window and door. Eventually he was drawn to the sprawling hulk of a parking garage. The entrance was fenced and adorned with warning signs, the openings in the first two levels filled with barbed wire. As he walked by, he thought he could hear movement inside, shuffling, a sigh of breath. The concrete pillars were cracked, the surfaces flaking, and yet he felt an enormous sense of, not solidity—what was it?—gravity, perhaps. It was the first time he was aware of the smell—oil, salt, vinegar—although it had a vague familiarity about it, reminiscent of aging boat docks, and birth. A row of store fronts was attached to the ground level of the garage along a cross street. All were vacant but one, the *Print & Copy*, a HELP WANTED sign in the window.

The owner was elderly, thin and tired-looking. A series of brown spots of varying sizes covered his arms and ran up his neck and the sides of his cheeks before fading into his thinning hair. They made a kind of pattern. Cooper thought of lizard skin. The man asked him several questions related to his experience. Cooper's answers felt rehearsed, but they seemed truthful. Yes, he had strong computer skills. Yes, he had experience with high-speed copies, printing, oversize laminators, trimming, pouch lamination, folding, and binding.

His new boss must have been desperate because he hired Cooper on the spot, trained him the rest of the day on procedures, and told him he was in charge until the next morning. The poor fellow seemed anxious to leave. Cooper felt no interest in stealing from his new employer, so that was at least one bit of self-knowledge: he was an honest man.

When his first customer arrived, he made himself smile and did his work without hesitation, so perhaps he indeed had the necessary experience. He hoped his ease with the tasks the job required would trigger clues, identifying memories, but nothing came to mind.

The first time the shop phone rang Cooper stuck his hand in his pocket searching for a cell phone. He didn't have one. It seemed likely he'd owned a cell before. He'd lost it or thrown it away. He grabbed the red handset off the wall. The caller asked for prices and hours of operation, which Cooper was able to read off a sheet on the counter. But he didn't like the customer's tiny voice inside his head and couldn't wait to hang up.

The night shift customers were generally polite, grateful to have a last-minute option for projects desperately behind, often due the next day. Inconveniently located miles from the interstate, the shop's only appeal was it never closed.

When his boss took over the next morning, he seemed inordinately pleased to find everything intact and more money in the till. Cooper left on foot, and after many blocks noticed the houses seemed vaguely familiar, although the people he passed did not. No one spoke to him. Eventually he knew to turn into a building, walk up the stairs, and go to a door at the end of the hall. Number 14. He went into his wallet and found the key behind a small leather flap.

The two rooms were clean and nondescript. No books, no pictures, no knick-knacks, the bed made and covered with an army green blanket. Nothing to remind him of anything. A small TV beside the bed. The several changes of clothing in the closet were like what he wore now, assorted colors but within the same muted tonal range, plain cotton trousers, both short-sleeved and long-sleeved shirts, a battered pair of tennis shoes, an older pair of rubber boots. A winter jacket and scarf hung from a hook. Cooper had the perception, both despite of and because of the paucity of material possessions, that he had lived here in relative anonymity for quite a while.

He searched the apartment thoroughly for anything which might provide hints as to his personality or origins. He did so carefully, not wanting to disrupt what his previous self kept in such meticulous order. But there were no personal records or correspondence of any kind, and no cell phone.

He did find a dozen or so sheets torn from a notepad in a trash can. They'd been filled with what he assumed was his handwriting—at least the gestures seemed familiar—but overwritten repeatedly with various pencils, pens, and crayons, so none of the writing was legible. He stared at these scribblings, searching for patterns, until fatigue drove him to bed.

When he arrived the next day for his second shift, Cooper discovered a few square yards of dead insects strewn across the sidewalk in front of the print shop, moths and butterflies, a few crickets, a handful of beetles. His boss told him to get rid of them. It wasn't a big deal. Cooper swept them up and bagged them, threw them in the bin on the corner past the last empty shop.

He arrived for his shift the following day to much the same scene: a killing field of entomological carnage spreading from the front of the shop to the area around the adjoining garage. Cooper dutifully took care of the mess. As the weeks went by this proved to be a daily occurrence, and Cooper started coming in early to clean up the corpses before his shift began. He was seeing fewer and fewer live insects in the area, but he knew they were there. He could hear them distinctly buzzing as if right outside his ears.

He wanted to tell his new boss it wasn't part of his job, like it wasn't his job to chase the homeless away from the front of the store. He might have been one of those homeless folks himself at one time. The margins of error were so narrow in life; one false move and you became a derelict wandering the streets seeking shelter and safety.

Cooper needed to keep this job. The consistency of coming to work every day made him feel alive. And his boss was too frail to take on such a chore.

But a month of dead birds, bats, and rats followed. He'd never seen so many dead in one place before. The bats had lost most of their heads, as if their tiny brains had exploded, but at least he could tell they were bats. The birds were unidentifiable as to species. Their heads had melted down the length of their bodies, and half their feathers were gone. The rats were reduced to lumps of meat and fur.

The cats and dogs came after, their hides disintegrated, faces erased, although some kept their eyes, wide open in alarm. A few other unidentifiable animals were part of the mix: a raccoon, a deer, maybe a large fox. Cleanup took Cooper hours.

He didn't know how long he could keep this up, never knowing what new dead thing would turn up next as the killings progressed up the food chain. He asked his boss what could be causing this, but the man shook his head, muttering "Death is everywhere."

Then it stopped. The problem appeared to go away.

Cooper had sufficient time to attend the first *Creating Your New Story* seminar before his shift started. It was held in a decommissioned elementary school not too far from his apartment. Although it had been repurposed as a community center, he couldn't find much evidence of use. The gym was full of shabby furniture and audio-visual equipment and the classrooms appeared hastily abandoned, with papers and books and in one classroom piles of hardened modeling clay on each desk.

A series of crudely lettered cardboard signs led him upstairs to the classroom holding the seminar. Cooper paid his ten dollars to a diminutive lady sitting by the door. Could she be the instructor's…the guide's mother? She didn't bother looking at him. Only a dozen or so seats were occupied. The guide dispensed with any sort of introduction. He sat at the front of the room facing them, still wearing the long gray coat, and read aloud from a paper held in front of his face.

"Our goal here is to see reality without assumption, without interpretation, without making up a story. But if we must make up a story, because we are all story makers by nature, perhaps we can at least make it a positive one, a tale which will comfort us during these trying times. If not that, then at least something interesting, something to get the blood flowing and shake us out of our lifelong sleep." The guide moved the paper aside, looked at Cooper, and smiled slightly. Not knowing what else to do, Cooper nodded. The guide's eyes widened, as if he hadn't expected a response. He continued to read.

"True self-knowledge is a rare thing, an ephemeral moment of clarity out of a lifetime of confusion. Most of us will never experience such a moment. I wonder if it is even possible. Because our minds latch onto pain, and pain consumes us and informs our stories about ourselves. Mental health involves countering those stories of pain with more positive ones. But they are still stories, still untrustworthy narratives of the truth that is out there.

"We cannot trust our memories of who we once were. Those times, that self, are all gone now. Look around you. See what exists in your world *right now*. Trust *that*.

"We can never be sure of the things we do not see. It is difficult enough to make an accurate assessment of what is right in front of us. We cannot believe what lives in the shadows, or trust what dwells in the darkness beyond. Not until we see these things with our own eyes can we know they exist.

"The first step is emptying our minds of the old narratives, the old notions of who and what we were about. We need to let a new consciousness push aside everything that was there and when those stories are gone, we will have sufficient space for our new truth."

The lecture drifted along in a monotone, the speaker rarely making eye contact with his audience. Cooper indeed could feel the thoughts being pushed out of his head, only to be replaced with boredom. Where was the guided voyage, the learning from each other? The ideas seemed familiar, even intriguing, but delivered so poorly Cooper's attention began to wander to the other attendees.

One elderly man was so intent on the ceiling Cooper looked up to see what was so interesting. Overlapping stains made a topographical map of the graying tiles. There'd been roof problems in the past. A drop of liquid splattered the old man's glasses. So not the past. The man's body began to palsy. When the quaking subsided. Cooper noticed the crustiness on the back of the poor guy's skull, like pavement requiring repair.

Cooper was aware of that peculiar smell again. Was it leaking out of the ceiling, or from the fellow's head? He heard the distant rise and fall of conversation, but he hadn't noticed any other people in the building besides the ones in this classroom. Then as if aware of his attention, the conversation stopped.

The two young men on either side of him appeared to be taking notes, so he assumed they were engaged with the lecture. But when he looked closely, he saw they each had one of the flyers, circling specific words, adding connecting arrows and various petroglyph-like doodles. One of the men turned the sheet over and started scribbling manically, creating layer after layer of words and symbols in the same space. The flyer tore, despite the thicker stock, and soon he was etching his writings into the surface of the desk like a thoughtless schoolchild.

Many of the other attendees were asleep, heads on arms on their desktops, heads in hands and leaning precariously into the aisles. He noticed then how poorly dressed many of them were, how dirty their hands and the backs of their necks.

The sole exception was a young woman dressed primly in a white blouse, black skirt, and red sweater. She wore her light-brown hair long and pulled forward making a collar around her neck. She seemed agitated, leaning forward as if to listen, then leaning back with shoulders slumped, looking around at the others, and like Cooper trying to see what they were writing. Once she glanced back at him and he was alarmed at how pale she was, her eyes like black coals in the snow. She smiled at him self-consciously and turned back around.

They were given a thirty-minute break at the halfway point. Many went outside to smoke. Cooper, who did not smoke (Had he ever?), followed the young woman out to the front of the building. He was intent on leaving and going into work early, but he waited, sitting a few feet away from her on the steps. She gazed at the dark street, the lamps coming on. She rubbed and scratched the back of her hands, in one instance drawing blood.

"What do you think so far?" he asked.

She twisted her legs around and frowned. "It's not what I expected, from the flyer." Then she stopped, looking as if she'd lost the thread of the conversation, or she'd heard something else and was trying to make sense of it. After an awkward length of time, she blinked and began speaking again. "I don't know much about these things, but he doesn't seem very good at this."

"He's not. He's a terrible speaker. He might as well give it to us in a handout and let us leave. In any case, I'm going to go. Life's too—" He paused. "Is it too short, or is it too small? Funny, I can't remember. But it was nice meeting you." He stood up.

"Wait…I'll walk with you." She practically jumped to her feet. "Is that okay? I can't…I can't go back to where I'm staying. At least not yet."

He hesitated. He didn't know her, and he wondered if this was a foolish thing to do, but along with his memory he had lost his sense of what was or was not foolish. "If that's what you want to do."

As they walked in the general direction of the *Print & Copy*, he wondered if she realized they were entering a *questionable* neighborhood and if he should caution her somehow. He expected her to stop and tell him goodnight at any moment, that she should be going home now, but she never did. "I'm Cooper. Stefano Cooper…you can call me Stef." Had he ever gone by Stef?

"Stefano—is that Italian?"

"Could be, I guess."

"You can call me Cathy." She paused, looking down, and then didn't continue. Since this had happened before he didn't say anything, and they walked quietly together. She tugged on his sleeve, and he looked at her. The way she nodded and rose on her toes she reminded him of an anxious child. "I think maybe I once thought I should be a Cathy. In the mirror at least, I think I look like a Cathy." They had entered the edge of the warehouse area. The prevailing architecture lost a level of refinement and visibility as they entered the darkening lanes between buildings. "Can you smell that? I thought I smelled it before, but it's stronger here."

"Then you smell it too, a little sour, and salty."

"No, more like a slaughterhouse," she said, wrinkling her nose. "Do they butcher cattle here? It smells like...old blood."

"Oh. One of these buildings might have been a slaughterhouse at one time. But I was thinking the ocean, and birth."

She frowned. "Well, birth can be bloody, I guess. A new life doesn't happen without pain."

There was more itinerant activity than normal, assuming all the figures moving through the shadows were the usual types he saw on these streets every day. She kept looking around and moving closer to him. Some of the figures had gathered in groups near the buildings. "We're only a couple of blocks from my work. I could ask my boss if you can stay. If you like."

"Would you? I *can't* go back there. I took ten dollars from his wallet for the seminar. By now he knows I'm gone and what I've done."

"Who is this man?"

They'd stopped beneath a streetlight. It provided a false sense of security. The brightness of the light kept them from seeing what lay beyond. The silver glare bleached her face. Her hair was thin on top, exposing regions of bare scalp.

"I have no idea who I am!" she blurted. "It's as if whoever I once was has been pushed out of my head! He found me in the park—no wallet or purse, *nothing*. Not even a watch. He said he'd take *care* of me." She made a bitter face. "Oh, he *has*. He says I don't have enough sense to be out on my own. I can't take care of myself, according to him. He's watched my every move for almost *two years*!"

Cooper didn't know what to say. He wanted to understand more of what was going on before making his own confession. *Two years?* He pulled her hair off her neck. She had symmetrical bruises on both sides, some dark, some yellowed. "I'm sure my boss will let you stay. Then you can tell me what you want to do next." They walked further into the maze of warehouses. He liked the closeness even though it made him uncomfortable.

"What's that by the dumpster?" She was already walking toward the green container before he could stop her. She halted several feet away from the pale form lying on the pavement. He walked a few feet past her. "Sometimes people dump dead dogs and cats down here. They treat this neighborhood like the city dump. I should have warned you."

With the skin gone and the skull smashed it was difficult to identify, but it was too large to be a cat or a dog. Perhaps a large calf, but the front legs were shorter and less muscular than the back ones. He nudged the body with his foot. It moved easily, weighing almost nothing.

"What is it?" she whispered behind him.

The left eye remained. It appeared human. "Nothing. Nothing. An animal carcass, too far gone to identify. We should go." He pulled her away before she could see the other soft forms lying on the damp concrete in the shadows but a few yards away.

Something about the parking garage was different, a bit more of a general lean, more cracked and collapsed perhaps.

Then he looked into those open spaces behind the barbed wire and saw people inside, hundreds of them rocking back and forth, their backs turned. He couldn't see past them. The gate blocking the entrance had been flattened, and there were other forms—he could see their legs and backs at least—milling about within. She stopped as if intending to look, but Cooper pushed her past the entrance and into the *Print & Copy*. It was foolish, but he felt safe inside this small space where he worked every day.

He was surprised to see the counter and the tables stacked high with orders waiting to be picked up. They had never been this busy before.

"You're early! Thank God for that!" Cooper didn't see his boss, then noticed a single bloodshot eye peering through the stacks on the counter. He went around the counter's edge and found the aged man slumped in his office chair, faint and shaking. Normally smartly dressed in a narrow black tie and a white shirt embroidered with his name on the pocket, his boss had stripped down to a sweaty tank-style tee. Seeing more of the man's spots reinforced Cooper's impression of *lizard*, but today they appeared liquid, as if painted on. "They've been coming in all day wanting these handouts and advertisements and pamphlets and whatevers. The oddest jobs. I told most of them to come back tonight for pickup."

"I can help." She'd come up beside him.

"Who's this? I'm not hiring."

"My friend…Cathy. She's…just visiting."

His boss waved his hand dismissively and climbed to his feet. "I don't care, really. It's your shift, whatever you want to do. I'm leaving now. If I don't show tomorrow, put the CLOSED sign up. I may have to take the day off."

She helped him make sure each order was in its own separate box. The old man had gotten sloppy. Some orders were just stacks of printed pages with nothing separating them. It didn't help that much of the text on these jobs were nonsense words with random illustrations of unfamiliar animals, individuals staring out of windows, and examples of odd architecture. Several of the booklets consisted of random abstract designs with no words. Cooper found the original order sheets and matched them with the jobs, printing the order number on the front of the box. She helped him move these boxes off the counter and onto the floor behind.

Now and then he paused to listen to the noises and conversation coming from the garage. At times it sounded like a variety of abstract music. He could not tell if there were instruments other than voices involved. She kept waving at her ears as if annoyed by flying insects.

As each customer came in, he had them check their order for correctness before accepting payment. As always, he proofread the jobs from a variety of angles. It made his head hurt. With each job some bit of text or image remained lodged in his thoughts and could not be removed.

By morning, the disgusting odor was back, stronger than ever. He ran to the bathroom a couple of times to empty his stomach. She had already given up, collapsed in the chair with her eyes closed. He wondered if he would have to carry her or call an ambulance. He was afraid to stir her, afraid she would not open her eyes.

The final job left from the day shift was more flyers for the Seminar, thousands of them in a variety of colors. Cooper couldn't imagine why they were needed, given the evening's sparse attendance.

The woman who'd taken their money at the door pulled up in a battered station wagon to pick them up. Cooper forced a smile. "He must be expecting a lot more students."

"He would never call them students," she replied, paid, and he loaded the flyers for her. She sped off without another word.

After sunrise he waited over an hour, but his boss never showed. He cautiously approached her, but she was already awake and actually smiling. She helped him clean up and then he hung out the CLOSED sign.

Once outside, he felt awkward, hoping she would speak first and tell him what she wanted him to do. But she remained silent, gazing at the buildings and the streets around them. He watched as lines of people entered the warehouses through front doors, side doors, even climbing up on loading docks and pushing their way through the dingy overlapping vinyl strip curtains used to keep insects out. This had never happened before. He was anxious to leave.

They noticed the fluid in the street at the same moment: a greenish, yellowish froth leaking from inside the parking structure and flowing across the sidewalks and down the gutters and spreading into the intersection beyond. It had that awful smell, but intensified. Cooper walked out into the street, stepping over the flow, turned around, and stared up into the garage. All those ones were still there with their backs turned, but motionless, and silent.

He walked over to her and whispered. "I can't let you walk away from here alone. I can walk with you, take you anywhere you want to go. A police station, or a hospital?" He should have gone to a police station when he first found himself here. The idea had never occurred to him.

"I don't know what to do," she said, avoiding eye contact. "Could I go with you to your place for a while?"

"Sure. I'm fine with that."

She looked directly at him. "But we're not going to have sex."

The statement shocked him. "I—of course not. You're perfectly safe with me." In fact, the idea had never occurred to him. In this new life of his he never thought about sex.

On their way to his apartment, they passed crowds heading in the opposite direction, toward the warehouse district and the print shop. He wondered if there was some big event about which he did not know. Certainly possible—he never paid attention to such things. He didn't even watch the news. Was it possible there was a sports arena in the area? But he'd never seen such crowds before.

It was a great mix. Many seemed in a holiday mood. Some looked as if they'd missed a few meals. He saw men and women and children in only their underwear, a dazed look about them, as if they'd come down with an unexplainable urgency and left their homes without getting dressed. Many looked confused. Many mumbled nonsense to themselves. His companion grew quite agitated. She clutched his hand and was now practically dragging him along behind her.

When they got into the apartment, she asked him to lie down with her. She looked so tired, so fragile. He was afraid she would collapse before she got to the bed. She wrapped her arms around him and lay her head on his chest. He couldn't move even if he wanted to. They both fell asleep.

He remembered how they folded themselves into each other, how nicely her hair smelled when everything else seemed so foul. How he couldn't remember her name, the fake one, or even his own. But this was a safe place away from those crowds, where he could hold on to something he could be sure of.

Cooper woke up with one hand in her hair, but his fingers went too deep, because she was far too soft.

He propped himself up on one elbow, not wanting to free his other arm from under her head. But she was too light, and the sudden motion made her float away. He heard her body land on the floor beside the bed.

He was painted with her. Most of the fluids had dried, but there was some dampness. He dragged himself over to the edge of the bed and looked down. The top of her skull had collapsed into this gritty mush. Everything else about her face appeared erased.

Hours went by, but Cooper couldn't quite catch them. He would have to clean up the mess. He threw the blanket and sheets over her and gathered what he could. She'd been right— she smelled more like slaughterhouse than ocean, and the stench was everywhere. He stripped out of his foul clothes and added them to the pile.

He showered until the water was too cold to tolerate. Still, he sprayed himself down with deodorant before slipping into fresh clothing. Even with the bedding the bag he put her in weighed almost nothing. She took up little room in the bin outside. It was already late in the day. What had he been doing?

He thought about going to work even though he suspected his workplace was gone. But he couldn't remember or imagine himself being anywhere else. He walked to the old elementary school and tried to climb the stairs. It was impassable because of all the people trying to get into the classroom. They all had their ten dollars and their flyers waving in their hands. A few shouted they'd be willing to pay much more if the old woman would only admit them.

Cooper gave up and left the building, heading back toward his apartment. He still had the vague notion he might go into work. Where else could he go?

Voices filled his head. There were many people around him, but few were talking. Now and then he stopped walking to listen. He couldn't be sure, but it seemed her voice had been added to the mix.

Crowds poured out of the buildings and filled the streets. It was like a kind of parade. Waves of people swept across yards and broke down fences, torn down bushes and pushed over trees. Most were silent but a few tapped on shoulders and shouted questions. "Have you seen me before? I don't know who I am! Is this the way? Please tell me this is the way!" Some appeared angry. Many looked genuinely terrified.

Cooper saw one man twirl around in confusion, as if forced into a kind of dance. He fell and the people walked over him. They stepped on his skull, and it crumpled as if made of plastic. Cooper paid more attention to the ground from then on. There appeared to be bodies everywhere, their individual features disappearing as they were trampled into nothing.

He saw much of the *Print & Copy*'s recent work in evidence. Hundreds of the flyers advertising the seminar in a multitude of colors. Several people had them pressed to their faces or stuffed into their shirts. Others were eating them. Cooper found it mesmerizing the way the type flowed from flyer to flyer and hand to hand, sometimes abandoning the sheets and falling into the street where shoes and bare feet trampled them and scattered the letters around.

The tide of humanity was difficult to resist, and he knew he was being swept toward the warehouses, toward that garage where something waited to be seen into being, and awakening to the consequences Cooper realized that was the one place he did not want to be.

He turned around and had to start fighting, punching people in the face and chest, and shoving them aside. They gave him little resistance, focused as they were on what lay beyond. He made it to a less-traveled street and wasn't sure where to go, just in any direction opposite where everyone else was going. The confusion of voices was dizzying. He kept shaking his head and was relieved to discover the further he traveled the fainter they became.

He ran through a park and up a hill. The area was heavily wooded and seemed to have been avoided by the manic mob. From the top of the hill, he was able to see a train station several blocks away with massive crowds pouring from the cars.

The woman at the counter was distracted, talking to herself, her mouth a confusion of tics. She printed out his ticket but did not know how to take his money.

Cooper didn't search the cars, but he appeared to be the only passenger on this outbound train.

Miles into the countryside he felt the shift, as if something massive had suddenly entered this world, or just as suddenly departed. He could not see it, so it was hard to say which. His mind was open, and he nervously awaited what might come in.

WITHIN THE CONCRETE

Carl pounded the wall in frustration, knocking the photograph further askew. The voices within the wall stopped for a moment as if waiting for his next move, then continued at a lower volume. He pressed his ear against the textured plaster and listened, eyes closed and one palm flat against the wall for support. The surface was so cool it was almost comforting. He felt as if he were praying, but he had no idea for what.

His knuckles were bleeding, and now there was a dent. He wondered if he had time to return the world to normal before Grace got home.

All day he'd heard this continuous stream of vague vocalizations. Both monologues and conversations, but he could make out few words. They might have been in some language he did not recognize; it was impossible to say.

The city attracted people from all over the world, but after forty years here, he didn't understand why. It wasn't a kind city. Perhaps it wasn't meant to be. Were cities expected to be kind? Were mountains? The city felt increasingly like a range of geometric mountains: primal, unyielding, uncaring. Whoever came here became instantaneously anonymous.

The voices might be the consequences of air moving through the pipes or trapped within the wall cavities. Or perhaps they were generated by expanding and contracting metals inside the structure. He understood little of physics, nor did he know much about construction or the sound-conducting properties of materials.

Possibly it was some rare auditory characteristic making itself known after a certain threshold of concrete had been achieved. Like every other citizen here he was surrounded by it, buried in it, concrete simultaneously reaching for the sky and descending hundreds of yards underground, covering every inch of visible earth, and over time damaging the atmosphere above. An aggregate of error and misguided planning lay hidden within concrete.

Whatever the mechanics involved, the voices continued just beyond the limits of his comprehension. Carl imagined people much like himself with heads pressed against the wall from the other side, palms caressing the plaster, mouths open and attempting communication. The voices were so persistent, almost desperate. But this was the building's outer wall. There were no apartments on the other side.

When Grace returned from her doctor's appointment, he would ask her opinion about the voices. She'd always had a sensible, practical way of looking at things. If she said the voices were nothing to worry about, he would stop thinking about them. Or if she thought they were a legitimate concern she could tell him who to call and what to do. After all these years he still could not believe his luck in finding her. The process by which people come together had always seemed a mysterious one. So had the process by which they come apart.

He gazed out the window at the building across the street. The window openings in the top six floors were bricked up. He couldn't figure out when this might have occurred. Scaffolding surrounded the building, and more openings were being sealed. Windows were disappearing from many other buildings as well.

Long ago he had stopped watching the news, so he didn't know if the suicide rate was still climbing.

What did the residents think about losing their windows? The buildings on this block were massive. He often wondered how many people they contained. If they all fled outside at the same time no one would be able to move. Yet as he gazed down at the streets below it appeared only a few had ventured outside. What if they couldn't leave, or chose not to? If he did nothing with his time but observe from this window, he might be able to estimate how many had been absorbed.

The mid-afternoon glare gradually dimmed. He hadn't realized it was so late. Grace was long overdue. He should have gone with her to the doctor's appointment, but she wanted to go to this one alone. He should have insisted.

Before he was distracted by the voices, he was hanging Grace's photo—it still tilted to the left. She was unaware when he took it last summer in the park. He managed to catch her slight, unselfconscious smile which he loved so much. He planned to surprise her with it when she got home.

Carl didn't own a carpenter's level. He'd leaned his head against the wall for a better perspective, and that's when he heard those first unexplainable conversations.

Her appointment was hours ago. He didn't have the exact address, but he knew the office was in the giant hospital complex downtown. He picked up his cell and dialed Grace's phone.

It rang and rang and the sound was everywhere. But no one picked up. Then his phone died. In a panic he ran from room to room as if expecting a solution to present itself. If the voices were offering a solution, they needed to speak more definitively. After a few minutes he fled the apartment.

Carl rarely left their building alone. He went out if Grace needed a prescription filled or some special food she thought might make her feel better. He felt less than competent on these streets.

He began walking, searching for a taxi or bus which would get him downtown. He passed scattered pedestrians, pale-complected, thin, some talking to themselves, all wrapped in their coats even though it wasn't cold. Their faces showcased startled eyes and open mouths, and he couldn't imagine what they must be seeing. After a few minutes he couldn't bear to look at them, and diverted himself with the storefronts lining the sidewalk, where similar pale figures lingered in doorways, or watched from windows, some crowded inside and filling the store displays, entire groups gawking as if he were the strange one.

The dirty gray sky descended between the buildings and spread through the streets. He tried to remember if there was a pay phone nearby. Hadn't they all been taken out? He vaguely recalled several bus stops on this street, but couldn't remember where.

A pallid figure made a beckoning gesture from a crumbling stoop and mouthed a few words. Carl made himself ignore it. After years in the city, he knew how to keep himself safe, and refused the invitations of strangers.

A bus appeared in the lane alongside him. He looked ahead for a stop but didn't see one. The bus was full beyond capacity, people jammed together in the seats and standing in the center aisle, a few clinging precariously to the outside by hanging onto half-open windows.

The bus stopped abruptly at the next corner and vomited passengers. Dozens streamed out of the buildings to replace them, making the bus overly full again.

Distracted, Carl veered into a wall, scraping his arm. The rusty concrete disintegrated onto the sidewalk in dry rivulets of red sand. He brushed off his clothes and stumbled on. He would have searched for a bathroom to clean himself up but couldn't spare the time. He ignored the advice whispered from beneath the sidewalk. If he remembered correctly, the entrance to the subway was a few blocks down.

The tall building ahead wore unstable scaffolding around the upper stories. The plank and pipe arrangement was overloaded with brick and workmen. A man appeared in a window opening, gazing at the street. Although Carl couldn't see the face clearly, he knew the man was staring at him. The man waved and Carl stopped. The man's head bobbed as if speaking, but Carl was too far away to tell for sure. Several shadows joined the man and they, too, began to wave, heads bobbing. They opened their mouths as if shouting, but their shouts did not reach him.

When the workmen reached that window, they began bricking it up, even though the figures inside struggled to push them away. Within a few minutes the opening was completely sealed. Carl couldn't help them. Something had gone wrong with the city, perhaps a multitude of things, but he had neither power nor time to understand it. There was nothing he could do. He continued toward the subway.

For the next few yards, the sidewalk was covered with barriers. Large square holes in the concrete left a narrow safe path between them. At some junctures Carl had to turn sideways and slide his feet to get through.

A worker's head in a yellow hardhat popped up in one of the square openings. Before Carl could ask what they were doing here the head vanished below. He tried to peer into the dark cavity, but vertigo forced him back. He heard a crowd of voices somewhere within that deep passage underground, but he dared not lean over for a better view.

Over the next block pedestrians leaned against the buildings with one ear pressed to the wall. Carl wanted to ask if they too heard voices but couldn't afford the delay. He needed to find Grace as quickly as possible. He couldn't imagine having to search for her after dark.

He walked another block and wondered if he'd mistaken the location of the subway entrance. He couldn't remember the last time he'd been there. It might have been years. A man was standing on the third-story ledge across the street. Carl glanced around for someone to tell. No one else was in sight. The man on the ledge kept shaking his head. It was unfortunate, but Carl had no time for this. He had to go to Grace. He continued walking and searching for the subway.

A small park filled the following block. He had a vague recollection of the tall fountain and the circular arrangement of benches around it. For a moment he wondered if it might be the park where he'd taken Grace's photo, but maybe that was in the other direction. The city had a number of these small parks, curated patches of nature meant to calm people down. But there was something artificial about them. They were a little too curated, like oversized window boxes. Dig a few yards into them and you hit another concrete layer. Not enough room for a decent root system for their failing trees.

Numerous sleepers lay in random spirals around the fountain and scattered among the trees. The grass was tall enough to obscure their clothing, so he couldn't speculate whether they were homeless or perhaps office workers on a lunchtime nap. Some were so still he thought he should check on them, but he didn't have the time.

Were they talking in their sleep? He didn't see their lips moving, but if he was quiet, he could hear the faintest breath of their voices drifting through the air.

In the distance the faded red arrow on the vertical SUBWAY sign pointed down. Carl would have to pass several buildings under construction, and one being demolished. The sidewalk was closed, but he thought he could discern a safe path through the wreckage. He maneuvered around several yellow barriers but then had to climb over debris streams flooding the sidewalk and spilling into the street. No one stopped him. The sky had darkened further, and he could smell the coming rain. He needed to get to the trains.

The side of one building had been peeled away. A honeycomb structure filled the building's exposed interior and within each cell men and women lay with heads protruding. Carl kept walking—he'd had the briefest glance and needed to keep moving—but had he misapprehended?

He was almost to the subway entrance when he turned around. Several huge black panel trucks were stopped in front of the devastated structure and workers were loading dust-covered bodies inside. The city was conspiring, it seemed, to keep him from finding his Grace.

Once inside the lobby Carl had no idea where to go. The facility may have been remodeled; he wasn't sure. He'd almost never ridden the subway, even before he met Grace. He'd never felt comfortable submerged beneath so much material. Five staircases went down, along with ramps, elevators, and several escalators. The signs were confusing, referring to various color-coded lines, landmarks with which he wasn't familiar, routes named after past mayors, but nothing to indicate where they might take him. A complex map of the underground system was mounted on the wall. It was pretty, but he couldn't follow a bit of it.

After wandering in circles he found some red graffiti scrawled beside a down staircase: DOWNTOWN!, with an arrow. He didn't have time to wonder if this was someone's prank. He took the staircase.

He came to a landing with ramps leading both up and down. He assumed he needed to continue downwards but remembered from trips in the distant past you sometimes went up a level to change trains. He listened for the sound of the trains, which led him sometimes to go up and sometimes to go down. After a while he couldn't decide if the trains were above or below him. He couldn't tell if the rush he heard was due to wind in the tunnels or some speeding mass. It was almost as if confusion had been the planners' goal.

Some walls were not square. The occasional bulge appeared where two concrete slabs joined. Spiderweb cracks spread through many of the corners, and a crevice of a couple inches had opened from floor to ceiling by a staircase. He wondered how many tons of concrete and soil were overhead. Whatever the figure, he knew it wasn't to human scale.

He stopped and closed his eyes. He could no longer hear the trains, but he heard waves of the deepest murmuration, the voices of thousands people buried inside, but he had no sense of their location.

There had to be someone, somewhere who understood exactly what was going on. Who knew the rules, the paths, the strategies required to negotiate this urban warren. Maybe several such someones, but Carl wasn't among their number.

He had the strangest sensation of being watched. It wasn't by the other commuters, who appeared to do their best to avoid him, looking away as he approached, sometimes stopping and facing the wall until he passed. He kept looking for cameras or other monitoring gear. He saw deep holes spaced throughout the overhead concrete beams and wondered how many hid cameras within their depths.

He followed the passages down as far as he could, finally reaching a vast area turned into a maze by cage-like fencing. The people wandering the maze, their bloodless faces frozen into anxious masks, did not speak. He called out asking where the trains were but received no answer.

He heard a rumbling and thought the trains had to be near, but soon came to a dead end. The roar increased in volume and he retraced his steps searching for a passage. As he ran toward the sound of the trains, he passed a series of closet-sized alcoves where people waited, or hid, faces obscured by their raised hands.

A narrow corridor branched off before a wall, and at the end an open elevator waited. Carl ran inside and pushed the single button.

The elevator brought him back to street level with only a short walk to the hospital complex. The medical offices loomed many stories above everything else downtown. He felt relieved, but disappointed he'd never found the trains. He considered the possibility they'd been replaced with sound effects as a cost-cutting measure.

The hospital was a stone mountain at one end of an immense concrete plaza. He'd been here with Grace several times. He supposed in any sizable city a great many people fell ill and needed to be hospitalized. It seemed even with the advances in modern medicine more people were sick than ever before, but perhaps the medical professionals were better at finding them.

Few people were out on the plaza: two teenagers walking hand in hand, an old man with a cane, a younger man in a gray uniform jumpsuit sweeping the concrete. Carl wondered if the poor fellow was expected to clean the entire expanse by himself.

The last time here he saw hundreds on the plaza: families and school groups, office workers, people streaming in for medical services. Was today a holiday? Since retirement he'd rarely kept track of such things. He imagined thousands sinking into the plaza leaving just their voices remained.

The tall glass doors appeared impossibly far away, although he'd never thought so before. He headed toward them as fast as he could, which resulted in some stumbling. He passed a concrete wall mid-way with metal plaques fixed to its surface. He presumed it was a memorial of some sort. Two women stood on either side of this wall, eyes closed beatifically, hands and one ear pressed against the polished surface. Neither said anything. They might have been praying, grieving some loss, or listening for each other. Anything is possible when you don't know the answer.

The last hundred yards or so featured a broad rose-colored walkway lined with concrete benches. A thin naked man had folded himself within the hollow space beneath one bench. He gazed at Carl with a frightened expression. Carl decided to say nothing. The entrance was in sight. He moved on.

Closer in the massive building resembled a warehouse more than a mountain—a weathered concrete block with windows so narrow and deeply recessed they were almost indetectable. Sideroads lead traffic into the back of the facility, presumably for unloading: those enormous black panel trucks he'd seen earlier, and a convoy of buses.

Inside, the first floor was one large open area. White painted concrete beams overhead were held up by numerous identical square concrete posts. Lit glass globes hung from a ceiling which was much too far away, miniaturizing the partitioned maze below.

A line of identical frosted windows faced the front doors. Each had a circular cutout with a narrow horizontal slot at counter level. Carl stopped a few feet away, straining to see through the cutouts, crouching for a glimpse of the figures behind the windows. He managed to make out bony, mottled hands, bits of keyboard, the occasional deep-set sleepy eye, a bruised ear, but nothing indicative of a receptive clerk eager to help.

He went to the window in front of him and knocked on the glass. A smoky mascaraed eye and narrow nose above a wrinkled mouth appeared in the cutout.

The mouth didn't appear to move, but he heard the rasped deliver. "Next window please."

"I'm looking for my wife. She had an appointment with Dr. Aronovitz."

"That office is closed now."

"But I haven't heard from her. Can you at least let me know if she's been admitted to the hospital? She's been ill."

"Our computers are down."

"When will they be back up?"

"I couldn't say."

Carl thanked her, although she'd been no help. He turned away, considering his next steps. On one side was a large waiting area with the usual assorted institutional chairs and benches. But there was booths along one wall, spaced a couple of feet apart. Within these spaces people stood with their faces averted. Some thumbed through magazines and some stood weeping into their hands. But in one a couple stood kissing with an intensity Carl remembered from his youth, when desire had ruled him, and not embarrassment.

As their numbers were called people left these spaces and went to the nurse standing in a distant doorway. But one man refused to budge even though his number was called numerous times. Two stocky orderlies came out and forced the man to walk between them as they guided him past the nurse.

Carl collapsed into a chair and tried to figure out what he should do next. It seemed he'd been better at solving things when he was younger. Now his brain was like cement slurry, right on the edge of hardening, after which no thoughts might escape.

Perhaps his raw panic had made him leave the apartment too soon. Maybe Grace was there now waiting for him. But he didn't understand why she hadn't let him know she'd be so late. It wasn't like her. He'd be so relieved just to find her safe. Not that he believed in this hopeful scenario. Something was terribly wrong here.

Someone had left a cell phone on the small table beside him. He looked around. No one appeared to be paying it any attention. He picked it up, turned it on, and was surprised to find it didn't require a password. He punched in Grace's number and waited.

The phone made a connection, but no one answered.

"Hello?" Carl spoke softly, then more loudly "Hello?"

He heard a soft, whistling whisper, as if the phone on the other end were falling through air. It never landed, and no one ever answered. He placed the phone back on the table.

Agitated, he couldn't bear to sit. He saw movement behind one of the frosted windows with no line waiting. He stepped up to the window and knocked on the glass.

"Please take a number and sit down," said the voice behind the glass. "Wait your turn. We all have to wait our turn."

"No, please. You have to help me." Carl struggled not to cry in frustration. The bureaucrats were waiting for you to lose control so they could punish you. They tormented the weepers the most. "My wife Grace is missing. We've lost all contact. I need someone to explain to me what's going on."

"Is she one of those in quarantine?"

"I don't think so. At least I wasn't informed. Has there been an outbreak?"

Pale lips appeared centered in the circular cutout in the glass. "Third floor. Ask for Doctor Smith."

There was a bank of four elevators. Carl dashed into one and pressed the button. When the car arrived, he stepped inside.

When Carl came out of the elevator, he appeared to be on a patient floor. A long hallway with rooms on both sides led to an oversized, gunmetal gray nurse's station. There was a short distance between doors, so the patient rooms had to be quite small. The ceiling was low; he could almost touch it with his fingertips. He assumed the above ceiling space held the utilities, the giant tubes of an HVAC system perhaps, or maybe it was a way to squeeze in more floors. He'd heard hospitals were always exceeding capacity. It required a great deal of space to hide the sick and dying.

He didn't know where the office of this Dr. Smith might be, and if the man was out on rounds Carl might miss him. To be safe he went room to room, hoping a quick glimpse might avoid disappointment.

The first room contained one large bed with room for little else. Several dust-covered, pale faces peeked from the folds of a gray blanket and stared at him before disappearing again.

There was much whispering beneath the covers, but they never reappeared.

In the next room a woman and three small children gathered around a man's bed. On the other side of the room five physicians in shiny steel chairs leaned forward, watching. Prayers might have been said, complaints or promises. He couldn't tell.

In the next room he heard soft noises with no apparent source. He entered the room, and realized a constant monologue was coming from within a tall metal wardrobe. He opened the wardrobe door. Inside an emaciated old man looked up, distressed. Carl apologized and shut the door.

In another room he thought the old man sitting by himself was looking into a mirror, but then the other old man moved. They were either twins or old enough to resemble each other.

He turned his attention to the rooms across the hall. The bed in the first room was empty but appeared recently occupied. The sheets were disheveled, and there were bits of gauze, bandage tape, and bloodstains on the floor.

The next door had a small, printed card taped to its center: DECEASED. The dead person lay in bed with a single sheet pulled over the face. Three men in low-slung hats and long dark overcoats stood at the foot of the bed, whispering among themselves.

Similar shrouded forms occupied the next five rooms whose doors had also been labeled with a DECEASED card. Carl stopped in the middle of the corridor, unsure how to proceed. He couldn't bring himself to go through the entire floor this way. Echoing voices rose and fell, drifting through the corridor like awful smells. Perhaps there were priests hiding in the shadows, delivering a succession of last rites.

He saw a nurse behind the distant counter and went there, ignoring the various patients crying out to him from their beds.

They called him by unfamiliar names; everyone seemed to think he was some relative or lover. But none were Grace. The nurse appeared startled to see him there and looked down.

"Can you direct me to Doctor Smith's office?"

"You have an appointment?" She busied herself glancing through the papers on the counter, but she didn't appear to read any.

"Of course," he lied.

She didn't look up. "Just keep going. Fifth door on the right past this station."

The first four doors were closed. The fifth was open, but the room was almost filled with fresh concrete, splashes staining the ceiling and the tile outside. A man's glasses protruded from the surface in front, crusted in gray bits of cement.

"You don't belong here, sir." Carl turned around. The nurse he'd spoken to earlier stood flanked by two security guards. He had no chance of outrunning them, not at his age, but he still raced toward the door marked STAIRS a few yards away.

Carl ran out of breath almost immediately, but his legs continued to move up and down. He heard the footsteps thundering somewhere above and behind him, their echoes multiplying until it seemed he was being chased by hundreds. He jerked open the door to another floor and stumbled through.

He was in a large room crammed with hospital beds no more than a foot apart with barely enough room for the patients to get out of bed and stand. One old man stared at him from beneath several layers of sheets and blankets. Only his shiny nose and eyes were visible. Carl sidled sideways between the beds looking for another exit. Taking the opportunity, he shouted "Grace!" but no one answered. Many of the forms were motionless. It was impossible to say whether they were resting or dead.

A door in a side wall led him down another staircase and into another large room. Here the patients were dancing. Many half-dressed, some naked. No one seemed to mind. One man held his partner up with the greatest of effort. The apparently unconscious woman hung limply, her feet dragging sideways across the floor. An audience of patients in hospital gowns and wheelchairs were arranged along the edges of the crowd, some clutching their intravenous poles. No one spoke. He tried to look at all the faces, hoping to recognize Grace, but there were so many of them, and so many who looked the same.

He heard footsteps coming behind him and headed toward the double doors at the end. On the other side was a loading dock, a multitude of those black panel trucks waiting. Body bags were being taken off those trucks, while other body bags were being loaded to replace them. More bags were stacked against the wall several columns deep, waiting. He felt the arms grabbing him from behind, the bag being slipped over his head.

Carl woke up on the plaza before the hospital doors. People were walking around him, trying not to make eye contact, although a few threw him coins. He gazed out over the plaza. It occurred to him how much it resembled a giant, toppled headstone.

Faint voices issued from the concrete like steam. Not strong enough to understand, but they had their effect.

In one section of the plaza workmen were replacing a damaged portion. He walked over but couldn't get past the ropes. Others gathered but they too were denied access. No one was allowed to get close enough to discover the secret which lay beneath the skin, the bricks, the rocks, and the concrete fill. People might be trapped within hidden vacancies far below the surface, but only those select workers and the ones who'd hired them would know for sure.

Such a huge volume of concrete, the weight of it seemed too much for even the planet to bear.

Carl ventured to the center of the plaza and stood there, listening. It seemed a good focal point to catch all the voices. Still, nothing sounded recognizable, and he could find nothing of Grace here at all.

He would have to return to their apartment and wait. He would charge his cell phone, dial her again, and continue to wait. There was nothing left to be done. Grace would contact him if she were able, and if she were not able, she would not. He might never know what happened, but this was true of most things. Grace had always been better at accepting these simple truths than he. In this world you did what you could do, and no one could expect more.

Had he forgotten something? Had she given him some information, some clue, and somehow, he had forgotten?

Carl fell to his knees. He imagined he could hear her breathing beneath the concrete. He began to sob, and he struggled to make himself stop, because he would never hear her as long as he made so much noise. He took a long, deep breath to contain himself, which made his entire body shudder. Deep within the concrete he heard himself weeping.

THE LAST SOUND YOU HEAR

Connor's grandfather leaned over him, cracked lips making a tortured "O." In that long moment all he could hear was the depthless pulse of the world.

His grandfather wasn't a mean man. He never raised his voice to Connor, and he certainly never raised his hand. The old man supplied his grandson with unsettling lessons in the strange and the obscure, the dark and the grim. "I want to prepare you," his grandad said. Exactly for what, Connor was never told.

Distant and isolated on the western edge of their desert town, his grandfather's house lay partially sunk into red rock and sand, a quiet retreat at the end of a dusty lane. Connor liked that he could hear no traffic here, except the occasional stretched rush of a plane far overhead, punctuated by some sleepless coyote's yip. His grandfather said there were other sounds to be heard further out in the desert, but Connor wasn't yet ready for them.

The house had three outside doors: a front door which made a terrible screech, a screened back door full of holes, and a side door into the parlor which Grandad called the *coffin* door. "After I die that's how they'll get my coffin in and out. But don't let your mother drag me out of here prematurely," he said with a wink. The original family home back in Massachusetts supposedly had such a door. Now his grandfather was happy to have one too. Connor's mom scoffed when he shared the tale, advising him to take Grandad's stories with a pinch of salt.

Starting when he was twelve Connor rode his bike every Saturday to his grandad's house. They had lunch and hung out. Hanging out meant a demonstration would take place, sometimes an experiment, always another lesson.

"That whole house is an experiment!" his mother said. True enough it was packed with projects, lab equipment and electrical gadgets, amateur taxidermy and yellowing charts on the walls, dusty books and art supplies and specimens in dirty jars and all of it disorganized, jumbled together, filling every room, covering the floor. Things rustled in Grandad's house, even though he didn't own any pets. Connor could hear a curious stirring whenever he visited, but he could never locate the source. "A fire trap!" Mom cried. "We shouldn't let you go over there!"

But she did. Connor's parents felt sorry for him, and he took advantage. The trip was never easy. Connor was frail and had to take his time. He'd been in the hospital for so many procedures he couldn't remember everything wrong or done to him, not that his parents shared everything the doctors said. His lungs had issues and his heart wasn't right. He tried not to think about it. Sometimes he just wanted to tell his grandad that learning new stuff didn't always help.

The bike was good exercise, and he was happy to get out. Mom and Dad hovered too much. His grandad cared, but at least he never made a big deal about it.

Connor usually took his time getting to his grandad's, stopping to talk to people, listening to the music from their radios, the conversations and the noises escaping their houses.

Grandad didn't mind waiting. "Our time begins when you get here."

He'd missed a lot of school, and rarely went anywhere, so although everyone seemed to know who he was, most were strangers to him. His mom and dad kept a quiet house; it felt like what he imagined church would be. Because of him, he thought, although he didn't think he understood all the ways how. Grandad said, "No one's to blame, especially not you. Your mom and dad have always been rather self-contained."

Visits with Grandad were never predictable. Once Connor interrupted him with a javelina (Grandad called them *skunk pigs*) spread open on the kitchen table, its insides hanging out in such a mess he wondered if Grandad had been looking for something. "Just in time. I have things to show you."

One especially hot afternoon Grandad took Connor out in his battered station wagon for a lesson in roadkill identification. Another time they traveled to a local carnival and Grandad lectured loudly on the morphology of circus freaks to the dismay of the small audience and the ire of the sideshow barker. Another day Grandad dumped a sack full of bones on the living room rug and challenged Connor to identify them. "I found them out in the desert. I hope none were friends of yours."

Then there was the lesson about—Connor wasn't sure what it was about—*sounds*, maybe. They were eating a late lunch. Grandad moved slowly that day. He seemed to have trouble deciding which plates to take out of the cupboard, and when he opened the refrigerator, he stopped and stared at its contents as if he'd forgotten why he was there. Eventually he turned around with a tomato in each hand and sat down at the table.

"I read recently that hearing is the last sense to go before you die. What do you think about that, Connor? Lying there, unable to see or feel anything, but hearing what people said about you?"

"It might be awful. Or good, depending on what they said."

"That's right. Very good. So, we should be careful what we say. We never know who might be listening. Someone might be dying in the next room, and our words are the last thing they'll ever hear. If you could choose, what's the last sound you'd like to hear? People telling you how much they loved you? When your grandmother was dying, I kept telling her how much I loved her, but I think she'd already moved on to somewhere else where my words had no meaning. You know, I think she'd have preferred listening to the ocean. I should have played her some ocean sounds."

"I'd like the desert, I think."

"Pardon?

"You asked me what sound I'd want to listen to. We're nowhere near an ocean, but we're surrounded by desert. But I have no idea what it sounds like out there—you told me I wasn't ready yet."

His grandfather didn't reply, but took a tomato and began sectioning it, positioning the oh-so-sharp blade precisely before levering the knife down to make the cuts. The old man seemed lost in thought, and it made Connor nervous watching him with the knife. "What sound does a heart make?" his grandfather asked.

Connor thought a while and answered. "We talk about heartbeats, so it's a beating, right? Beat *beat*, beat *beat*, like that?"

"The heart is a *pump*, Grandson. Let's test it, why don't we?" As if performing a magic trick, his grandfather pulled a stethoscope from his coat pocket, slipped the diaphragm between his shirt buttons and with one hand, held it to the skin above his heart. He handed the earpieces to Connor. "Listen and tell me what you hear."

Connor struggled to get the ends into his ears. His grandfather used his free hand to adjust the tubing and the earpieces until they fit.

Although he couldn't have explained why, Connor felt uneasy doing this. He didn't know what would happen if he said "no" to one of his grandfather's instructions. He'd never tried. It took a few seconds, but eventually Connor could hear the heartbeat. "There are two different sounds."

"And they are?"

Connor listened some more, and said, "it sounds like a *lub*, followed by a *dub*. The dub is louder."

His grandfather removed the diaphragm from under his shirt and held it in his hand. He smiled at it as if he were holding his actual precious heart. "Excellent. The *lub* is the sound of the tricuspid and mitral valves closing. The *dub* is the sound of the aortic and pulmonary valves closing. At least, that's the English version. What sound do you think my heart would make if we were, say, Italian?"

The question made no sense to Connor. "The same, I suppose. It's not as if your heart knows Italian."

"It's not your heart, you see. It's whoever is listening, and the language they're accustomed to hearing. Our native language inevitably conditions the way we hear sounds. For example, those of us who speak English believe a cat says *Meow*. But if you were Vietnamese, you might hear *Meo*, or *Nyan* if you were Japanese, and *Niaou* if you were Greek. And Italians, I believe they hear something similar coming out of their cats, *Miao*. An Italian would hear my heart saying *tut ump*. And someone from India is likely to hear *dhakdhak*. Isn't that an odd sound for a heart to make?"

Connor had to admit it was. "Would all Indians hear that sound?"

"Good question! You know, I'm not sure. I suspect most would. I think that's what they would expect to hear and so they would hear it. They would see it written out in their books and as visual sound effects in their newspaper comic strips. But I wonder if not all Americans or Englishmen would hear *lub-dub*. For some it might be *thump thump, ba boom*, or even *ba bump*. There are always eccentric individuals, outliers who march to a different drummer, so to speak. They might perceive sounds differently. So, for people from other countries, a range of perceived sounds *should* be possible for them as well."

Connor closed his eyes. *Lub-DUB. Lub-DUB.* He could hear it almost immediately, and without the stethoscope, coming from deep inside his chest, but also from somewhere else, from multiple *wheres*, as if his heart had no definite location, but existed everywhere. It gave him a chill. There were other sounds as well, in languages he didn't understand, and clicks, and rubs and pops and moans, signals about what was, and would be happening to his fragile body.

He opened his eyes and looked at his grandad. He felt dizzy, and his face and limbs were cold. "Does a healthy heart sound different from a sick one? Could a doctor tell if something was wrong with you by listening?"

His grandad looked at him curiously. "The stethoscope is a diagnostic tool, so yes, although a professional might not be able to detect some subtle condition with the instrument, major malfunctions would be as obvious as, say, flat notes to a musician's ear." His expression went odd for a moment, his eyes staring at something beyond Connor's head. So clear was the impression Connor started to turn around and look for someone behind him. "Wait!" his grandfather cried. "Try listening to the heartbeat again."

His grandfather handed the shiny diaphragm to Connor, who stared at it a moment fearfully. It felt alive in his palm. He adjusted the earpieces for a good fit. He slipped the diaphragm beneath the shirt. It was so cold. Connor concentrated as best he could for a long time, his eyes closed, but heard nothing, in any language. "Are you sure it's making good contact with your skin?"

His grandfather didn't reply. Connor gazed into the white, tightly wrinkled face, the eyes fixed and staring. Connor was used to his grandad's dramatic, feigned reactions to events, and considered this another example. His grandfather made no sound at all, his lips frozen into a hideous O-shape.

Lost within the ghosts of other languages, Connor gathered up the sounds native to this place much as a beachcomber might gather shells. He examined each one, not sure what to make of them, all the open-throated *howls* and bitten *yips* and slippery sounds of things moving across and through desert sands. He had never visited any sort of beach, and now he feared he never would.

He still heard the occasional, barely detectable *lubs* and *dubs*, and even *tut umps*, distant and without definite location.

He did not return home immediately. Because Connor had had so little freedom most of his life, he and his parents agreed these Saturdays with Grandad would be "free" days in which Connor could come and go as he pleased. He imagined the decision had not come easily. But they were free days for his parents as well. On Saturdays they didn't have to keep track of him, they didn't have to be responsible, they didn't have to worry (although Connor knew of course they still did).

The land beyond Grandad's ramshackle residence was wide-open Arizona desert. This was outside the town limits, and as far as Connor knew no one lived here. Grandad said the ground was alkaline, which meant it wouldn't grow much. "Nothing for the plants to feed on." Where the surface soil had blown away it was caliche, hard as cement and six feet deep. Grandad said you needed a jackhammer to break through caliche.

Connor climbed onto his bike and rode out into the desert at the same time the sun was falling and setting the distant mesas on fire. It was an easy, frictionless ride. He could barely feel the seat or the pedals. He'd left Grandad's with way too much energy and felt a need to pedal as fast and as far as he could to burn off whatever was running through him.

Lub-DUB, lub-DUB, lub-DUB. He couldn't hear it or feel it, so he made this rhythmic sound in his head. The sensation was both a thrill and a terror.

It remained hot in the desert even after dark, like that time his mother left the oven on all night, and they woke up to the smell of burnt air. Peddling as fast as he could brought no relieving breeze but only increased his impression the world around him was burning. So much moisture cooked out of his skin his arms looked like wax paper. He imagined he could see through the skin into his interior works, all those bones, veins, fluids, and muscle.

The adults in his life had always warned him not to touch anything in the desert. Everything there, he'd been told, was out to hurt you. Things which cut or bit or stung blended into the landscape and sometimes you didn't know what they were until it was too late.

Tonight, Connor believed he could and needed to touch everything. Even the tarantulas and scorpions, maybe especially them, and even the intense spines of the cholla. He wanted to feel them all, and hear what they had to say, even if he didn't understand their language.

He took his feet off the pedals and the bike seemed to surge forward on its own. The sounds of the deep desert rushed through him all at once: wind whistling through the short malformed trees, the screech of some predatory bird, soft whisper of lizards moving through sand, frogs, crickets, and maybe a cactus wren, the put-put-put of an owl, the sharp crunch of a hoof, javelinas snuffling and digging, all drawing out and distorting as the bike pushed him beyond the limits of his native tongue.

Connor wasn't sure how long he was out in the desert. He recalled several changes in the light. He knew it was always hot, even though he didn't necessarily feel it.

He had no idea what time he arrived home. The neighbor's big collie kept barking at him. The dog had always been quite friendly before. Mr. Baxter came out, shushed the dog, and looked around. He stared right at Connor but didn't say anything. Connor wanted to apologize but couldn't quite come up with the words. Mr. Baxter would tell Connor's parents about the incident, and they would give Connor all kinds of grief about it. Maybe they'd ground him. It made Connor sad to think he might not be able to see his grandad for a few weeks.

He didn't have his bike with him. He had no idea what happened to it. Had he dropped it there in the shadows at the edge of the yard? Exhaustion had finally visited him. He'd go to bed, and when he woke up, he'd go looking for his bike. Hopefully his dad didn't find it first, wake him up and yell at him about how careless he was with his things.

Connor started to go inside when he saw the coyotes out in the street, staring at him. Three of them stood in the middle of the cracked asphalt, their heads turned in his direction, the lead one sniffing the air. Coyotes almost never came into town. He wondered if they had followed him here out of the desert. He wasn't sure they were dangerous, but it felt creepy the way they looked at him, so he went inside.

Mom and Dad weren't up yet. Connor went into his room and lay down on his bed with his clothes still on. The fan in front of the window turned slowly. His mom must have turned it on to make his room more comfortable. She did things like that. He never had to ask; she just knew to do them.

Lub-DUB, lub-DUB, lub-DUB. He kept listening for the sounds, but he didn't hear them. He could only imagine them. He wondered if this had always been the case. There were other sounds in other languages, surrounding him and closing in, but suddenly frightened he tried not to hear them.

Even though he was exhausted, as soon as he lay down, he knew he couldn't fall asleep. He stared at the ceiling. Outside the sun was climbing the sky, and his fan was fighting the rising heat. It wouldn't win, but it didn't need to as far as he was concerned.

The sun went higher and then out. It came up again and repeated itself while Connor kept his eyes open. Deep down in the earth the core of the world went lub-DUB, lub-DUB, as if the planet had a human heart. Connor could hear nothing else.

Mom didn't call him for breakfast. She came in and made his bed, straightened his room, turned off his fan which was now making a whining noise. She didn't speak to him. Connor guessed he'd really messed up this time.

He came out of his room and watched his parents eat a meal. More than a few meals. They weren't talking to each other. They stared at their plates and cut their meat and gathered their peas on their forks before shoveling them in. They had always been quiet, reticent people, but this was extreme even for them. It made Connor ill to watch, although he didn't feel the illness in his stomach. The sickness was somewhere else. Had they argued? He'd never seen them stay angry this long. It seemed he may have spoiled things for everyone.

He walked outside to look for his bike. He couldn't find it anywhere. He checked the garage, thinking maybe his dad had brought it inside, but it wasn't there. For a moment he wondered if maybe the coyotes had taken it, one perched on the seat to steer, the other two holding on and working the pedals. That would have been something to see, almost worth the cost of losing his bike.

Grandad had once talked about the language of coyotes, how they created their songs out of a series of yips and howls, changing pitch and tone to create songs lasting almost half an hour. Maybe he could learn to use their language to ask for his bike back.

A coyote's heart was tucked in right behind its shoulder joint with its lungs. Grandad once told him a dog's heart beats much faster than our own. Connor wondered if the same thing were true of coyotes. No calm *lub-Dub* for them, but a rapid repetition like a frantic moth trapped inside a glass.

It wasn't Saturday, at least Connor didn't think it was, but he felt an urgent need to go see his grandfather. Since he didn't have his bicycle, he would have to walk.

As had been his habit, he meandered through the various neighborhoods, waving to people, seeking some entry into their lives. Today they paid him no attention, going about their business without a glance in his direction. Connor didn't mind. Sometimes people get so busy they can't see what's right in front of them.

But their animals noticed. Their dogs and cats and once, a goat. Pets stared at him, hackles raised, their owners recognizing something had changed in their world, but with no idea what.

It saddened Connor, and sometimes he waited for someone to say something, or nod. He witnessed the day change from light to dark to light again, waiting for an acknowledgement which never came.

The days grew longer, hotter, until even the shadows burned. His own shadow burned completely away. He didn't mind. He could always borrow one from a house or maybe a tall Mesquite.

At Halloween the kids streamed by him in packs, howling like coyotes, their bags full and spilling candy. Some stopped and looked around, and he thought to touch them but never did. At Christmas the saguaros were wrapped in strings of colored lights and the doors decorated with strings of dried chili peppers. He was surprised one morning to see the crisp white coating everywhere—he'd seen snow once—it looked like frosted candy and disappeared once the sun peeked above the mesas.

Grandad's house was a different color from what it had been yesterday, softer, paler as if imperfectly remembered. Connor thought it might be the angle of the sun, now a brilliant white star behind streaks of cloud. Grandad could have explained the science of it and might even have arranged a demonstration during which they both might have taken a dangerous look directly into that burning globe.

But once in the yard Connor could see the frayed boards and the worn paint streaked with gray bleeding through, paint strands like fallen curls of white hair scattered around the weathered brick foundation. Connor's bike was still propped up against the front porch where he'd left it, its tires disintegrated, and the metal frame dull and rough with corrosion. He went up on the porch and before he could knock, he was inside.

His grandfather always kept a careless house, but Connor had never seen it so destroyed. Tables were overturned and what remained of specimens and experiments reduced to trash and strewn through the rooms. Cracks in the floorboards collected dirt where thin patches of weeds grew like gray hair. Most of what Grandad owned was missing. There were deep scratches in the floor and wide scrapes where shovels might have been used to remove collections he'd spent a lifetime putting together. Just like Mom said would happen to Grandad's stuff in the end.

There were still creatures living here, mingled in the trash, and hiding beneath the floors. Connor could hear their frantic hearts.

In the back of the house, he found the old man sitting in the corner within the crumpled carcass of an ancient pink chair. The ravaged face and the collapsed shoulders, the translucent bag of skin with nothing inside. His grandfather appeared to be napping. His eyelids floated. His cracked mouth fell open into a thin-lipped gasp. He was wall-eyed like a fish dragged from dark waters. Connor listened for the pump, the *lub* and the *dub*, but heard nothing.

"You came back." The words drifted side to side, but Connor still grasped their meaning.

"Is it the wrong day? It looks like it might be a bad time."

His grandfather laughed. With no sound coming out it looked like a seizure. Then he stopped. "Every day is Saturday now. Come closer and let me look at you."

Connor stood before him. He reached out and touched his grandfather's bare arm. It appeared thinner and more fragile than he remembered. It felt like nothing, even when he gave the flesh a little pinch. Maybe this was some new trick, some misguided lesson. Connor could have performed more of a test, shaken the body or even slapped the face, but of course he would never do such a thing.

"So, what kind of sound does my heart make now? Is it a *lub* and a *dub*? Or something softer, almost inaudible?"

Connor recalled all that nonsense with the earpieces and the ever-so-cold steel diaphragm. "Really? That's what you want to do? Where's your stethoscope?"

"I have no idea. Long gone I suspect, like most everything else I owned. But you shouldn't need something so primitive, not in your current condition. Just listen."

Connor lifted his head and closed his eyes. Far beyond the limits of this room he could sense a distant pulse, but he didn't hear it. "Nothing at all. Just like the last time we tried this."

Lub and *DUB* and nothing more.

"What do you remember of the last time?"

"I was," Connor began. "Was it yesterday, or was it longer? Maybe it was longer. You handed the diaphragm back to me. I didn't want to finish the lesson. You'd made me uncomfortable, like always, Grandad. I just wanted to go home. But I made sure the earpieces were firmly placed in my ears. Then I slipped the diaphragm inside the shirt, and against the skin. I remember it was cold."

"Because it was your shirt, Connor. Your skin. You were searching for your own heartbeat."

The *lub-DUB* he now heard was not in his body, or in his grandfather's, and maybe not even in this world. But he couldn't stop hearing it. "Did I make that awful rattling sound people do at the end?"

"No, there was no time. You didn't linger, you didn't struggle. It was a simple moment of quiet surrender. There may have been a detectable sighing sound, but as much as I debated those moments later, I could never decide for sure."

His grandfather was off the floor, out of the chair. Connor could see his face and hands, but nothing more. "They blamed me, of course. And maybe I deserved it, I don't know. On the other hand, when I left almost a year later, out my coffin door mind you, I made such noise it shook the house."

Grandad moved them both along, through the house and then beyond, although Connor couldn't determine the mechanism involved. "Come now. You're just in time. I have some interesting things to show you. We have much more to see, you and me. There are songs only the rattlesnake and the Gila perform. And the dreams of the tortoise and the ring-tailed cat are like no others. And I must tell you everything, I mean everything about the tiny Kangaroo rats."

INTO THE WHITE

The meteorologist predicted snow. This time of year, the meteorologist was usually right.

When he was a small boy, and the snow depths were legendary, his father would watch the rising accumulations of white from their front window, now and then repeating, "Well, we needed the moisture," until the snow stopped, and he pulled his snow suit and boots on, and went out into the silence to shovel and scrape and take back their small world. His mother, who hated the snow, muttered from the kitchen, "I hope he doesn't have a heart attack." Even as a child he understood the risk was significant.

His father didn't have the heart attack, but both his mother and father died in their sleep one winter while he was in college, their bellies full of pills and wine. They did not leave a note. That home full of questions and empty of answers was the house he lived in now. He'd always imagined he would one day marry and have children, but reality let him down. He had been and still was, alone.

He had a college friend, a woman, who loved him, but not the way he loved her. Every week they exchanged messages on the internet, and every other year they visited one or the other's home. He imagined more but understood the danger of imagining someone else's thoughts and feelings. He would not risk that ration of love they shared.

Sometimes they reached out over the phone, but the phone calls always felt strained and left him yearning for more, so eventually they dropped that method of communication. They still sent their messages back and forth, intimate acquaintances on opposite poles of the world. She was not the solution to his life.

The last few years had seen increasing amounts of snow. It filled the shallow places as if they did not exist. It erased the roofs until only the walls were visible. Some months the snow lasted so long he could not remember what lay beneath it. At least he could still wade to his mailbox, and for the rare occasions his groceries could not be delivered he kept a well-stocked pantry.

He stopped looking outside his window. He knew he would see little more than white, little more than trees and posts rising from the white, little more than houses half-buried in white as far as he could see. He sometimes heard the echoes of children playing, and if he searched for them from his windows, he might see a few distant dots coming together, falling apart, gliding over the snow as if on wings.

He did not mind, not looking out. It gave him more time for reading, consuming the books which fed his imagination. He read until he fell asleep in his chair, then when he woke up again, he read some more.

He wasn't aware it was still snowing. A fine white mist suffused the air. Over the next few days, it grew thicker, heavier, and when he finally rose from his chair and gazed outside, he could not see the distant line of trees, and he could not see the fields in front of those trees, and he could not see past the road separating his land from those fields. He could not see the road itself. By nightfall, the icy air was full of flakes the size of his head, as if reality were disintegrating to disclose the unimaginable whiteness beyond.

He'd been awake too long, and now he was experiencing the consequences. At some point what had been an adding to had become a taking away.

The next morning the world outside his windows was completely white, soundless, and vaguely threatening. He slipped on his father's shabby old snowsuit and battered boots and walked outside.

The snow was deep, but his boots barely sank in. He knew there would be no mail delivery today, and not likely for any subsequent days. He wanted to know if there were other people in the world, or anything at all to see, and so he began walking.

In a world of all white, he couldn't say in which direction he was traveling. In a world which was all white he couldn't tell if any progress was being made.

He heard ice rattling and snow cracking, the distant explosions of collapse. In a world without obstruction, sound traveled far. When it finally arrived it was amplified, and painful.

The sky was so intense it became a dream scorched into his now. Smoldering shadows moved through the mist like memory. The clarity left him snow-blind. It became a burden to see. The snow continued to fall, the flakes becoming embers behind his eyes.

This was the world without pretense. This was the world as it was, with everything humans imagined removed.

Occasionally he came across pools of melt lying on top of the snow. Staring into those pools made them shimmer.

The white air was a perfect screen to receive his memories, an endless chronicle of yearnings, couplings and uncouplings, searches for solutions never found. He had run out of ideas. If he could have interrogated his parents, he felt sure they would tell him his birth had been a tragic accident. His had been a long journey and approaching the end he had outpaced his capacity for joy.

A mass exodus of animals crossed his path. Other than the steady crunch of his own footsteps, their hoofbeats, paws, and claws created the first sounds he had heard in days. He felt an overwhelming urge to follow them into extinction, but they were too swift for him, and soon disappeared into the mist.

He wasn't sure where he was relative to the world he had known. He had forgotten much of it. He knew there were streets far beneath him, road signs and intersections, bridges perhaps, on and off ramps, superhighways. But here in the world of white, he had to make his own way. He had to create his own path forward.

His boots hit something solid, and he tumbled off his feet. He crawled around and found it: a brightly painted piece of wood. Digging further, he uncovered pieces of a merry-go-round beneath the snow, brightly painted horses, the riders mannequins the size of children.

Further along he discovered upright posts protruding from the snow, burnt and broken trees looking like shattered bones wedged into the snow, like the bones of dinosaurs, like the bones of ancient cities.

A sudden wind came up. The world moved by him so fast it whistled. His snowsuit began to shred. The emptiness washed over him, embedding itself in his flesh. He saw blood upon the snow.

Ahead of him the sky began to tear. He thought at first it was the Northern Lights, but he came to believe it was something quite different.

THE OLD MAN'S TALE

We all seek a kind of understanding. How the world works, and our place in it. It doesn't have to be true.

Dan heard a disturbance of birds, maybe some cats and maybe something else, deep within the dark shadows beyond the parking lot. It sounded harsh and desperate, and it was difficult to say what was going on. No one else seemed bothered. Perhaps they'd become used to commotion. An old-fashioned word—did anyone else still use it? He was a few months shy of seventy-four, so he figured he had a right to use an old word or two.

He was surrounded by people, although he couldn't see them in any detail: the dark silhouettes of fellow pilgrims and storytellers against the fading crimson light. He was determined to believe none of them meant him harm, which during these times seemed a major leap of faith. People were less trusting than they used to be, and far less kind. Lies and deception, hatred and fear, the worst in people had taken control. Dan was confused and angry most of the time. It was safer to hide your pain and suffer in silence. There had been numerous shortages this past year, but the most critical might have been empathy.

His eyesight had deteriorated in recent years, the decline accelerating over the course of this trip. This might have been a result of his diabetes and kidney disease, or something yet undiagnosed. He couldn't be sure if the things he saw were a symptom or a revelation. Dark silhouettes stood at the edges of things, making of the night a Rorschach. He thought he'd feel better if he saw their mouths.

The face a few yards away was that of the organizer. Dan had been skeptical—he never responded to either unsolicited mail or phone calls—but Jane had been so excited by the invitation and the possibility of finally seeing the Grand Canyon, and the last thing Dan wanted was to disappoint her.

He'd been afraid the stories from the other travelers might disturb her, but she insisted on being beside him as he told his tale. He kept reaching out to make sure she was there. Once he thought he saw her moving through the crowd, but he must have been mistaken. She wasn't speaking to him now. He had no idea why. It was a typical problem in marriages. Somehow, he was expected to read her mind.

After more than a year with only Jane and doctors to talk to he had a lot to say. "Do I just start? How much time do I have? If you want me to keep talking, I'll keep talking. I have nothing better to do, not at my age."

Somewhere a fire was burning. He could smell it although he couldn't see the flames. It seemed too warm for a fire; he supposed it was for atmosphere. Or maybe it wasn't a literal fire, but simply his sense of the world burning. So many wildfires had raged this past year—Australia, California, his home state of Colorado—they'd left this acrid remainder in his nasal passages he couldn't shake. Climate change, worse by the day. One more thing to make him feel helpless.

"I've never been to Arizona before, so I'm not used to the heat. Yet here I am wearing my sweater. Old men depend on their sweaters. When you're old that icy hand is always trying to slip in and steal your heart. My Jane—" He gestured in her direction. "—used to say we should move here when we got old. I tried to laugh off the idea, because I couldn't bear the thought of living somewhere with so much empty space."

There was movement in the crowd. He couldn't pinpoint its location because of all the shadows. He hadn't realized so many were in attendance. They moved little, which made them good listeners he supposed. He felt self-conscious being the center of attention, being overweight, being old. His CKD caused him intermittent pain and would probably end his life prematurely.

"I can't drive anymore, not with my vision, and Jane's been too ill, so we had to take the bus from Denver to get here. I spent a lot of time going to the bathroom on the bus. I worry I might smell like pee. Is that too much information? With all our scientific advances, you'd think they could help people like me."

Sometimes he had accidents and he wanted to cover his face and weep like a small child. He shouldn't have brought it up. Jane had to be embarrassed, but she didn't say anything.

"It's a long trip with a whole lot of nothing to see. Even less for me, I guess. So, I must use my imagination. Someone points at something in the distance and says 'Ain't that a beautiful mesa!' I always agree, because in my mind's eye, it *is* grand. I see most things as being much better or much worse than they are. In that regard, I suppose I'm like everybody else on the planet."

His cell phone started ringing from inside the small backpack on the bench beside him. He stared at it. "I'm so sorry." He looked around foolishly thinking he might see the caller. "I thought it was dead. It's *been* dead. My son gave it to us for emergencies. I never charge it. These things don't charge by themselves, do they? I don't know why I brought it. I never use it. The only people who ever call me are con artists." He opened the pack being careful not to jostle the contents and pulled out the phone. There was no name, and he didn't recognize the number. The phone went dark again. He dropped it back into the pack.

"My wife Jane has always wanted to see the Grand Canyon. She's been after me for years to go. I told her I didn't want to drive all that distance and spend all that money to see a damn hole in the ground. I said it harshly because I wanted to discourage her from asking again. I told her I didn't care how big it was, or that it was prehistoric. After a while she stopped asking because she knew my mind was set." It felt strange saying this in front of Jane, but he was sure she already knew.

"It's the only time I've ever lied to her. The truth is the idea of being on the edge of that canyon always terrified me. I've seen pictures, and I'm *seriously* afraid of heights. Once we got there, I knew I would refuse to go anywhere near it. The Grand Canyon is a place where the world is broken, where it shows its wound, so why would I want to see that?

"I've always regretted disappointing her. Then this last year, this Covid year, watching people we knew getting so sick, watching neighbors and relatives dying—when Jane's sister passed, we couldn't even attend the funeral. Her brother was the designated mourner. He took a shaky video of the barebones burial and sent it to us in an email. Jane watched it over and over, crying. I was afraid this was the thing that was going to break her. I was scared to death to go anywhere, but she still had to leave the house for doctors' appointments, tests, and treatments. If she saw someone without a mask, or buying a hoard of TP, water, hand sanitizer, she made it her mission to give them a miserable day. I understood completely, but it still shocked me. Jane is the kindest person you'll ever meet, but this last year of constant stress and disappointment has worn her down to the basics. We knew the world wasn't ending, I mean we all understand this isn't the end times, am I right? But that knowledge doesn't travel very deep. We still feel on the lip of oblivion, I can't be the only one.

"We were so grateful when your invitation came. I immediately told her we would go, *had* to go. Just to see something eternal when so many people we knew were dying, losing their jobs, fracturing inside. For the first time in a long while I experienced excitement. I hadn't taken a long bus trip since my college years.

"I'm rambling. Forgive me, but I haven't talked to other people in a while. It may take me some time to remember how. Am I the only one who thinks the world has fundamentally changed?

"Do any of you still watch the news? I stopped. I can't watch that crap anymore, all those alternative versions of reality. The deliberate lies and the stupidity, and the goddamn delusion. You don't know these people, so you don't know which it is in their case. I'm just an old man with no influence or power. Before, I was a young man with no influence or power. It seems all we can do is witness and tell the truth about what we've seen. But no one wants to do even that anymore.

"Jane complains that I tend to lecture. That's not what I'm trying to do here. Old guys like me, sometimes when we talk to people it sounds like a lecture, I'm not sure why. I'm simply trying to explain myself. Let me back up a little.

"Nine months ago, I was sitting in our back yard, trying to figure out this emergency cell phone our son Blake gave us. I've never been good with cell technology, and the screen is too small for me. Blake didn't leave us his number when he left town, so who was I supposed to call anyway, some stranger? We didn't even have an address to send him a letter. I've always had trouble connecting with our only child, and I take full responsibility for that. But Jane has been such a good mother—didn't our son want to know how she was doing?

"There was this small pile of garbage against the wooden fence on the side of our yard. Our next-door neighbor tossed it over like this was a normal thing to do. Some spoiled food, some upholstery foam, discarded mail, pieces of a doll and what used to be a stuffed toy. Something new every day, and I cleaned it up every day before Jane could see it, because it upset her so much. Our neighbor wouldn't even talk to me, said he knew nothing about it, then he called me senile. It was a smallish outrage to add to the many humiliations I've experienced the past few years.

"We used to use the backyard all the time before Jane got sick. We used to have barbecues. We would sit out there and listen to the birds. But it had begun to feel unpleasant and uncomfortable. The back fence is chain link and you can see the yards and the trees south of our house. At one point I glanced up from that damn cell phone, and I saw this dark figure standing by the fence, either on our side or the other, I couldn't quite tell. I stared at this person, waiting for him or her to move. After a tense few minutes with no change, I assumed it was an optical illusion, or maybe just a shadow, and I turned my back and walked away. I slept poorly that night, worrying over it, and wondering how I could have left without investigating more thoroughly.

"So, the next morning I went into the back yard and checked it out. I didn't find anything, no footprints, no sign of a disturbance of any kind. But as I was going back into the house, I sensed something behind me, and I turned around. Just for a second I may or may not have seen several more human shapes in the yard, on both sides of the fence, but they weren't there a second later. Puzzling, but easy to dismiss when you have eyes as bad as mine.

"Then a couple of days later I was convinced I saw the silhouette of a man climbing over our side of the wooden fence to get into our neighbor's yard. I should have told him, but after our disagreement, I was reluctant to knock on his door. Instead, I considered getting Jane out of the house and checking into a motel, but how could I explain why? The last thing I wanted to do was scare her. So, I did nothing. I decided to wait, thinking maybe it was just me seeing things. I thought maybe I wouldn't have seen anything if I hadn't been so upset about everything on the news.

"About a month or so passed. I was out in the yard again trying to decide if the lawn needed mowing. I don't do much yard work anymore. I usually hire a teenager if I can find one. Jane was inside resting from her chemo. She was really sick the first part of the year, then she got better, then she was sick again. Most of the summer we took a cab to get her blood transfusions every few weeks. We watched a great deal of TV together, sitting on the couch and holding hands. That's how we spent Thanksgiving and Christmas. That's how we watched the insurrection, and then the inauguration. We were sitting on that couch watching when the 500,000 deaths from Covid were announced. And we watched that George Floyd video again and again, trying to understand why it happened, and knowing it had happened many times before. We felt helpless as we watched it, and feeling helpless made us feel ashamed.

"But that was ahead of us. On this day, while I was trying to decide if I could let the lawn go another week or two, and if I could just ignore the weeding until next season, I noticed movement near the top of one of the trees beyond the chain link fence. A mass of leaves obscured my view, but something was changing, shifting, and causing the top branches to bend as it began its descent. I didn't know what it might be, I just had a peek of something, and as I followed this movement down the tree, I experienced an overwhelming feeling of dread. I can't remember ever feeling so afraid over apparently nothing. I waited for whatever might appear at the bottom of the tree. But what dropped out of the lower limbs wasn't a form or even a shadow, but some sort of distortion in the light, a visual ripple which quickly dissipated.

"Now, this could have been a combination of some sort of wind through the tree branches along with some play of the light. But the presence felt undeniable. I looked at the nearby trees, and after a few minutes I was sure something was sitting in the top of a second one, and now it too was slowly coming down, a few leaves, some bits of branch and the negative spaces in between, descending in unison, a kind of camouflage in motion. I still had no idea what it might be, but I felt threatened, and I didn't want to be there when another one reached the ground, and so I retreated inside.

"For the next week I spent a period each morning observing the trees. That experience of a barely detectable presence followed by motion and descent repeated itself day after day, until I couldn't stand to watch anymore."

Dan paused his story to allow for questions or complaints, any kind of reaction from his audience at all. There was none. He did notice slight movements, and he had a sense of being watched, so he assumed they were still present.

"I've read that some ancient peoples believed the spirits of the dead manifested as birds, perched in the treetops and observing the living below. Not that I believe this, but if it were true, imagine their anger over how we've handled things. All the damage we've done, all the promises broken or simply forgotten.

"I tried not to think about what I'd witnessed. I didn't need something new to worry about. I didn't tell Jane." He put his hand out, thinking his touch would let her know he was sorry for that, and for talking about her so openly, and his fingers grazed the backpack. "In fact, I've never told anyone else about this. You people, you're the first."

Since Dan began this tale his surroundings had changed. The light from the fire was more evident, casting yellows and reds through the shadows. Dan thought he could make out a few more faces, although he couldn't see their expressions. Not knowing how his audience was reacting to what he told them was disquieting.

He couldn't be sure who or what they were. In the darkness almost anyone could have slipped into the crowd, sat down, or stood at the back. Visitors might have been among them, phantoms, witnesses, those presences crept down from the trees. Some might even have followed him from Colorado. He didn't know how any of this worked, so anything was still possible.

He probably shouldn't have told them. They might be able to have him committed. He'd heard Arizona was not a good place to be mentally ill. He should have rehearsed his story with Jane first. She could have advised him what not to say.

"It's been a strange and demanding year. I'm not claiming to understand what I saw. I'm just putting it out there. I'm a rational human being trying to deal with the irrational, these phantoms at the periphery of my vision, like someone just arrived, or someone just left, or someone's waiting there, ready to do some damage, cause some mischief. I don't want to say it's related to the pandemic, but maybe everything is, if you think about it.

"People have changed so much the past few years, don't you think? Things will be fine for a while, then these pockets of—I don't know—*derangement* appear, and they spread through the population.

"I thought Jane was oblivious to it all, then one day she grabbed both of my hands and stared at me in this intense, almost scary way. 'It's that awful man they elected. People now think it's okay to say anything that pops into their heads.'

"My wife has never been a political person, so that was a lot for her to say. She wanted to go to the Women's March the day after his inauguration, but she'd been too ill. A friend gave her one of those pink knitted hats and she wore it around the house for weeks. She'd lost some of her hair, and it kept her head warm.

"We have seen so many terrible images. Those poor refugees. Children abandoned in the desert, or their bodies washed up on shore. You've seen those pictures too? Or am I crazy?"

He waited for an uncomfortably long time. Finally, someone in the distance said "Yes," and another "Yes, I think we've all seen them."

"I think of those children as another kind of arrival. Like the entities up in the trees, like the reminders from history. Welcome them or try to keep them out, it doesn't matter. They're still going to come. It doesn't matter how angry you are, how unpleasant, it's a matter of physics. The true facts of history are going to rise to the top however deeply you try to bury them. If people's houses are burning, they're going to find somewhere else to live. The way I see it, fires are burning all over the world.

"I've had difficulty sleeping for months. Has anyone else lost sleep?" A murmur traveled through the crowd. "Underneath everything were my worries over Jane of course. But laid over those were the soft whispers, the sensation of something touching the hairs on my arms, and I'd feel around for insects on my body which were never there. More than a few nights I listened to the sound of tree limbs brushing across the roof of our house, and then I remembered we had no trees in our yard.

"Then sometimes there was this faint crackling within the walls. Sometimes a rhythmic pulse of something moving through the rooms.

"I was relieved to have this opportunity to escape the house, to travel somewhere I'd never been before, where I knew no one. We were both so eager, so ready to go. Jane could hardly contain herself. She planned for this trip for months.

"But then on the morning of departure I couldn't make myself walk out the door. The taxi was waiting, horn blaring. It was the trip we'd been looking forward to so much, and yet I couldn't budge. For some reason I could not imagine ever returning from this trip. I felt as if I were about to go to my own funeral.

"Jane had a grip on my arm so tight it ached. She kept whispering in my ear that I'd promised her, that I'd made a commitment. So I hurried down to the cab before I could change my mind again. I held it together pretty well on the ride into downtown Denver.

"I'd packed light—a few changes of clothes in a single backpack because I couldn't carry more. I'd loaded the pack with lots of brochures for every place we were going to or through. I love brochures, don't you? I'd already read them once and I planned to read them again on the bus. I'm a planner, always have been. I always refer to a map even when I've been to a place a dozen times.

"Jane kept whispering words of encouragement, bits of poems and song lyrics, anything to distract me from my anxiety. Gazing out the window I felt out of place, watching people walking around so close to each other, some with masks and some without. I wasn't even sure what the current rules were, although I knew masks were required on buses.

"I looked for those visitors and found them, those other presences crossing the street, sitting on porches, stepping out of bushes. They manifested mostly as color shifts and staggered outlines. For me this was confirmation the phenomenon wasn't restricted to our neighborhood.

"I hadn't been downtown in years. But it was much as I remembered, vast concrete stretches with little green, a few shiny new buildings and fewer of the old gray ones. Shabby figures pushed their grocery carts from corner to corner. At first I thought these might be the visitors, but they were too crisply defined, and I realized they were homeless people. We passed an entire encampment arranged along a parking strip: a variety of small tents, carts, boxes, and trash bags filled to overflowing.

"The driver said something crude. It was brief and offhand, and I could have let it go, but it angered me. 'So, what's your solution?'

"The driver stared at me in the rear-view. 'Don't have one, I just know it's wrong to let them live in a public area. Isn't that why we have elections? To put people in charge who know what to do?'

"I felt Jane's hand on my arm. I said 'I wish the ones in charge would do a lot of things, but they don't. The economy leaves lots of folks behind. On top of that the climate's changing. We pretend there's nothing we can do. Pretty soon it will be our own family members, moving, trying to find safety. Maybe you. Maybe me if I live that long. We need to do better if we want to save ourselves. We could start with those folks out there.' Okay, not those exact words, but something like it. Yeah, sometimes I lecture people. I guess I don't mind if it's important.

"When we arrived at the bus station we had to wait a little while before boarding. I kept stalling. Jane had to push me. I was afraid once I left on that bus my life would never be the same. It increasingly seemed a terrible idea, leaving the safety of home to go somewhere completely unknown.

"Some people were being cautious in the station and on the bus, and some people not. There were a few who behaved as if the pandemic had never occurred. Before we got to the interstate ramp the bus driver slowed down and parked on the side of the street. A few yards away the police had pulled a man out of his car and were talking to him forcefully. Some of the passengers stood up and held their cell phones up to the windows on that side. Others beat on the glass. One of the officers glanced over, then turned away. Jane kept telling me I should do something, so I got the dead cell phone out of my pack and held it up to the window. I felt uncomfortable doing that—a few years ago I would never have imagined such a thing, but the world has changed, hasn't it? I don't know if the officers were going to act inappropriately; maybe they were just doing their job. These days you can no longer assume the best, can you? Eventually the bus started up again and everyone sat down.

"Signs on the bus reminded everyone that masks (except when eating and drinking) and social distancing were required. Seats and hand surfaces were regularly sanitized. Another sign had a diagram explaining how cabin air was continuously replaced every five minutes. It looked very scientific, as if NASA had been involved in the engineering. These details and more were described in colorful brochures. I added one to the large collection in my backpack.

"The first four seats behind the driver were taped off so no one could sit there. These measures reassured me at first, then I saw that although many passengers wore their masks, many did not. Some had pulled their masks down in order to complain to each other about the *arbitrary* rules. One of those complaining with his mask down was a preacher, presumably.

At least he had a bible in his hand which he continuously quoted from.

"The driver wasn't enforcing anything (except for that no-sit space directly behind him). I understood—the man wasn't paid to be an enforcer and it would probably be dangerous for him if he tried. They expect people to cooperate and be on their best behavior during a crisis, but that's not how people act.

"I pulled Jane closer as we escaped the southern limits of the city and the bus headed for Colorado Springs and points beyond. The foothills grew closer, then fell away again. The stretches of flatland increased their spread, and even though there was a great deal of development south of metro Denver, I was impressed by all the emptiness. Some people like that sort of environment, the wide-open spaces with your nearest neighbor miles away. I never have.

"Although I had a definite destination in mind—this place, and the canyon beyond—I wasn't convinced we'd actually arrive here. I imagined the driver taking us as far as possible into nothing before the fuel ran out.

"I was still conscious of those ghostly visitors, but there was no evidence of their presence on the bus, and although I looked for them out in those dry, burning stretches, I didn't see any indication they were there. A silhouette standing and watching from a distant house doesn't count—it could just be some curious resident—although I saw quite a few more of those than I expected. I attempted to see into the windows of passing cars. Of course, you can't see much unless they're traveling at the same speed. Sometimes I'd see some shadows in a back seat, but those could have been anything.

"Maybe we were too far away, traveling too fast, but I suspect their preference is to manifest within the company of human beings. By themselves I imagine they must behave quite differently. But around us, it must be like visiting a foreign country, getting used to the culture, trying to understand customs which to us feel quite strange. I have no evidence for any of this. We human beings shouldn't develop convictions and beliefs based on feelings alone, but that's what we do. The human animal is a fiction machine.

"We made ourselves a little island, Jane and I, there in the middle of the bus. All around us people were chatting. It seemed no one was traveling alone, or if they were they'd made conversational friends with a speed I could only envy. I've never been good at talking to strangers, not ever. It's not that I don't like people. I just feel separated from them, and that attitude has only deepened as I've grown older. Even on this long trip with Jane she did most of the talking. I listened, and occasionally offered some perspective, usually a negative one. Jane was used to that and mocked me playfully for my grumpiness.

"We whispered our conversations. We didn't want to disturb the other passengers, and we didn't want them to hear the secrets we shared only with each other.

"Occasionally people would turn and stare at us, even though we were whispering. Maybe they wondered what all the whispering was about, or they'd forgotten there was such a thing as privacy, or that it is considered rude to stare. There were several children on the bus, and they stared the longest, until their parents made them turn around. This was usually followed by whispered conversations of their own. I didn't try to listen. At least I know how to respect people's privacy.

"Since I've gotten old, I've noticed sometimes children point and snicker at me. I think it may be because none of my clothes fit. They haven't fit for a long time. I don't know how to make them fit or even what *fitting* means. Now I can't seem to make myself care. About either the fit or the snickering. I try not to judge.

"If I've learned one thing from this past year, it's that I'm not a bad person. I'm a good person, just not a great one.

"To be honest I felt ill the entire trip. I still feel a vague sickness throughout my body. It's *chronic*, I suppose. My lower abdomen, my chest, my constant trips to the bathroom. The bus bathroom was horrid, as I expected it would be, but I had no choice. I had to spend a lot of time in there. Each time I returned from the cramped bathroom I looked for Jane, and if I didn't see her immediately—and sometimes I didn't—my anxiety surged.

"When the stress became too much, I took a nap. This has always been my go-to solution. Once I opened my eyes and saw a much younger version of myself sitting in the seat across the aisle. He blinked, obviously alarmed. He was from long before I met Jane.

"Another time I awakened to see insects crawling through the bus, and even a rat or two. I thought I should tell someone, probably the driver, but what could he do? We were in the middle of a trip. I kept my mouth shut and went back to sleep. When I woke up again, I wasn't there. It was past my sell-by date, and I was a shadow staining the seat.

"I woke up again, now confused about where I was. Then I felt Jane's hand on my arm and saw her leaning over me. 'Have a good rest?' She must have said that same line hundreds of times during our marriage, and it was always comforting.

"I get confused a lot these days, and it sometimes takes me awhile to realize I'm confused. I always have more questions than answers."

Dan had been talking a long time. He stopped and took a slow drink from his water bottle. He worried this might have been a mistake. He might develop an urgent need to go to the bathroom. Were they allowed to take bathroom breaks during the middle of a story? 'Allowed' probably wasn't the right word—there was no coercion here, except the need to avoid embarrassment.

He was so tired of this, having to schedule his life around his unreasonable bodily needs, the toilet, his fatigue, his bouts of worry and anxiety. It was humiliating. None of those had been considerations when he was young.

It was almost pitch black. None of the parking lot lights were on, and the fire had burned out. A thick mass of variegated darkness hung in front of him. He assumed people were inside the darkness ready to hear the rest of his tale.

He turned his head to look for Jane. He couldn't see her, but he heard her whispering to him. He couldn't make out all the words, but he knew they were of love and encouragement. Fortified, he continued.

"Northeastern New Mexico is dominated by a broad region of volcanic fields. Capulin, an extinct volcano, is well east of I-25, so we bypassed it. But I still had brochures. It's strange to think about volcano activity in the US, especially near one's home. Ancient cinder cones and petrified lava flows, and the land itself looks burnt and alien. There was active volcanic activity in New Mexico during the time of the Paleoindians, can you imagine? Not being able to trust the ground beneath your feet or the sky over your head? Yet maybe that's not so different from now.

"There's something vaguely romantic and emotionally familiar about the apocalyptic landscape there, but it made me uncomfortable. A smoky mist eased down the highway, soon enveloping the bus. A charred stench drifted in through the vents until the driver shut them. Unable to see past the windshield the driver pulled onto the wide shoulder. We all stopped talking and stared out the windows.

"I saw several thin, upright shadows wandering the cloudy plain across the road, appearing and disappearing as a pale yellowish film slowly drifted through. They looked like people walking away to some unknown destination. When the bus started up again we passed a few empty parked cars a hundred or so yards down the road. I heard someone say we should stop and check if anyone needed help, but the driver ignored the suggestion.

"I saw a few animals along the road, both small and large, several rabbits and prairie dogs, and something which looked like a small antelope. I couldn't identify the rest. They might have been anything, I just knew they were covered in fur, I think. It was perhaps emblematic of the boredom of long bus rides that anytime a passenger made such a sighting they called it out and we all strained to look.

"An argument erupted several rows ahead of us. A young girl accused the preacher of touching her under the cover of his open bible. There was shouting and a great deal of shoving and I leaned over Jane to protect her. A few minutes later the bus stopped, and the preacher was thrown out onto the shoulder of the road. It happened so quickly I didn't have time to think about whether this was right to handle things that way, but everyone seemed agreed, and the driver did allow it to happen. In any case I couldn't have done anything.

"We stopped in Las Vegas, New Mexico. Jane thought it funny such a small, dusty town had the same name as that glamorous city in Nevada. According to the brochure part of *Easy Rider* was filmed here and in the old days outlaws like Billy the Kid walked the streets. I thought it would be an interesting place for us to spend the night and catch another bus the next day. I was exhausted. I wouldn't have thought sitting on a bus could be so tiring, but it did me in. Jane, who was the sick one, who had been reduced almost to nothing, never complained. I felt ashamed of myself, but it couldn't be helped. I couldn't bear to be on the bus another minute.

"We walked a short distance from the bus stop to a small motel. It was depressing in its adequacy, but it was close by, and I didn't have the energy to find another. I strapped on my backpack, and Jane and I walked around a little before having dinner at a small western-themed café. She chattered the entire time, but I couldn't really follow what she was saying. I guess I was too tired. I had a strong feeling others were walking with us but explorations into my peripheral views revealed no one. So, I assumed this town had visitors too. This was strong confirmation these phantoms were everywhere, as far as I was concerned. Witnessing, perhaps judging, because why else would they be here?

"Despite decades of living in Colorado I've never felt like a westerner. People at the café were watching me eat, at least I think they were. Jane kept telling me to ignore them. I told her I couldn't stand it anymore. I paid up and left. I've always thought we should have retired to a small town like that—it didn't matter where—I thought we'd feel safer. Jane says small town people aren't necessarily better. I guess there are no safe places anymore.

"In the parking lot of the motel a shadow stood beside an old dusty automobile. It looked like it had traveled miles and years to get there. The figure was still standing there when we walked away from the motel the next morning. The bus stop was more of a truck stop—trucks were parked everywhere, and I walked cautiously between them to get to a place where we could wait for the next bus. It wouldn't do to be run over now. I don't dread death, but I don't want to die because I've acted stupidly.

"A large open air flea market filled the block across the road. Not all the sellers had protective awnings, and they looked miserable in the hot sun. I worried that maybe I'd read the schedule incorrectly and we'd be stuck with no way to either continue our trip or to get back home. Sometimes I think worrying is my job, and it's Jane's job to reassure me and calm me down. Within a few minutes a line of waiting passengers formed behind me and the bus arrived. It looked identical to the previous bus, but I felt good about facing a new set of passengers. I noticed a man staring at us from the middle of the flea market as we boarded the new bus. I couldn't see the man's face, and I couldn't make myself stop looking at him.

"The new bus was already crowded. After we settled in a man came up to me and asked me if I would slide over so the man could sit down.

"I was bewildered by this. I kept looking at Jane, thinking she should say something, but she just stared at the man with a big smile. I finally said, a little shakily I'm afraid, 'But there are only two seats here!'

"The man kept looking at me, scowling. I began to feel panicky. Where was the misunderstanding? I pulled Jane closer to me. The man looked back toward the driver, sighed, and much to my relief found himself another seat toward the back. Maybe I should have been more patient, more understanding. He might have had some sort of mental problem, some emotional issue. We all need to be patient during times like this.

"I noticed one man on the bus had a bloodied face. For a while I watched him. He acted as if nothing was unusual about his appearance. Other people stared, but no one asked what happened, or if he needed medical attention. I overheard someone say they shouldn't allow certain kinds of people on the bus, and I wondered if we were going to have another incident like the one with the preacher. I guess people don't take chances these days, on planes, or anywhere else. Jane whispered that the man deserved his privacy.

"For long stretches the other passengers were quiet, but now and then everyone seemed to be talking at the same time.

It confuses me when too many people speak at once, and this inability to distinguish conversations happens to me all the time now. There are times, it seems, Jane is the only one who will talk to me or bother to wait for my answer.

"Several passengers had canes, both young and old people, and sometimes they'd tap them on the floor when they were unhappy. I heard a lot of cane tapping on this trip. I also own a cane. Sometimes it helps me get around. I forgot it at home.

"The air conditioning went out for a while. It became extremely hot, and my nose began to bleed. I was so embarrassed. I didn't know what to do. The next time I went to the bathroom I used up all the paper towels trying to clean myself up. I felt terrible not to have left any towels for the next passenger who needed one. I thought I saw someone staring at me from the bathroom mirror, but once I focused the figure was gone.

"It turns out it's only about 125 miles from Las Vegas, New Mexico, to Albuquerque, where I'd planned for us to spend our second night. I thought it would make the trip much more interesting for Jane. But I'd always thought the two places were further apart. When I realized my mistake, I felt overwhelmed. I thought I'd ruined our entire trip, and this was probably the last trip Jane and I would ever share. I had to lie down. I don't know what I was thinking. I guess I wasn't thinking. I stretched out on the floor in the center aisle of the bus."

Dan couldn't see anything now, not the audience in front of him, not the parking lot, not the motel, not Jane, not even the stars. Yet he still felt surrounded. He felt pressed to continue, and so he did.

"This created a great deal of excitement, as you might imagine, with concerned people bending over me and asking what was wrong. I explained I was just a little tired. A couple of nice men helped me back into my seat. One of them gave me a bottle of water, for which I thanked him so profusely it appeared to embarrass him.

"I could see that my clothes were a mess: greasy marks on my trousers, my shirt tail out, dirty and torn. I was so embarrassed. I wanted to go clean up, but I was afraid I couldn't do it properly in that small bathroom. I'd likely spill water all over myself, and maybe I'd look as if I'd peed myself. I didn't want to take that chance. I looked down at my hands and I was troubled to see my father's hands. He had this same thin skin, stained and stretched so that you can practically see the veins inside.

"How do you know when you're old? I really don't know. I guess when everybody tells you. I look at other old people—with their white hair, all their wrinkles—and I think they're a lot older than I am. But most of the time it turns out they're younger.

"Suddenly I wasn't aware of Jane being anywhere on the bus. I twisted around, I looked everywhere. I didn't see her. Had I left her behind at the last bus stop? We hadn't stopped anywhere since Las Vegas. I started to cry. I've become so like a young child. I made myself stop because I simply couldn't afford another scene. Stopping like that, holding it in—I wanted to scream.

"Then my foot kicked my backpack which had fallen to the floor in front of my feet. I picked it up and hugged it tightly, afraid to let go.

"Jane came up behind me and put her hand on my back. She often did that when I was upset. I would recognize her touch anywhere. *It's okay*, she said, and then everything was for a spell.

"In Albuquerque, the bus driver instructed everyone to sit quietly while the police came on board. I was sure they had come for me because of that incident lying on the floor. It had only been a brief episode of confusion, but I was afraid I'd be unable to convince them of that. Sometimes if you make too many mistakes someone takes charge of you. Then you have no choice but to do what they say.

"The officers wore clear face masks, but there appeared to be no face behind the mask of the female officer. They walked past me and grabbed the man with the bloody face and pulled him out of his seat. As they led him away, he gazed around at the other passengers with a disturbing grin. He appeared to fix his attention on Jane, and she tried to hide behind me.

"I like the bus station in Albuquerque. It has that early-Mexican look, with modern adobe and rounded arches everywhere. But it doesn't appear to be in a great part of town. Rather than finding a place to stay for the night Jane and I waited for the next bus. No one bothered us, which was a blessing. Jane was tired and not in a good mood. She had some harsh things to say about my behavior on this trip.

"The final leg from Albuquerque to Flagstaff, and then to here was over seven hours. It was the longest leg of the trip, taking Interstate 40 north of the Acoma Pueblo, the oldest continuously inhabited community in the United States according to the brochure, and the Zuni Reservation. I would have liked to spend some time there but by that point I was focused on this destination, this meeting, telling you this story. I was honestly afraid I would give up if we stopped for any length of time. I missed home, my own chair, my own window on the world. I didn't want to be anywhere else.

"I wondered if the driver shared my sense of urgency, because right out of Albuquerque he picked up speed and seemed to be driving much too fast. As the bus began to rock ever so slightly, I could see that the other passengers were nervous as well. At one point I remember thinking we would crash. I closed my eyes. Jane knew I was in distress. She began to rub my arm.

"Eventually he slowed down, and over that long, monotonous stretch I was able to reclaim some sleep, although pieces of disturbing dreams would now and then jar me awake. I dreamed of Jane when we were younger. We're always younger in my dreams.

"Sometimes when I woke up, I wasn't sure where we were. Had I finally gotten into the taxi, or had I insisted we stay home? Did we actually receive your invitation? Then I'd recognize the interior of the bus, but I didn't see Jane and I would wonder why I would take such a long trip without her. I couldn't figure out if the bus had gotten to Arizona or if we were still in New Mexico. I've never been here before, so I didn't know if there was much difference between the two states. It's a long way if you're unfamiliar with the route. I don't really like going places I've never been before. If I must, I always bring a map. It seems safer that way. But I wasn't driving. A stranger was driving. He could have taken us anywhere. Our future was outside the bus, ahead of us, and there is no map for that.

"Sometimes I sensed Jane sleeping beside me. If I'd had a blanket, I would have covered her with it. I had nothing. I could do nothing for her.

"I remember at one point we were headed directly into the sun. The bus was rattling, and both the sky and the land outside were red. The sun was so bright I couldn't see the driver, but I could see the other passengers: dark, not quite opaque, and not quite human. They were visitors, and my companions on this journey into a frightening interior.

"I still don't know why they appeared. Maybe they didn't want to miss what's going to happen to the world. Or maybe it's just the right time for it. I wonder sometimes if the virus came because it was the right time for it."

He stopped and looked around. The world was still thick with darkness. He shouldn't have been able to see anything. And yet he did. Hundreds of forms all made identical by the shadows. From the way they held themselves he understood they were all focused on him.

"This might have been a terrible mistake coming here. I mean, think about it. I tend not to trust people I don't know, and I know nothing about any of you, but still I've come all this way based on some random invitation I received in the mail. How foolish is that? This could be a cult and I might be about to come to some terrible end." He made a half-hearted laughing noise and it startled him, not having heard himself make such a sound before. "You're not a cult, are you?"

No one replied. He sighed. "I suppose I don't care at this stage. Jane and I, there was never anything special about us. We weren't famous people. We lived the kind of life that ends up in a thrift store. But it's the life we had. It wasn't one of those stirring romances they make big movies about, but it was the love we had.

"I remember, as a child, those summer afternoons of endless play and discovery. The way time stretched in those days, everything lasted for years. Me, and my friends, and all those potential friends I never saw again. We'd make these grand plans and talk about the great things which would happen when we got together again, until we wore ourselves out, and one by one I'd see my friends being taken from me, sometimes by means not readily apparent, and I'd wonder what had happened to them, until finally I'd be standing there alone, and needing to find my way home. I never thought I'd ever feel such things again, and yet here I am."

His dead cell phone began ringing from within the backpack. He looked around apologetically but couldn't see faces clearly enough to apologize. Finally, he opened the pack and retrieved his cell. He stared at the screen. The number displayed made no sense to him. He tapped the screen and put the phone to his ear.

There was a brief burst of static, then her voice, distant and distracted. *You were supposed to come visit, weren't you? You were supposed to be with me. Why didn't you come?*

Shaking, he put the phone back into his pack. He let his hand linger a moment, then removed the dull metal cannister from his extra clothing and set it carefully beside his feet.

"Jane died a couple of months ago. She had Covid those final weeks, but she would have died anyway. It just meant I couldn't be with her. I begged them, but I hadn't had the vaccine yet. I have it now, in time for this, but too late to hold her hand. That's the one thing I promised her, that I would be sitting there holding her hand at the end.

"There are so many things I regret, thoughtless things I said to her, and other things I should have said but didn't. Marriages are built on things unsaid as much as anything else.

"She never told me what she wanted done afterwards. She always changed the subject. Then I couldn't ask her anymore, and she couldn't answer. I think her mind had already traveled a far distance ahead.

"I didn't know what to do. I didn't have her to tell me what the right thing would be. But I knew she hated missing this trip, and I figured both of us could still go. Every place along the way I told her what things looked like, as best I could imagine. I whispered, but maybe sometimes I whispered too loudly. We didn't travel much during our marriage, and that was my fault.

"I'm going to scatter her ashes at the canyon. She would have liked that. It will mean—oh Hell, I don't know what it will mean, but that's what I'm going to do. I hope no one objects."

No one said anything. Dan didn't know what he would have done if they did.

"It's too bad we can't leave our sorrows there, isn't it? If everybody drove to that giant wound in the earth and could toss their sadness inside, and walk away to get on with the rest of their lives, wouldn't that be a great thing?"

He pulled one of the many brochures out of his backpack. "It says here if you threw the body of every human being who ever lived into the Grand Canyon, as if it were one giant grave for all of human history, you'd fill less than point two percent of it. Isn't that, isn't that remarkable?"

WHENEVER IT COMES

It was a long year of quiet dread. I lost my job. I lost my nerve. I stayed home and watched over the house and my family. I made my wife uncomfortable, but I believed she knew I had their best interests in mind.

At first, I saw no one outside, not even the neighbors. They kept their curtains closed. Sometimes I could hear their children screaming inside. I had no idea if theirs was an expression of bottled-up excitement or pain. My own children remained as still and quiet as possible. I asked them to pretend they did not exist. I wanted people to believe no one lived here anymore. Sometimes I believed it myself.

It broke my heart trying to keep our children safe. I didn't want to tell them the world had become a dangerous place. As parents we made mistakes, sometimes terrible mistakes, as all parents will. Yet our children still looked to us for answers.

I didn't understand how things worked anymore. I didn't believe anyone did. I no longer trusted people, least of all myself. No one knew for sure what lived inside the human heart. No one knew how this would end.

The air went from beige to gray to nothing at all. Sometimes we could see distant cities and mountain ranges and the possibilities which lay beyond. No one had ever seen such skies, and we gazed at them from our windows, hoping we were safe behind the glass. The sun could see everything and shone its bright judgment across the world. The animals came out of the woods and nibbled on the edges of civilization. Pets retreated inside and refused to leave.

Unable to bear our solitude, some of us exited our homes and wandered the sidewalks. I spoke to no one. Our neighbors appeared changed. I told my wife and children to stay inside and never, ever, answer the door. I was embarrassed by my words. Sometimes I didn't recognize my own thoughts. I didn't want to give orders to anyone, but it was a time of desperate behavior.

My father was one of those who fell ill. My elderly mother was hysterical and spoke nonsense over the phone. I was afraid of what might happen to my family while I was gone. I explained again to my wife and children what to do if there was a knock on the door. Stay inside. Whatever you do, don't answer. I took a long and circuitous route to my parents' house, without stopping and avoiding the major population centers. When I arrived, I learned my father was dead.

My mother and I were the only ones at my father's graveside service. Others stood watching from a distance. Some seemed familiar, but they were too far away to know for sure. Where did these spectators come from? None had been invited. After the funeral my mother came to live with us. Her house sold quickly, and she chose to trash most of her possessions rather than see them go into a thrift store. She said she needed nothing at this point, nothing at all.

My father wanted to come too, but my father was dead. So I told him no. That he would even ask made me angry. I had my children to consider.

We drove for miles without seeing another car. When we did encounter another vehicle, I slowed down for a better view. The people inside were never what I expected. They stared at us as if we were the strange ones.

Once home I searched the house to see if anything had changed. I asked my wife if there were visitors while I was gone but her answers seemed evasive. My children acted as if I'd never left them. They ignored my mother and continued to play with their invisible toys.

The city stopped picking up our garbage. They lied when they claimed basic services would not be affected. Food continued to be delivered. They would leave it on the front step, and I retrieved it when I thought no one was watching. Whatever packaging or scraps were left I buried in the backyard. Sometimes I thought my neighbors were watching me from behind their curtains. Sometimes it seemed everyone was holding their breath.

I could not remember the last time I saw a plane in the sky, but the air was full of birds, sometimes so many they collided, and their dead bodies hit the house in syncopating drumbeats. I told my children it was hail and to stay away from the windows.

Every morning I insisted we make some feeble attempt at normalcy. We all sat at the kitchen table for breakfast. My son Billy was infected with a new frenetic energy and could not sit still. He kept getting out of his chair, walking around the kitchen, and prattled on about this, that, and everything else. My mother, who listened intently, both smiled and frowned at random. My little daughter Caroline remained silent. She had not spoken in over a year.

My wife left the table and walked down the hall to the living room. She asked if I would join her there. She said there was something important she needed to tell me.

I didn't want to leave. This was supposed to be our family time. Billy was telling my mother a long and complicated tale. She smiled and nodded but I didn't think she understood anything he was saying. Caroline stared at her pancakes and sausage, the steam rolling off them in waves and dissipating into the bright kitchen air. I worried she might be starving herself.

I left the table to join my wife. As my mother was the only remaining adult, she was now in charge of the kitchen. I walked down the hall to the front of the house. I felt a powerful urge to turn around and look at my children.

My wife was talking but I couldn't focus on what she was saying. I glanced down the hallway into the kitchen. My mother was sitting with her back to me. I heard the sharp rise and fall of my son Billy's voice. I could not see Caroline.

My wife told me she needed help keeping the house clean and orderly the way I liked it. She said I had to stop staring out the windows and making everyone nervous. She needed help keeping things organized, especially now the entire family was home all the time. She needed help in the garden. She told me the garden was like a jungle and the yard was almost as bad.

I said "I thought we agreed we wouldn't be going outside anymore. Don't tell me you've been going outside."

Someone knocked on the back door.

"Don't answer it!" I shouted. "Mother, Billy, don't answer the door!"

My wife kept talking. I had a hard time giving her my attention. I didn't catch all her words. There's something else I must tell you, she said.

Someone knocked on the back door again. "Don't answer!" I cried. I saw Caroline cross behind the table headed toward the back door. "Billy, don't let your sister answer the door!"

I started toward the kitchen, but my wife held my arm. A few days ago, my wife continued, when you were napping, someone came to the door.

"Tell me you didn't answer it. Just tell me that."

It was a man, just an ordinary man, she said. He wanted directions to the Willises'. I pointed to the house across the street, and I closed the door. That's all. Nothing else happened. Everything is perfectly fine.

I heard the back door open. I heard my son, still chattering on. My wife said I know I shouldn't have, but everything's fine. Everything is perfectly fine.

"Mother? Who's there? Don't let him inside!"

I know I shouldn't have, my wife kept saying.

I heard those big shoes, and then Billy calling Dad! Dad! The Shut-Up Man is Here!

But my wife was still talking, trying to explain herself. I kept hearing those big shoes moving around, and Billy had stopped talking altogether, and my mother was no longer in her chair.

My wife said she knew she shouldn't have opened the door. Where was Caroline? My wife said it was one little mistake. But everything was perfectly fine.

"Shut up shut up shut up!" I shouted, with fists clenched and eyes closed. I shouted this over and over until the house was quiet again.

I turned to my wife to apologize but the front door was open, and my wife was not there. I gazed into the kitchen, but the kitchen appeared empty. That's when I realized this house was no longer ours, but belonged to whoever, or whatever, comes after, whenever it comes.

MEMORIA

During the untold hours, he is all memory and imagination. If he has a body, he is unaware of it. The same was true during certain periods of his life.

What he remembers most about those final years was the fear. They never put it into words, but he could see it in Diane's face, and in his own in the mirror. Now he cannot see his reflection, and it is just as well. He imagines an appearance with no expression, pebble eyes under a film of gray, a mouth fallen open and full of shadow.

He remembers friends and relatives erased, one now and again, then two or three, then entire groups of everyone he knew, gone. The grief that came after. The numbness. He remembers worrying over what an illness actually meant, a weakness in a limb, a headache, an abdominal pain, a lost thought, a missed connection. He remembers her asking, *How do you feel?* He remembers taking longer and longer to answer. He remembers getting old.

He remembers wanting to ask her, *What was the point?* After all that effort, he couldn't decide how everything added up. She'd always been the optimist, the one with the comforting answers. *What did it all mean?* But he didn't ask. He didn't want to hurt her.

He remembers hearing things in the middle of the night. He could never decide if the sounds were new, or the same noises he always heard. There were always sudden drafts. Was a window open? There were always doors opening and closing.

He remembers smelling smoke. He remembers getting out of bed and searching the house but never finding the danger. Diane slept so soundly, it became his job by default. To turn the lights on. To turn the lights off. To walk through the house like a memory, listening, smelling, trying to find a path through the dark.

They gather outside the windows and beat on the glass. He is afraid they will wake her, but she is oblivious. They want him to come out. They no longer require warmth, or shelter, or food, but they do crave companionship. But his love lies here sleeping, and he is reluctant to leave her side.

He wants to close the curtains, so he doesn't have to see their faces, but cannot. Their lack of features is unsettling. He tries to raise his hands to feel his own face but cannot find either his face or his hands.

Diane remains motionless on the couch. He cannot tell if she is sleeping, or resting, meditating, or dead. She has spent most of the past month this way, body covered, eyes closed. He cannot see below her neckline. Her body could be anything, the body of a fish, or a leopard, the body of an aging woman who needs her rest. The clock, ticking, is the only sound in the room. He waits for her to rise, or leap, or swim away.

He watches her through darkness and through day, until she stirs, first her head and then her shoulders, shifting, slipping from the blanket, her face turning toward him, but not seeing, eyes blinking away dead tears. Her mouth stretches into a yawn.

Her cell phone on the coffee table rings and rings, but she doesn't answer. Eventually it dies, becoming yet another useless artifact.

Diane climbs from the couch with the blanket wrapping her like a shroud. She is smaller than he remembers, thinner, paler. He is beyond all worry, and yet somehow he worries. A few wisps of colorless hair fall across her forehead. She moves with small steps into the bathroom. He waits outside.

He hears the toilet flush, the water running. He follows her from the bathroom into the bedroom. He waits for her to go to the closet, to put something on, but instead she stumbles to the bed and sheds the blanket, and for a moment she is but a figment of flesh before crawling beneath the covers. He watches the sheets rise and fall. Her breath expands to fill the room. He leaves before she gathers him into a dream.

He remembers leaving this house many times but always returning. He remembers wondering if he would ever leave this house again. He can be in two places at once, or even three. So much is possible when you are done.

The house is smaller than he remembers. It seems much dirtier than before, or perhaps he has more time to notice. He feels the walls, ceilings, and floors bleeding dust into the air, the tiny deteriorations of frame and sheathing, furnishings, and flesh.

A fuzziness collects on the edges of things. Time drifts through the rooms, settles into episodes of decay, moves on. He listens to the creatures beneath the wallpaper, the creatures inside the wood, the creatures above and below. These rooms are never completely dead.

During the long night, he gazes from the windows and cannot see the stars. During the endless day, reflections of nothing paint the walls. Outside their house, birds are frozen in midair. The clouds are unmoving.

He watches their neighbors departing their houses, crossing the lawns, moving along the sidewalks. He cannot remember which are living and which are dead. He wonders at the busyness of the living, their preoccupation with appearances, their almost constant disappointment.

He follows the sunlight as it moves through the house, keen for its touch.

Most of his possessions still remain: books and clothing, a few favorite foods, letters, souvenirs, the old dresser from his college years. He doesn't know why she keeps them, or if she will keep them for long.

Diane sits at their modest kitchen table, spooning mac and cheese into her mouth, but he can find no pleasure in her face. He is not sure when was the last time she ate. It may have been days. He resides in the chair across the table, his old spot. She still uses her same chair, leaving his open. But it does not feel like an invitation.

He watches her chew. She has difficulty swallowing. He remembers warning her the bites she took were too large and potentially dangerous. More than once he witnessed the blankness come into her pale eyes as she began to choke.

He has a vague memory of how food tasted, although he recalls the warmth of it better, the heat in his mouth and as it went down. He imagines opening his mouth and tasting the departures, all those moments gone and now irrelevant. Feeling foolish, he stops and tries to keep his mouth closed. He has no idea if he has been successful.

She closes her eyes as if she no longer wants to see. He can imagine much, but he cannot imagine what she must be thinking.

Unable to watch any longer, he turns away and moves into the living room. A novel lies on the coffee table, an overdue bill stuck somewhere in the middle as a bookmark. He'd left it beside the bed, never finished. She has moved it here, by the couch where she sleeps and reads. Does she intend to read it? Will she start from the beginning, or from where he left off?

He studies the cover. The words. He can no longer read.

He spends an age watching the light slip away, the shadows which settle and stay. A distant sound finally arrives. Outside the window, there is a sudden explosion and a flash of brilliance. Everything—what lasts, what does not last—is frozen in silver. The rain outside appears impossible. Why did he never realize this before?

He is drenched in memory. He tries to choose but one to take with him and cannot.

She is crying because he said something that hurt her. He was careless and wishes he could take it back. Now he knows nothing can ever be taken back.

The night of her miscarriage she is lying in the hospital bed, heavily drugged, and he hovers over her. He knows she is alive, but her resemblance to what he imagines death must be thoroughly shakes him. They never try again after that.

The jokes that fell flat because he was trying too hard to make her smile. The jokes he was so proud of because they made her laugh.

That day in a bookstore when they first met. He didn't understand her taste in literature, but he wanted to.

Their first kiss. She kissed him, of course, because he was too shy.

The bright-blue dress she bought in Mexico. The spring afternoon they were married in the mountains in front of all their friends. Her parents refused to attend.

That small indentation on the left side of her back.

The many times she forgave him for being a fool.

When they spent hours together in bed.

When they couldn't stop touching.

All these moments gone to light and air and nothing.

His is an instability spreading everywhere.

Acknowledgments

"Everyday Horror" originally appeared in *Qualia Nous* Vol. 2, ed. Michael Bailey, 2023

"Fish Scales" originally appeared in *Black Static* 80/81, 2021

"Gavin's Field" originally appeared in *The Mammoth Book of Folk Horror*, ed. Stephen Jones, 2021

"An Gorta Mór" originally appeared in *Consumed: Tales Inspired by the Wendigo*, ed. Hollie & Henry Snider, 2020

"Black Wings" originally appeared in *The Dark Magazine*, April 2022

"Bags" originally appeared in *Close to Midnight*, ed. Mark Morris, 2022

"Late Sleepers" originally appeared in *It Came from the Multiplex*, ed. Joshua Viola, 2020

"A Thin Silver Line" originally appeared in *The Unquiet Dreamer: A Tribute to Harlan Ellison*, ed. Preston Grassmann, 2019

"Inappetence" originally appeared in *The Alchemy Press Book of Horrors 3*, ed. Peter Coleborn & Jan Edwards, 2021

"The Winter Closet" originally appeared in *Three-Lobed Burning Eye*, #36, July 2022

"Privacy" originally appeared in *Mooncalves*, ed. John J.M. Thompson, 2023

"Monkeys" originally appeared in *The Mammoth Book of Jack the Ripper Stories*, ed. Maxim Jakubowski, 2015

"When They Fall" originally appeared in *Literally Dead*, ed. Gaby Triana, 2022

"The Things We Do Not See" originally appeared in *Black Wings VII*, ed. S.T. Joshi, 2023

"Within the Concrete" originally appeared in *Parsec #5*, November 2022

"The Last Sound You Hear" originally appeared in *The Dark*, December 2021

"Into the White" originally appeared in *Vastarien* Vol. 5 issue 2, 2022

"The Old Man's Tale" originally appeared in *The Canterbury Chronicles*, ed. David Niall Wilson, 2023

"Whenever It Comes" originally appeared in *Weird Horror* #4, March 2022

"Memoria" originally appeared in *The Deadlands*, May 2023

MEET THE AUTHOR

Steve Rasnic Tem was born in Lee County Virginia in the heart of Appalachia. He is the author of over 500 published short stories and is a past winner of the Bram Stoker, International Horror Guild, British Fantasy, and World Fantasy Awards. His story collections include *City Fishing, The Far Side of the Lake, In Concert* (with wife Melanie Tem), *Ugly Behavior* (crime), *Celestial Inventories* (contemporary fantasy), and *Figures Unseen*, his Selected Stories. His novels include *Excavation, The Book of Days, Daughters, The Man in the Ceiling* (with Melanie Tem), *Deadfall Hotel*, Blood Kin, and the recent *Ubo*.

Steve Rasnic Tem's short fiction has been compared to the work of Franz Kafka, Dino Buzzati, Ray Bradbury, and Raymond Carver, but to quote Joe R. Lansdale: "Steve Rasnic Tem is a school of writing unto himself." In 2024 he received the Lifetime Achievement Award from the Horror Writers Association.

NOVELS

Blood Kin
Deadfall Hotel
Excavation
The Book of Days
The Mask Shop of Doctor Black
Ubo

WITH MELANIE TEM

Beautiful Stranger
Daughters
In Concert

The Man on the Ceiling
Yours to Tell: Dialogues on the Art & Practice of Writing

COLLECTIONS

Absences: Charlie Goode's Ghosts
Celestial Inventories
City Fishing
Decoded Mirrors: Three Tales After Lovecraft
Everything Is Fine Now
Fairytales
Figures Unseen
Here with the Shadows
Out of The Dark
Rough Justice
Scarecrows: Appalachian Tales
Thanatrauma
The Far Side of the Lake
The Harvest Child and Other Fantasies
The Hydrocephalic Ward (poems)
The Night Doctor and Other Tales
Twember
Ugly Behavior

Curious about other Crossroad Press books? Stop by our
website: http://crossroadpress.com
We offer quality writing
in digital, audio, and print formats.

Subscribe to our newsletter on the website homepage and
receive a free eBook.